THANATOS

GUARDIAN SHADOW WORLD - BOOK 4

KRIS MICHAELS

WWW.KRISMICHAELSAUTHOR.COM

CHAPTER 1

Night settled around London, cloaking the city in darkness. His target would be returning shortly. Decreasing traffic, both on foot and in vehicle, slowed the punctuation of the night sounds on London's Kensington High Street. The antique Victorian chair, covered in a tastefully woven silk brocade, protested mildly as he carefully leaned back, closed his eyes, and listened to the vehicles and the occasional talkative pedestrians pass by the front of the house. As was typical of all the men Thanatos stalked, Benjamin Wellington was a creature of habit. Every Thursday, without fail, the man smoked cigars and drank expensive brandy while talking with his compatriots at an exclusive gentlemen's club located near the Egyptian Embassy. The weekly habit provided the access that would end the man.

He shook his head, silently decrying the miasma of intentional ignorance that swirled through society. Wellington had murdered hundreds if not thousands in a life-long effort to build the perfect biological weapon. For years, just as the designer labels that cluttered Wellington's upstairs closets fabricated a sense of respectability for the bastard, the "humanitarian" cloak the man wore had shielded his nefarious acts. Finally, that shroud had been yanked back and the monster revealed. For the crimes Benjamin Wellington had inflicted upon those who had no defenders, the international tribunal known as the Council had sentenced him to death. As the instrument of the man's eradication, Thanatos awaited his prey.

His surveillance and reconnaissance were complete. There were no holes in his plan, however, humans although predictable, could surprise a person. He didn't anticipate Wellington changing his routine, but it might happen. Preparations were drawn for that eventuality, too.

Headlights broached a small crack of the heavily draped window. He listened as Benjamin bid his driver good night. The guard at the front of the house opened the wrought-iron entry gate. Muted conversation between the two men could be heard. The front door opened and closed. His target hummed as he walked down the marble-tiled hallway. The click of his Italian leather shoes went from sharp staccato taps to muted reverberations as he stepped onto the luxurious carpet outside his office.

The door opened and Benjamin headed straight for his bar. The heavy wooden door closed with a soft click. He watched from a darkened corner of the office as Benjamin stopped and flicked on a small lamp. The man moved to pour his drink. Motionless, Thanatos waited until the abomination in front of him settled behind his desk and opened his computer. The light from the monitor displayed the frown on the man's face when his laptop didn't activate. He reached for the phone.

"All means of communication from this room have been disabled."

Wellington startled, sprang to his feet, and moved to face him.

Thanatos turned on the table lamp next to him. His handgun and the suppressor on the end of its barrel made a deadly statement. A small movement of his weapon motioned Wellington backward.

His mark's eyes shifted to the duress button at the side of his desk. The man stood slowly and moved a few inches toward what he obviously believed was assistance.

"Who are you? What do you want?" he quavered.

"I am destiny. You have been judged and found guilty. Your sentence is to be carried out tonight." Thanatos lifted a small straw and blew forcefully. A small silver dart nailed the man in the leg just above the knee.

Wellington jerked and grabbed at the dart, pulling it free from his body.

It didn't matter. The effects would be almost instantaneous.

"What have you done? Why are you doing this? I've done nothing wrong."

"I've seen the bodies. I've followed the money. My handlers have proof, and you have been judged. Tonight, you cease to exist." He drew a deep, easy breath. This portion of his mission could prove difficult. *Could.* His specialty required the man to leave a note. Some were easier to convince than others, which necessitated the drug-laced dart.

Once they understood their demise was imminent, his targets tried to bargain for their lives. Wellington was no different.

"I'm a very rich man. I'll triple whatever they're paying you." The quavering tone no longer existed. The man's persona shifted, and his cloak of respectability fell as dust onto the ground.

"The dart isn't poison. It's a drug called Devil's Breath. Please, do sit down."

His target blinked several times as the chemicals worked. The chemicals stripped his free will. Suggestions, even from his killer, became commands. Wellington struggled, his eyes blinked rapidly and his muscles shook, but he finally sank slowly into his chair.

"You will use the pen and paper in front of you to write your suicide note."

The man shook his head. "I don't want to kill myself."

Obviously, a strong mind. Thanatos wasn't impressed. The Devil's Breath always won.

"I'm sure the thousands you murdered didn't want to die, either. Pick up the pen."

The man reached forward and picked up the pen he had prepositioned on top of the desk. Wellington's hand shook as his mind fought the suggestion.

"Who sent you?"

"Consider me an avenging angel."

"Strange. I would've thought you'd have been sent by one of my competitors, not the Council."

"Write the following. To whom it may concern, I can

no longer go on living as I have been. I am haunted by those I have harmed. Forgive me my sins."

He watched the man scribble the note on the paper and instructed him to sign it. The vague note, written in Wellington's hand, would lead to an investigation into the bastard's crimes. He'd positioned that proof where the investigators would find it.

Thanatos stood and the man's eyes rose to meet his. "Will you kill me now?"

"I believe you understand you will be killing yourself."

The statement didn't necessitate an answer. The man nodded and licked his lips. "I have heard of you. The Angel of Death. I thought you were a myth. The others... nothing was proven."

Of course, nothing had been proven. He was the best in the world and his scenes were pristine. A fact, not a point of pride.

"May I make a last request?"

"You are hardly in a position to ask for anything."

"The request is not for me. I have no regrets about what I have done. When I started experimenting years ago, my goal was to develop a vaccine against Ebola. Through experimentation on human subjects, my research developed several strains of the virus more effective and far safer to handle than Ebola. Money can be made with these altered viruses, but no bioweapon is useful without an antidote or vaccine, which is another lucrative side business.

"Bioweapons are radically unpredictable. The demand for specific antidotes arose and my team determined the best way to produce the required counteragent was by in-vitro gene manipulation to produce an inherently immune individual. That work years ago provided a viable birth. Throughout her infancy, we tested and exposed her to various strains of common diseases. She survived them all. The tests grew more aggressive as she aged. Almost ten years ago there was a demand for materials that could wipe out villages. We had more demand than product. She lived through a year-long research program that should have killed her.

"The woman is remarkably normal. The researchers who raised her told her she was a carrier of a rare cancer and testing on a routine basis was a requirement if she wanted to live. She is quite compliant." Wellington chuckled. "We make new bioweapons, we expose her to them, and using her immunized blood as the basis of the remedy, I make vaccines. The entire spectrum of the war machine is an endless source of profit."

"You sick fuck."

Wellington shrugged as if his opinion was inconsequential.

That man had exposed infants and the unborn to the worst nightmares known to man. Wellington mentioned one living, but there must have been many more who died. He rarely wished for latitude in the way his kills were dictated. Tonight, if it wouldn't compromise every intrinsic value he'd managed to hold on to, he'd gut the motherfucker and watch him bleed out.

He narrowed his eyes. The man almost sounded... proud? "And what does this have to do with your request?"

"My, how shall we say, customers, will actively seek my research vaults and the treasures they hold. Unfortunately, once I'm gone, the truth about my experiments will eventually be revealed. Capturing and regulating this woman and her unique immunities are in my competitors' best interests. If they can't control her they will kill her." The man's words slurred toward the end.

"So why are you telling me?"

"I have no desire to wholly destroy the population of the earth. Without this woman and the antibodies she produces, if found and released, two of the diseases we manufactured have the potential to end all human life. I have taken measures to ensure they are destroyed should I die, but there is always a chance my preventative measures could fail."

"What is her name?"

"Eve Salutem."

"Where is she?"

"Somewhere in the States."

Thanatos narrowed his eyes. The bastard or his researchers had a sick sense of humor. Eve, the name of the first woman in the Christian Bible, and *salutem*, the Latin word for health. He weighed the conversation. The gasped words of a dying man could very well be a lie to pull Guardian into a trap. On the other hand, if the bastard was telling the truth, an innocent woman would be in the crosshairs. Additionally, if her blood did in fact provide an antidote to such horrendous diseases, the world needed her. A conundrum. One he'd deal with, after his work here was finished.

"It is time." He opened the small bottle he'd earlier

placed on the side table and dropped the tablets it contained into his palm. He crossed to the tumbler of brandy and slipped them into the liquor. "Drink it all. It's quick, effective, and relatively painless. Unfortunately."

This method of execution was rarely satisfying. Only the target and he knew of the emotion, the regret, the struggle at the end of life. The biological weapons this bastard had produced had slaughtered over a thousand men, women, and children, a thousand souls who deserved retribution.

The man lifted the glass and drank. Benjamin choked and gasped, his survival instinct trying to override the drugs that already coursed through his system.

The empty tumbler hit the desk awkwardly and rolled away from the man's hand. His eyes closed and his breathing became shallow pants.

Thanatos carefully unscrewed the suppressor from the barrel of his weapon, and holstered his gun, closing his jacket to hide the weapon. The suppressor slipped into the inside pocket of his suit jacket. Finally, he retrieved the small silver dart and placed it in a plexi-glass vial in his pants pocket. It was a waiting game now.

Benjamin's guards had retired for the evening. The duress button at his desk and the phone lines to the den would be reconnected when he slipped out the back after Wellington took his last breath. The lovely garden hidden behind the house was a perfect escape route. There were no motion detectors, cameras, or dogs to hinder his departure. Strange how a vile and evil person such as Benjamin would assume a wrought-iron fence, an outdated alarm system, and a complacent guard on the premises, provided safety.

The man's hand waved without any control and then hit the desk blotter with a thud. He stood in front of the desk and waited as the man drew his last breath followed by a rasping, strangled release of air with no inhale. The suicide note, the dead man, and the manufactured setting were perfect, as usual. He placed the emptied bottle of prescription painkillers beside the crystal tumbler that had held the man's brandy. The prescription was written by a doctor who had recently passed away. Wellington's fingerprints were on the bottle and the date on the script was falsified, but all suicides needed an established means of death. The opioids from the vial, which were now in Wellington's system, checked that box. Thanatos gave the office one final sweep. Suicide note, overdose, and evidence. Yes, two plus two equaled four, and pointed to obvious conclusions.

He strode across the room and pressed his ear to the door. Nothing moved, no sounds. He opened the door, slipped into the hall, and after he restored the office's connectivity, disappeared through the small garden. As he emerged on Kensington-High Street near Royal Albert Hall, he smiled and acknowledged a passing couple. He gazed up at the bright moon and drew a deep breath of cool September air, his assignment complete, and another monster slayed. Warding off the chill of the evening, he shoved his hands into the pockets of his wool overcoat and slowly began to stroll down the avenue.

His hotel bar was packed. The stale smell of alcohol, mingled with a confusion of perfumes and colognes, twirled throughout the forced air of the establishment. The murmur of voices reached a moderate din that resembled a flock of babbling geese. The posturing, preening and pretending people went through to construct social contacts reeked of desperation. He'd never fit in with the living. The charged energy of people trying to be what they weren't disgusted him. He'd stripped that veil of pretense long ago. Where he went, death followed. The dark trail he left absorbed the filth of the world. His purpose, his curse.

The unsuspecting people who laughed and drank around him were blessed by their ignorance. If they knew the evil he embodied, they'd run in terror. He was a driven man, but not for the justice he dispensed tonight. No, his motivation was revenge. Vengeance for horrendous deeds perpetrated decades ago against unsuspecting innocence. Yet, here he was, acting normal after once again sweeping the filth of humanity down the sewers of polite society. He literally flushed human waste away from the people who sat in this room. Hatred for those who preyed on the weak had become a constant companion long ago. That emotion fueled his need for revenge. He lived in the filth and cloaked himself in respectability. Thanatos glanced at his reflection in the mirrored surface near the hostess stand. The defining line that separated what he did from who he hunted had diminished to the finest thread. Recently he'd reminded himself he was a specialist who was called on when needed. Not necessarily a redeeming quality.

He took possession of a table near the front window which overlooked the street below. London's double-decker buses stopped across the way, emptying and gaining passengers, as the city's public transit pulsed through its streets.

Life moved on, people went about their routines, clueless about the atrocities who lived in their midst. He ordered a drink and pulled his phone from his pocket to send a text. Carefully considering the words he fed into the phone, he tapped out a message. He never spoke of his conversations with the dead. The shrinks didn't know about them and he'd never volunteer the information. Yet each dying word of the people he was responsible for extinguishing engraved themselves into his mind. He could recall each threat, plea, and bribe, that had ever been thrown at him. Never had any of the abominations he'd terminated asked for something to benefit another human. It was an anomaly he couldn't disregard. No, strike that, wouldn't disregard. So, he hit send and waited for the message to be delivered. Once he received notification of receipt, he powered down his phone and returned it to his pocket. Its weight, coupled with that of his suppressor, felt familiar and grounded him in his reality, one of action, of justice.

He leaned back in the plush baby blue chair and stared out the window. Benjamin's words rolled through his mind again, unwanted and unbidden. He lifted the scotch the harried waitress had deposited in front of him and took a sip. With determination he flushed the night's activities from his mind. He had a flight in the morning. His work here was finished. Regardless of the dead man's plea or the actions taken by Guardian, his mission was complete. He was an enforcer, not a caretaker. The woman's future was not in his hands, and neither was her demise, because he didn't exist. He was a Shadow. His life was spent as a faint memory, a nondescript association that most people couldn't recall with clarity. He was a ghost, and the Angel of Death. His job here was finished, but the world was full of abominations like Mr. Wellington. It wouldn't be long before he was called on again. Until that time, his obsession and his reason for still walking on this planet would fill the void.

CHAPTER 2

Bengal strode through the corridor of the underground bunker in South Dakota. He'd flown in several days ago to work with Anubis on several projects. His focus however was on the information Jewell had provided him based on Thanatos' unusual text. Unusual, because it was the first time Thanatos had ever put an addendum on a mission complete notification. That in and of itself was enough to cause an immediate reaction. He glanced at his watch and hurried his steps. Thanatos' aircraft had landed in the States almost an hour ago. Getting to a secure phone so they could have this conversation was his priority. He opened the facility's communication room door and shut it behind him.

"What was Jewell able to find?" Anubis turned from the wall-mounted monitors to regard him as he entered.

"Eve Salutem. We've searched every variation of the name. There were four possible women found. One is dead, two are over the age of fifty, and the fourth lives in

Rochester, Minnesota. She's an elementary school teacher. She has an apartment she can't afford on a teacher's salary and access to a sizable bank account, but nothing that would trigger audits from federal entities. Everything is below the established caps for fiduciary reporting, but Cyber was able to determine deposits are made from an offshore account. We have been unable to weed through the shell companies behind it. Yet." He dropped in the chair next to Anubis and pushed the folder in his hands across the table.

Anubis flipped open the document and read the information on the woman. "I wonder why Thanatos said she was a person of interest."

"Good question, and it is why I had Jewell drill down on this woman's past. What's interesting is before she appeared in Rochester, she didn't exist."

Anubis nodded and continued to rifle through the ream of paper before him. "She's not with an agency. If she were, she'd have a manufactured past. Perhaps she's in a witness protection program?" Anubis shook his head, answering his own question, "No, WitSec doesn't use offshore accounts, and again, she'd have a past, although a crappy one."

"Hell, at least WitSec attempts to give them a past. There's nothing here before she entered college and got her degree in early childhood education. Eve Salutem is, quite literally, a non-person. Her social security number was taken from one of the many who died in Hurricane Katrina on the Gulf Coast. I'm surprised the Social Security Administration hasn't flagged the woman. But then again, if somebody manipulated the computer systems within the Administration, they wouldn't make the connection."

"We've seen that happen many times. It's not as if the Social Security Administration is foolproof." Anubis closed the folder and leaned back. "Where is he calling us from?"

"The safe house just outside DC. I wanted to make sure there was no way anyone could infiltrate the conversation."

"Good idea."

THANATOS SHUT the door behind him and flipped the switch securing the safe house's communication room. He turned the key on the phone sitting on the desk to encrypt his telephone call and dialed the number to the South Dakota complex. He'd expedited his return and hastened to the safe house due to the text message he'd received from Bengal.

The phone rang once before a male voice—that would be Anubis—answered with a curt, "Standby."

He leaned back in the chair and closed his eyes, listening to the line go through the encryption process on the other end.

"We are secure. Explain what you know about Eve Salutem."

Thanatos repeated the conversation he'd had with Benjamin Wellington. He finished his report, "I can't see how Wellington would let a resource like this walk around free. It is possible she is complicit. The likelihood the bastard was lying to me is high, but I believed you should make that determination."

There was silence on the other end of the line for a moment. No doubt he'd been muted. It didn't matter. The less he knew about the situation, the better. Clouding his thoughts with extraneous information not germane to his current endeavors was useless.

"Thanatos, Archangel is online."

Interesting. "Affirmative." He acknowledged the addition of his boss.

"According to the information we've been able to retrieve, it appears Eve Salutem is actually a person of interest. Unfortunately, I'm not inclined to believe your latest assignment's information without validating it. The feeding frenzy we're seeing on the DarkNet would lend credence to his words, but all sources are talking about an asset locked away inside a vault."

He nodded, although his bosses couldn't see him. "The individual indicated his competitors believed he had an antidote to the chemical weapons he sold them stored in his vault. I'm assuming none of them knew about the woman. Although, if she is donating samples routinely, there is a trail. Where there's a trail, the rats will follow."

"Exactly our conclusion. You have an appointment for your go/no-go evaluation in forty-five minutes. The doctor will meet you at the safe house. Assuming you pass, you will be on the next plane to Minneapolis-St. Paul. From there, you'll pick up a vehicle from one of our assets in the area and drive to Rochester, Minnesota. Your assignment is to get close to this woman. Perform a detailed background and surveillance. Watch her like a fucking hawk. If she is, in fact, who we believe she is, you'll be responsible for bringing her in. Alive."

Thanatos leaned forward; his eyes narrowed as he stared at the phone in front of him. "Alive. Interesting, but I don't believe that word is in my job description, sir."

"And I don't believe I asked." Archangel's gravelly voice snapped back. "Guardian is in the midst of a massive reorganization. Each of us are taking on more responsibilities and extending our reach. Your psychological evaluation says you *can* play well with others. So, you're going to get a chance to do just that." There was a definitive click on the line.

"So my question would be, do you have balls of steel or a death wish?" Bengal's laugh grated on his last nerve.

He wasn't in the mood for levity. Maybe his psych eval did say he played well with others. The fact of the matter was he preferred not to play—at all. People weren't his favorite past time. Oh, he *knew* people. Perhaps that's why he preferred not to associate with any.

Anubis fired off, "Report in with a text as to the status of your flight. When you get to Rochester, access your Shadow account email dead drop for instructions."

"You're assuming I'm going to pass the evaluation." And yes, he was thinking about throwing it, but if he did, he'd be taken out of commission. He wouldn't allow that. He needed to be in the field.

"I know you too well, my friend. I also understand the specific issues having to integrate yourself into this woman's life will cause you. We'll work out a solution at this end and hopefully have it waiting for you when you call in. She is your assignment. Deal with it."

Thanatos closed his eyes and shook his head. He hated having his stateside time compromised, but he'd been directed to perform duties within the scope of his ability without compromising his morals. Or rather moral. He only had one. He wouldn't lie. For anyone, for any reason. He also wouldn't back down on his pursuit and Bengal knew it. Finding that bastard was his reason for drawing his next breath.

He rubbed his brow feeling a headache developing—a massive fucking headache shaped like a woman. "I would rather not deal with this type of assignment. I don't do well with those who have a beating heart."

"I have no doubt you will be able to handle any eventuality. Get your ass through the appointment, get on the plane, and text when you're there."

The line clicked several times before the dial tone bleated across the connection. He returned the receiver to its cradle and turned the cryptology key, ending the connection from his device. He glanced around the safe house. Impersonal, beige, muted. The structure resembled his life. Impersonal, colorless, muted. He drew a deep breath and stood, pushing the emotional mess of his thoughts away like garbage. When dealing with Guardian's doctors, a colorless life was a safe one.

"But Miss Salutem, what if he doesn't come?" Rachel

clung to her fingers and her eyes glistened with unshed tears.

Eve knelt down so she was eye level with the little girl. "There's no reason to think that. Your daddy has always picked you up, hasn't he?" She pushed Rachel's bangs out of her eyes.

The little girl nodded and turned her attention to the empty street. Standing near the front drive through where students were picked up, they'd watched all the buses depart, the cars filled with children and parents, and even the majority of the teachers—all departing at the end of the school year for a summer of fun. Rachel's father still hadn't shown. Rachel had recently lost her mother to cancer, and she knew both the little girl and her father were struggling. She'd need to decide what to do with the tiny girl, soon. The office workers would be leaving and when they did, her access to the telephone numbers for Rachel's father would also depart.

The idea suddenly hit her. "Were you supposed to go home with someone else today, Rachel?"

"No. Sandy's mama said they had to see Sandy's grandma, so Daddy was supposed to come get me today." A single tear fell down the little girl's cheek. Rachel sniffed back others, suddenly pointing down the long avenue that led to the school. A lone sedan hurled down the road.

"Is that your daddy's car?" For some reason she thought Rachel's father drove an SUV, not a sedan.

Rachel jumped on her toes still pointing at the vehicle heading toward them at break-neck speed. "It's his new one. We got it last weekend. I picked the color."

The vehicle decelerated quickly and pulled into the parking lot, driving through the empty parking spaces. It stopped feet from where they stood. Rachel's father threw the vehicle into gear and slammed the driver side door open. He raced around the front of the car and dropped to one knee opening his arms for his daughter. "Baby, I'm so sorry."

Rachel flew into her daddy's arms. Her tears streamed down her cheeks. "I thought you forgot me."

Eve watched father and daughter. Rachel's father closed his eyes and squeezed his daughter to him. "Never, baby. I tried to get here sooner, but I had a flat tire." He looked up at where she stood and shook his head. "My phone is dead and for some reason my charger doesn't work in this vehicle. I had no idea until I tried to plug it in. I'm so sorry I'm late. Thank you so much for staying with her."

She smiled. "These things happen to all of us. I'm just glad you were able to make it, safely."

Rachel released her father and turned back to her, flying over the asphalt that separated them. She wrapped her arms around Eve's legs and hugged her tightly. "Bye, Miss Salutem!"

"Goodbye, Rachel. Have a nice summer!" Eve gave the small girl a hug before she pulled away and raced back to her father. Rachel's dad raised a hand and waved as he helped his precious cargo into her car seat in the back.

Eve waited until they pulled out of the parking lot before she turned back to the school. She glanced at her watch. Today's schedule was blown to pieces, but it was the last day of school, so to heck with her schedule. Her sneakers squeaked as she walked down the lonely and suddenly quiet hallway to her classroom.

"Hallelujah! Free at last!" Her fellow teacher, Lori Hutchinson, shouted as she exited her classroom with her hands held high above her head and a cheesy grin plastered across her face. Her exclamation garnered several remote laughs from the few teachers who were still working in their classrooms. The students may be gone, but the staff had final grades to record, and lesson plans to adjust and store for the following year's instruction. Additionally, she wanted to take down all the decorations from her classroom and place them in the storage container for next year.

"What amazing plans do you have for this summer?" Lori bounced into her room and plopped into her chair behind her desk.

"Nothing special." Which was the truth. Due to her medical condition, she never traveled farther than thirty minutes from Rochester. She smiled at her friend. "What about you and Mark?" Lori's husband was the high school football coach. They normally travelled for two weeks during the summer. Honestly, she was more than a little bit envious. Seeing the country was a dream she'd never realize... and that was okay. If she could stay healthy and teach here in Rochester until she died of old age, she'd mark that as a success in a life well lived. According to her doctors, that probably wouldn't happen.

"We're going to Vegas, baby!" Lori nearly levitated out of her seat. "We have reservations on the strip. We're going to see several shows. Then I'm gonna make Mark take me to Hoover Dam. I want to see absolutely everything."

"That sounds amazing. Make sure you take lots of pictures for me." She picked up the eraser from the tray in front of the chalkboard and wiped away the last remnants of the school year.

"I'll SnapChat with you the entire time. Are you sure you don't want to come with us? Mark wouldn't mind. He wouldn't have to endure shopping that way." Lori kicked her legs back and forth. She never stopped moving.

"No, you know me, I'm a homebody." She often wondered if that were true. When she dreamed about what she would do if she were healthy, she imagined herself as an adventurous and defiant woman who feared nothing and took on the world.

"Okay, I'll call every day to check on you. You should probably find a man to do that for you, by the way." Lori popped out of the chair and grabbed another eraser, aggressively rubbing the chalk off the green board. She sent Eve a sidelong glance and sighed, "I didn't say that to be mean, you know. You're so darn pretty, and you sit home all the time alone. I could set you up with one of Mark's friends."

Eve groaned. "I don't need anyone to check on me. How many times do I need to tell you I'm happy being single?"

"Probably as many times as it takes for me to believe you don't want to find a boyfriend!" Lori laughed and dodged the loaded eraser full of chalk she chucked in her friend's direction. Lori danced out of her classroom with a loud, carefree laugh. That woman was such a force of nature. People called her bubbly. She would agree. The effervescence Lori exuded was something nobody could compete with. Not that she really wanted to. She enjoyed her life and was thankful for every day she woke up happy and healthy. It was a blessing she didn't take for granted.

Her childhood memories were of hospital rooms and treatments. Her parents had abandoned her after she was born. The doctors assumed, as she did, that the bills and the uncertainty of her survival was too much for them to bear. If it wasn't for her benefactor, Mr. Wellington, she'd probably have died in infancy. But thanks to him she lived, and for that reason, she was eternally grateful he'd footed the bills for her medical care.

She placed the last piece of construction paper into its proper box and shut the lid. Gazing around her classroom, memories of smiling faces, laughter, and vivacious young people filled her thoughts. The innocence and intelligence of youth amazed her daily. Guiding these young children along the path to adulthood was a privilege.

She finished closing up her classroom and turned off the light. The sound of her door shutting in the empty building resonated with an echo. It seemed she was the last one to leave. She could understand the other teachers desire to start their summer vacation. They had families and plans. As she opened the door to the teacher's parking lot, she inhaled the warm spring air and once again lifted her eyes heavenward. The splendor of another day would always be special.

Eve drove out of the parking lot and headed across

the Zumbro River to the food co-op where she could obtain the organic foods and produce her physicians required her to eat. She hadn't been sick in years, and according to her doctors, the disease was being held at bay, partly because she exercised and ate right. But the fear was always there. She trembled at the thought of becoming ill again. Not that she could actually recollect most of the time she'd spent in the hospital. The doctors had kept her sedated to help her deal with the illness— an illness they claimed she'd beaten. Cancer was such a devastating disease. She'd done her research and even though her cancer was extremely rare and there was no documentation currently on the web, she'd researched similar illnesses. Unfortunately, the recidivism rate wasn't in her favor. So, she followed the doctors' directions to the letter. She ate right, exercised daily, and had found meditation helped to relieve a bit of the anxiety exercise didn't eradicate.

When she entered the store, she gave her normal smile and wave to the cashiers. Grabbing a buggy from the long line, she spun through the produce section and grabbed what she needed. Standing in front of the butcher case, she examined the fresh Alaskan salmon. Baked and kissed with crème fresh and dill, they would be delicious. As she waited for her turn, she felt a presence beside her. She shifted and glanced to her right and blinked. No, she wasn't hallucinating. A striking man glared at the salmon as if it had insulted him. He had sandy blond hair with a reddish hue, blue eyes and the type of peaches and cream skin every woman dreams about and very few were gifted with—all of that and a face with features that could have graced a magazine ad. His lean build towered over her five feet six inches— when she wasn't wearing her heels. Eve pulled her gaze back to the salmon with some difficulty. Men this handsome didn't frequent her little slice of Minnesota, or if they did, she hadn't seen them.

Today had been a field day for the school, so she was wearing a pair of tennis shoes and blue jean capris with her school polo. Her hair was pulled back in a high ponytail. Usually she looked more professional and for some reason that was important at the moment.

"Who was next?" Terry, the regular butcher behind the meat counter, almost shouted the question.

All eyes turned toward the handsome stranger beside her.

He glanced up and did a double take at the female crowd. He swung his attention back to Terry. "I have a few questions, if you don't mind."

Oh, dear God in heaven. The rich, dark timber of an Irish brogue rolled from Mr. Magazine Model. Eve melted—as did the five other women who'd been drawn to the meat case. Eve doubted they *all* wanted to buy salmon.

The delicious looking man pointed at the fish. "Can I fry this?"

Terry's eyes popped open. "Fry it? As in pan fry or deep fry?"

He cocked his head, frowned, and looked back at the fish. "Coated and crispy served with malt vinegar. Or should I get the white fish?" He crossed his arms in front of him. "I'm longing for some fish and chips, a little taste from the other side of the ocean. I have the chips covered, and the malt vinegar, but I'm afraid I didn't pay attention to which fish I needed."

"I'd suggest the cod or halibut if you're going to fry the fish." Terry pointed over the display. "Frying the salmon would ruin its natural flavor."

"I'll take a healthy portion of whichever you think is best. I'm afraid up until now, my cooking repertoire has been limited to frozen food or frying. My work usually has me traveling, and I rarely cook at home. I have created some memorable kitchen disasters when I ended up in the same spot for an extended period."

"So, you're here for a while?" Terry pulled a huge fillet of cod from the cooler and portioned it into fillets.

"For the foreseeable future. I've been reassigned to Rochester."

She stood silently beside him and snuck peeks when he turned to watch Terry.

"Well, I hope you enjoy your stay in our fair city." Terry handed him the white paper wrapped bundle of fish. He turned to her and she stammered for a moment, finally rebooting her non-functioning brain before she gave Terry her order. She turned and smiled at the sexy man next to her. Admittedly, it was a way of getting one final look at his strong shoulders and broad chest. She felt herself blush.

The man's eyes scanned her from head to toe before he nodded at Terry and turned away.

She followed his progress toward the front of the store until Terry's voice interrupted, "Eve, you taking this or not?"

CHAPTER 3

S he jumped and swung back to the counter. The blush she had felt earlier was nothing compared to the torrid heat that flushed her face now. At least three other women had that smug 'I know what you were thinking' look on their faces. Perhaps they did. She smiled at Terry, took her package, and made haste back to her basket. By the time she returned to her apartment, she'd convinced herself that the tall Irishman wasn't a Celtic god come to earth, although his body was heavenly. She stopped in her tracks halfway to her apartment door, dropped her head back, and stared at the afternoon sky. She did not just think that. She drew a deep breath and sighed. She sounded like the romance novels she read. The shifters, the fae, the delicious vampires, warlocks, and even the intergalactic warriors, now had a face. Lord have mercy, she'd fallen over the edge. Perhaps it was time to put the Kindle away.

She juggled her groceries, purse and keys. The apartment door across the hall opened, startling her.

"Well now, are you stalking me, lass, or can I chalk this up to a coincidence?" Her Irishman put his hands on his denim clad hips and raised his eyebrows.

She stood speechless.

The apartment across from her had been vacant for almost a year. Rent in this building was almost prohibitive. Had she not had the bank account set up by her benefactor, she wouldn't have been able to afford to buy the one she lived in.

"Do you need some help?"

His question startled her into action.

"No, thank you very much. I, ahh... I have this." She had it. *Really. Kinda.* Her hands shook from the strain of the weight of her grocery bags as she reached for the apartment lock with her key. Damn her for trying to get everything in one trip. It was the almond milk, potatoes, beets and squash. They weighed a ton.

"My name's Dolan. It appears I'm your new neighbor."

The heavy weight of her shopping bags suddenly disappeared. His large hands easily held the straps of the canvas bags off her shoulders.

"Oh! Ah, thank you. I'm Eve. Eve Salutem."

"Have you lived here long?" He nodded at her apartment.

"Oh, in the building?" Of course, in the building. God, she was acting like one of her students. His eyebrows raised and he nodded. She adjusted the keys in her hand. "For awhile now. I was able to buy it. I don't rent." She shook her head at her ridiculous flush of nonsensical words. "I meant to say that, yes, I've lived here since I started college."

"Pricy digs for a college student."

"Yeah, that's true. My benefactor purchased it for me. Otherwise, on my teacher's salary, I'd be living in something much more modest."

"Benefactor?"

"Long story but suffice it to say Mr. Wellington is a saint who has been a constant blessing to me."

"Indeed. It is good to have kind people in your life."

"Right?" She unlocked her door then extended her hand for the grocery bags.

HE RETURNED the canvas shopping bags and smiled politely. "It was good to meet you, Eve. Have a nice evening."

"Nice to meet you, too." She watched as he unlocked his door and slipped into his apartment. Oh, my, he was spectacular. She shook her head and scurried into her apartment before someone caught her imitation of a statue.

Curiosity about her new neighbor thrummed through her long after she'd put away her groceries. Her nightly run on her treadmill didn't alleviate the case of the snoops she'd suddenly developed. She showered and came up with a spectacularly silly idea. She prepared a double portion of fish, cooked her brown rice with the aromatics, prepared the red and yellow beet salad, and set another place at her small table. Well, what was the worst that could happen? She was being neighborly, right? It was still relatively early, maybe he hadn't started his own dinner.

Lord, was she really considering doing this? She spun and leaned against the counter of the kitchen. There was a reason she didn't date, but this wasn't dating. It was being neighborly. She could offer friendship. It was the right thing to do and she'd sworn an oath to herself she'd always do the right thing. Be the type of person everyone should be–kind, empathetic, loving.

Memories of the doctors who weren't nice, who didn't seem to care if the treatments hurt, would always sway her to be the best person she could be. It was wrong of her to consider her saviors cruel, but a few of them... she shuddered and rubbed her arms. Sometimes at night, the earliest memories she had of life growing up like some kind of exhibit in a sterile hospital room made of glass walls still terrified her. They were probably magnified by childhood fears because everyone who had come into contact with her wore self-contained, hazmat suits. All she'd ever seen were people's eyes above their oxygen masks, and truth be told, she still found those orange suits scary. The medical personnel had said it was to protect her, that her immune system was so compromised even the common cold could have killed her, but yes, the memories of those doctors would always send her anxiety to a new level.

No, kindness *was not* overrated. She checked the fish. Dinner would be ready in five minutes. It was time to bite the bullet and invite him over. She wiped her hands on her jeans. Why was she so nervous? It was a simple matter knocking on his door. If there was some way to determine he'd already eaten, she'd just apologize and leave. If not, she'd invite him over for dinner. It was the neighborly thing to do. Those words repeated on a continuous loop through her head, bolstering her and edging her toward the front door. She stopped on the way out her door and glanced at her reflection in the mirror. She made a face and rolled her eyes. There was nothing impressive about her. *No, no, no.* This wasn't about impressing the neighbor. This was about welcoming him and being neighborly. She drew a deep breath, grabbed the handle of her front door, and yanked it open.

THANATOS LEANED back against the expensive leather couch. His computer sitting on the coffee table in front of him was split into six screens. He had a clear view of the parking lot, both apartment building entrances, the hallway outside his door, her living room and kitchen. The tiny cameras would never be found. They had been installed for her safety, *if* she was an innocent. The fact she knew of Wellington led him to believe she wasn't. She'd obviously been paid, and paid well, for her services. Hearing her describe that disgusting excuse of a human as a saint and a blessing? His gut tightened. God, he'd wanted her to be innocent. He'd watched her for days now and had hoped the woman was legit. However, people never ceased to confirm his belief in the worst of humanity. If she was in bed with Wellington, the camera footage and his surveillance would document her duplicity.

He'd studied the material Guardian had provided. The woman had no past. Her future was predicated upon a stolen identity. Granted, her big hazel eyes and friendly smile were disarming, but it wouldn't be the first time an assignment had used subterfuge. His eyes landed on the computer again. The woman was in the kitchen. He leaned forward. It appeared she was talking to herself. Nothing audible, but she was having a conversation at least mentally. He watched as she moved toward the front door and then stilled. She put her hands on her hips and dropped her head back, staring at the ceiling. Her arms went up in the air and then through her hair. She spun and walked back to the kitchen checking whatever she had in the oven. Once again, she walked into the front room of her apartment. She headed to the front hall and then stopped in front of the mirror. He chuckled at the face she made at herself. Suddenly she spun on her heel and jerked the front door open. She marched across the corridor and... yep, the sound of his doorbell rippled through his apartment. He carefully lowered the lid of his computer, putting the equipment to sleep. Rising from the couch, he turned on the lamp and made his way to the front door.

She smiled hesitantly at him. "Hey."

"Hello."

"Hi... crap, I said that already, didn't I? Okay, well, I know it can't be easy being in a new city. Would you like to have dinner with me tonight? I made tuna." She shifted her weight from one foot to the other drawing his attention downward to her bare feet. She was wearing blue jeans and a thin cotton top. She was a tight little package; he'd give her that. Attractive in an all-natural kind of way. The typical girl next door, right down to the ponytail she had swept her hair into.

She lifted her hand and rubbed the back of her neck before she looked up at him. "If you haven't had dinner yet, I made enough for two. It isn't fancy, but…"

Indeed, he could smell the delicious aroma that drifted from her apartment. He leaned against the door-jamb and crossed his arms. Was the invitation legitimate? *Doubtful.* More likely a ruse to work some private agenda born from her association with Wellington, or simply an opening to solicit sex. Women liked to play games. *You don't want to dance with the devil, little girl.* He knew the steps, orchestrated the music, and had built the dance floor. Maneuvering her into the position he needed her to be in would be child's play, if or when the time for such manipulation came. Lucky for her, it wasn't now.

"Thank you for your invitation, but I believe I'll decline."

Surprise and a touch of hurt flashed across her expression. "Oh. Okay. Well, welcome to the neighbor-hood, and I'm sorry I bothered you."

"No problem." He kept his features blank. Silence stretched between.

She motioned toward her open door. "Yeah… Okay… Well, if you ever need anything." She turned an inter-esting shade of red as she backed away from his door. The woman spun and raced into her apartment, quickly pulling her door shut.

Thanatos closed his own door and strode back to his computer, flipping the lid up and waking the screens. He watched her reaction to his measured, deliberate rebuff. She leaned against her apartment door, dropped her head into her hands and stayed there for several minutes. He clicked on the camera that held her image.

Was she... crying?

He zoomed in as she wiped tears from her cheeks and straightened her shoulders. Well, fuck him standing. It would appear her invitation hadn't been subterfuge. Had his refusal of her invitation actually hurt her? What an interesting... anomaly.

He could count on ten fingers the people he trusted. Only recently had he extended his trust to some of the significant others of his fellow Shadows. This woman he currently monitored reminded him a little bit of Lycos' woman. Not physically, but both women exuded an aura of innocence. He knew and understood Bethanie's past. If what he had been told about Eve's past was true? Then that fringe of fear he detected could very well be real. Unfortunately, trust was a hard thing for him to extend. A very hard thing. This woman, Eve, could very well be sexually frustrated by his rebuff rather than hurt. Regardless, her feelings weren't his concern. His assignment wasn't to coddle the woman.

He animated all six screens and leaned back, watching the building for a moment. Eve moved to the kitchen and removed the meal from her oven. She carefully partitioned a portion of her meal onto a plate and sat at the small table to eat. He watched as she pulled a notebook out of a drawer in the kitchen and wrote in it, before cleaning her kitchen. She put the leftover food into plastic containers and then placed them in the refrigerator. She turned off the light and stopped in the living room to pick up… was that a computer, a small tablet perhaps? He enlarged the screen and then chuckled. An e-reader. He watched as she turned off the light and headed back to where her bedroom and bathroom were located. He'd refrained from monitoring her private areas as there was no way to enter them without his cameras recording the access points. Violating her privacy wasn't necessary to obtain the information he required.

Once he was satisfied she'd settled for the evening, he accessed his dead drop Shadow account. Routinely, his handlers, and for that matter some of the Shadows he worked with, would drop a draft into the account. There were two currently waiting for him. He clicked on the first.

*Uptick in DarkNet chatter. Interest in vault material. Bounty on medical personnel who were believed to work at vault. Anticipate continued interest from competitors. Information provided by target cannot be validated **or** dismissed as inaccurate. Parameters of assignment modified to authorize emergency actions if necessary.*

He read the paragraph several times. His handlers couldn't validate Wellington's statements, nor could they dismiss it. The woman would need to be the source of information. At this point, that Wellington's "competitors" had not found the vault, nor any personnel connected to it, was good. He had time to monitor the woman. He deleted the draft and clicked on an alias email account he'd built to communicate with the unsavory assets he used to help track the bastard who'd killed his parents. The only email in the account read:

DNA samples from new sources available. Running the sample obtained by the police against new sources. Will contact when/if progress is made.

Thanatos leaned back and stared at the email. It was the first indication in years of movement on his parents' murder case. He had exhausted every avenue to find their murderer, the man that had taken his parents and obliterated his innocence. With the new ancestry DNA programs available to the general public, Thanatos had reached out to a contact within Guardian. Several cold cases had been reopened due to the popularity and access to the DNA. Nobody read the entire privacy statement the vendors meticulously wove around the gaping holes in their intent to provide privacy. Access to the new DNA samples provided a small glimmer of hope.

He reached forward to close out of the email program when he saw a new draft pop into the Shadow account. He double clicked immediately.

You once helped me, now I'm returning the favor. I have searched every platform available to obtain information on your current assignment. The facts have been forwarded to my husband and his associates. The rumors, whispers, and holes in data I will leave with you. Delete the files attached and use our program to wipe your system so they cannot be re-created. If you ever need me, I'm always watching.

This communication could only have come from Bengal's woman, one of the ten people he trusted completely. The files attached were nothing, and yet everything. Medical records indicating a test subject. Well, calling the documentation medical records was a stretch. It appeared Jewell had patch-worked various memorandums and deleted files, and extrapolated connections in random emails. The way the woman's mind worked was phenomenal. If he followed the breadcrumbs as she had, a physician's group funded by a Wellington shell company had been very busy. The records attached dated back to the early nineties. There were pictures of microfiche documentation and photocopies of other electronic files. How Bengal's woman had obtained the information was beyond him, but shown in this manner, the documentation *could* substantiate what Wellington had told him. Eve *could* have been the test subject these people had written about—a female infant, then years later, a female adolescent. The files recorded the test subject's responses in medical jargon that meant little to him but obviously meant a lot to the medical professionals doing the research. *Unique metabolic resistance.* That term was used over and over again.

He read the information one more time before he deleted the files and used Guardian's proprietary application to wipe his system. He deleted all the drafts in his inbox and closed out his account. After a cursory check of the camera systems, he leaned back on the couch and put his feet on the coffee table.

Protection mode wasn't one he was comfortable with. Granted, he had stayed with Bethanie and Ethan while Lycos took care of a threat to his family, but that was an anomaly in his life. He'd kill anyone who went after the people he cared about, and yeah, he was a sucker for kids. Bethanie and Ethan were important to Lycos and he cared about Lycos, therefore, by extension, he cared about Bethanie and Ethan. Plus, they'd been defenseless.

Okay. Perhaps protection mode was something he was familiar with, but not comfortable with, per say. He shrugged his shoulders when he admitted that truth to himself, but being told to ingratiate himself with a subject for the purpose of protection? Well, that was... not going to happen. Not now. Perhaps before she'd admitted to knowing Wellington, he'd have followed orders and attempted to spark a casual personal relationship, but there were too many inconsistencies to assume the woman was a victim and not an accomplice.

He laced his fingers together over his stomach and closed his eyes. There was a time when he believed in the good of humanity. Long ago, he'd belonged to a family, had friends, and plans for the future. A singular act of violence had ripped that away.

THANATOS GLANCED at his vibrating phone. He glanced at his computer monitors again before he picked up the phone and leaned back.

He lifted it and swiped the face. "I find your recent habit of checking up on me tedious."

Bengal chuckled. "Suck it up buttercup."

"So eloquent."

"We all can't be Saville Row, now can we?"

He glanced down at the clothes he was wearing. He hadn't worn Saville Row in almost a month. His clothes screamed small town America. "What do you want?"

"You know why I'm calling." Bengal's voice lost all traces of levity.

"Of course, but I won't deny you your opportunity to rant."

"Rant? Well, if you insist. You were ordered to get close to that woman."

He rolled his eyes. "I've spoken with her." Not that he'd arranged the meetings that happened almost three weeks ago. The woman stayed after normal hours at school. He'd actually needed groceries that night. He'd tried to ignore her, until he couldn't. Damn it. "As my report indicated, she knows Wellington. Why am I still here?"

"Because we can't confirm she knew what Wellington was. She told you he was her benefactor and everything we've seen since she appeared validates that statement. You have disregarded orders." Bengal snapped the words at him like he was firing a weapon. Controlled, direct and deadly.

"Her innocence is... questionable." Which shined a new light on his mission.

"Her innocence or duplicity is not a factor in this situation. You have a job to perform."

"If you don't like the way I'm doing the job, pull me." The tedium of watching the woman, waiting for her to slip, could be handled by someone else.

"Not happening. Look, I understand that relationships are hard for you. I get why you don't want to go there."

Thanatos popped off the couch, his grip murderously tight on the phone. "You have no right to speak of that."

"I've read your file. I understand why you don't want to get close–"

"You *understand*? You understand what it is like to watch your mother be raped and murdered, to watch your father be sodomized and killed and then suffer the same fate yourself? You understand what it is like to wake up in a hospital, wishing you were dead? Do you understand what it is like to be admitted to a psychiatric hospital at the age of ten because the world expected you to 'get over it'? Tell me what happened in your past that would have prepared you to understand, even remotely, what I went through."

The silence over the connection held for a few seconds before Bengal cleared his throat. "I'm sorry for what you went through, my friend. I didn't mean to make light of it, but regardless of our pasts, or maybe because of them, we have jobs to do. We've expended thousands of man-hours scouring everything about Eve Salutem. Nothing, absolutely nothing, indicates she's complicit. You need to get close to her. You need to stay close. The DarkNet chatter is amping up."

"You said that last week, and the week before and if she is in fact innocent, you don't want me close to her." He was death and if she were innocent? No, there was no good in this scenario. Best to keep his distance. He paced through the living room into the kitchen and back again.

"How would you feel if this woman is innocent and something happens to her?"

"I'm watching her."

"Not close enough. You know from experience the smallest opportunity is all that is needed. Do your job, Thanatos." The words registered as what they were, a warning from one friend to another.

"Is there anything else?"

"Not at this time." The line went dead and he dropped the phone on one of the chairs in his living room on the way to the couch. He dropped into the soft leather and closed his eyes.

His father had tried to defend them, but he was no match for the predator who'd forced his way into their home. He'd been tied and gagged, but not blindfolded. He watched the man violate and kill his mother. And then... his father suffered the same fate. Sometime during the process of their deaths, he'd stopped crying. He'd stopped screaming for help. He'd gone numb, but every detail of that animal's actions was etched into his memory. For hours after his father'd stopped struggling, he watched the man clean every trace of what he had done from their home. When the man came for him, it was almost as if it was happening to someone else. Why the man left him alive, he'd never know. The police never found that monster. The only evidence the man had been in their home was a small amount of DNA they found on him when they did their rape exam.

After almost three months in a hospital, confined to a psychiatric ward, his aunt and uncle took him in. They tried to step in and be there for him, but when nightmares become reality, factions of the psyche break. Some people are better at fixing those disconnects than others.

He learned to 'fake' the correct answers. Smile when it was expected. Act normal. But internally, vengeance and images of his parents' deaths consumed him. The man who killed his family would die by his hands. It was a vow he made to himself long before he'd ever heard of Guardian.

He'd carefully crafted skills that would help him become someone who could kill without a trace. He'd worked on accents, mimicking others' voices and inflections. He'd learned how to become invisible in a crowd. He knew and understood what mannerisms drew attention and those that didn't. He never found the man, although he would look for that motherfucker until the day he died. Now, instead of revenge for himself, his sense of justice required he extract vengeance for others; the innocent, the weak, those unable to protect themselves.

The first person he'd killed was a pedophile. A judge released him due to tainted evidence. Newspapers screamed for a retrial, but where the legal system had failed, he didn't. The man died by his hands. The police arrested him on suspicion of murder. He wasn't particularly worried—simply bored. He'd spent lots of time in his cell, lying on his back and staring at the ceiling. The police did not have the physical evidence to tie him to the murder because he had learned that lesson from his parents' murderer. No, they had footage from the security camera of him entering and exiting the building around the timeframe of the murder. It was enough to hold him. That's how he met Demos.

How the man had ever known his hatred and anger could be utilized for good was beyond him, but that man and Guardian had been his salvation. Here he was, fifty-three assassinations later. Thirty-four of them by means of forced suicide. The nineteen before that he'd used various means, but the requirements of the Council dictated his skill set evolve. He, unlike his fellow assassins, listened to the dying words of those who had been condemned. Thirty-four people. *Thirty-three* events where the guilty had spewed hatred, fought their destinies, and raged against justice. The anomaly of Benjamin Wellington was beyond his ability to deny. So, twenty years and fifty-three assassinations later, he found himself on a couch in Rochester, Minnesota.

No doubt destiny, as well as his handlers, had put him in this place at this time. Now what the fuck was he going to do with it? He took a deep breath and stood up. He knew exactly what he was going to do. He would do his job, to the best of his ability, then once again escape into the shadows, where he belonged.

CHAPTER 4

E ve stopped in her tracks and groaned, "Oh, sweet heavens, no."

"What?" Lori grabbed her arm and looked past her, searching the sidewalk in front of them. "What's wrong?"

"That's him. I swear every time I leave my house, I run into him!" She turned her back on her handsome neighbor and started walking the opposite direction. She really didn't need a drink. "Come on, we can have something at my apartment."

Lori grabbed her arm and planted her feet, stopping her forward movement. "No, no, no and besides, you don't have caramel sauce. I want a caramel latte." Lori spun her back toward the coffee shop. "Come on. I'm sure you got it all wrong. You're the nicest person I know. There's nothing wrong with us going into that shop and having a cup of coffee. Besides, I want to see this guy." Lori grabbed her hand and started pulling her toward the corner shop.

Eve shook her hand but was unable to dislodge Lori's grip. She hissed, "Stop, seriously."

Lori stopped pulling and turned around. "This has been eating at you for almost a month. You *have* to talk to this guy."

"No, I really don't. I invited him to dinner. He didn't accept my invitation, Lori. Not only didn't he accept my invitation, every time I've waved at him or when I've made eye contact and smiled, he has out right ignored me. I'm not going to push myself on this guy." The man's refusal to acknowledge or talk to her was baffling. Yes, it bothered her. It hurt to be rejected so soundly.

"Well then, suck it up. Come on. I really want my caramel latte. We've been shopping all day. I'm dead on my feet, and I still have to pack for Vegas. I need my caffeine. This guy isn't going to be the reason I don't get it." Lori grabbed her arm again and proceeded to pull her into the coffee shop.

It was just her good fortune that her neighbor was in line directly in front of them. Good fortune? Not really. Lori linked her arm with hers and smiled. She mouthed 'watch this' and tapped the man on his shoulder. Oh, no. Could she just melt into the grout lines between the tile?

"Excuse me? Hey, I know you don't know me, but my name's Lori Hutchinson. My best friend here, Eve? Well, yeah, she's been feeling like shit for the last month because you totally shut her down when she was simply trying to extend a neighborly hand to someone new in the area. Now, I find it very hard to believe you have so many friends you couldn't use one more, but I guess we all have our issues. I want to see my friend here have a nice summer vacation. She's been moping around because she thinks you're pissed at her. We need to get this over with. Right now. Are you pissed at her?"

She slowly turned her head toward her friend. Her ex-friend. Her head shook from side to side but there were no words to describe the morbid embarrassment that flooded her entire body.

Her neighbor turned and examined Lori. He then looked at her and lifted a single sandy blonde eyebrow. "I'm not sure I understand why your friend would believe I'm pissed, which is a term I don't particularly like, by the way. I'm in Rochester for an indeterminate amount of time. I don't tend to socialize while on assignment. Sorry for busting your romanticized fantasy of being a good neighbor. So, if you will excuse me, ladies, I happen to be on a tight schedule this afternoon. I'd like to get my cuppa and leave." He tried to turn around, but Lori grabbed his arm. His features shifted into a mask of anger which froze both Lori and her. Lori dropped her hand from the man's arm.

Before her friend could make matters worse, she attempted to rectify the situation. "I'm very sorry for bothering you. I hope you have a nice day. If there's anything I can ever do for you, don't hesitate to ask." She grabbed Lori's arm and yanked her out of the coffee shop before anything else could be said.

"Holy smokes! That accent was amazing!" Lori jogged to keep up with her.

She spun on her friend. "That's what you're thinking? I can't believe you!" She pulled her hands through her hair and shook her head. "Why did you do that? Why would you ever think that I would be okay with you doing that?"

"Girl, that guy is a total douche. Sexy as all get out, true, but a total douche. I did you a favor by bringing his attitude to the surface. You don't need anything to do with that asshole." Lori lifted a hand as she started to speak. "Seriously, you need to let this go. The man is a total jerk."

"Look, he's probably simply a very private person, and as handsome as he is, strange women probably come on to him all the time. It must get old. I get it. I'm sure he's a nice person."

"You couldn't prove it by that douchey asshole in there." Lori pointed to the door of the coffee shop and practically yelled the words as her neighbor walked out of the door. Eve closed her eyes and groaned. This man would never, ever speak to her again.

EVE WALKED off the elevator and headed to her apartment. She'd left Lori's house after her friend had apologized for the fiftieth, or perhaps sixtieth time. The fact she still cared what her neighbor thought about her had baffled both Lori and her husband, Mark. Because of course, Mark was briefed on the entire event, to include her snubbed attempts at being friendly. Mark suggested she move, or get a boyfriend, or both, which was not helpful at all.

She shoved her key into the lock and twisted it with a force the poor mechanism didn't deserve.

"I don't believe I've ever been called a douchey asshole before."

She squinted and slowly turned toward her neighbor's voice. "I don't know how I can apologize for that. Sometimes the things that come out of her mouth." Eve dropped her hand from the lock and turned around.

The man leaned against his door with his keys dangling from his hand. His eyes traveled over her. It wasn't a sexual examination, rather she got the feeling he didn't know whether or not he could trust her words. Finally, he shrugged and straightened. He extended his hand, "Shall we try this again? My name is Dolan McDade. I've recently moved to the neighborhood. It's a pleasure to meet you."

She let out a breath she wasn't quite sure she knew she'd been holding. Extending her hand, she replied, "Eve Salutem. My last name is Latin because I was named by my doctors. I never knew my parents. And that is probably more than you ever wanted to know about me." Lord, there she went with explosive diarrhea of the mouth again. "Sorry, I ramble when I'm nervous." She smiled nervously and attempted to retract her hand, but he held it firmly in his.

"And I am obviously a douchey asshole, so we can let our quirks cancel each other out. I doubt that we'll see each other often, as my schedule is hugely erratic, but if we do, I'll make sure to speak. I hope you have a good evening, Eve." He released her hand, turned, unlocked his door, and walked through to his apartment. The door shut softly behind him. She turned and opened her own apartment. A small smile spread across her face as the weight of the disagreement slid from her shoulders.

THANATOS DROPPED his keys beside his computer and flipped open the top. He'd spent yet another day trailing Eve. The woman was the antithesis of what he'd expected and once again he questioned her duplicity. Honestly, he had no idea if she was working with Wellington or not. The hours he'd trailed her did little to persuade him she was innocent, but those same hours didn't convict her either. The six panels of the surveillance video populated the screen as soon as he woke it. He hit rewind on cameras one, two, three and four, replaying them at fast forward from the point they both left the building this morning. He scanned the screen to ensure no one cased the apartments or the streets outside. *What was that?* He clicked the mouse to start the real-time surveillance. That black van had been present yesterday, and the day before. He switched cameras, looking for an angle on the license plate. The best he could do was a partial. He jotted the information down to send to Guardian after he finished reviewing the rest of the video before he worked out.

He hung from the chin-up bar he'd installed in the apartment. Sweat streamed down his back and saturated his cotton shorts. He tensed and pulled himself up again. Each pull up built upon the last. He wasn't bulked with muscle like Lycos or Asp, but he would match his physical fitness against any Shadow or Guardian on the planet. His life and the lives of so many others depended on him being in top physical condition at all times.

His phone chirped from its perch beside his computer. He glared at it over the chin-up bar. He finished his set and dropped from the steel bar in a controlled, graceful movement. Using a kitchen towel as a rag, he wiped the sweat from his face before he lifted his phone.

"Operator Two Seven Four."

"Sunset clearance, fifth operative."

"Standby, Fifth operative."

A barked order followed his response immediately, "Standby while I switch to secure mode."

He'd checked in earlier this afternoon on a secure line. He had no idea why Bengal would be contacting him at this hour, but waited for his superior to key whatever system he was using to protect the connection. His portion of the conversation wouldn't be secure, so he needed to keep whatever he said concise and cryptic.

"I need you to listen up. I don't know what the hell is going on with you, but you were told to get close to that woman."

"What the ever-loving fuck? I can't get any closer."

"I read the transcripts of your briefs. Your monitoring is strictly arm's length with zero personal interaction and no physical threat deterrence in her domicile or daily activities. Two words. Professional. Assassin. She'd be dead before you could stop it."

"Never fucking happen." The audacity of Bengal to challenge his ability to do his job tossed a red flag in his face.

"I never thought I'd see the day when you directly disobeyed an order."

"I have not disobeyed an order."

"You have skirted the intent. Two weeks ago you were directed to make contact and to ingratiate yourself into the woman's life. Do you recall that conversation?"

"My directions were specific. I was to quote—'Get close'—end quote. I am. I'm three fucking feet away." What Bengal said was true. He was keeping a distance between himself and the woman. He didn't need personal interaction to ensure her safety.

"Then you know about the battery of tests she will be undergoing tomorrow at a private clinic on the north side of town, correct?" Bengal's sarcasm dripped from his sharp words.

"Would it matter?"

"With the amount of chatter we're monitoring on the DarkNet? Yes, it matters. Tell me you will be at her side when she goes to that appointment."

"Of course." He'd made plans for the eventuality he would need to be in her presence. He could mobilize that plan immediately without her being any the wiser.

"I'm worried about you, my friend." Bengal's words were low as if he was trying to keep them from someone else in the room.

"Explain that."

"Your attentions to other matters have become a distraction."

"I've managed them to this point." He'd never hid the fact he would continue to hunt the man who murdered his parents. That obsession had not interfered with his past missions, and would not with his current one.

"I need to be sure."

"Why?"

"We may have a familial connection on that DNA sample. Guardian has never stopped looking for the man either. I know you're tracking him on your own, but our assets are faster, and more trustworthy."

He sat back on the couch and dropped his head into his hand. Holy fuck, he was shaking. They may have a familial connection. He would finally have a solid lead on that fucking animal.

"My friend, do you know why I left the Shadows?"

Bengal's voice carried a weight of emotion Thanatos didn't want to register. The question, however, forced a response from him. "You failed a go/no-go evaluation."

"True. I did it on purpose."

That he hadn't known. "Why?"

"The most dedicated among us can lose our way, side-tracked by personal vengeance and private vendettas. I purposely failed my evaluation because if I hadn't, I would have turned into a darkness I would never have been able to find my way out of. Rarely are we afforded an opportunity to walk away from the pasts that haunt us. I forged that path through my own pain. Don't walk further into darkness, my friend. You were sent there to protect this woman. Watching her from afar only handicaps that effort. I don't care what you have to do, but assume the full mantle of the responsibility of this assignment. I'll contact you as soon as we have more information on that possible lead. But know this, no matter what we find, that vendetta will wait until this assignment is complete. That woman is the most important thing in your life at this time. Our friendship cannot stave off the repercussions of your failure to follow orders."

"You assume too much, my friend. My performance of my assignment has not been compromised in any way by the current parameters I have set. The most important thing in my life will always be avenging my parents' deaths. That fact is well-known. Do not presume to threaten me, Bengal."

There was a sigh, soft, yet audible. "My dear friend, as you know, I never threaten."

The audible click at the other end of the connection ended the conversation. He turned off his phone and tossed it onto the coffee table. His eyes fell unseeing on the computer screen. Bengal had issued a warning. Another misstep and Guardian would turn him loose. He'd never given the organization reason to do so before. His old friend was correct. Monitoring this woman had never been his priority, and although he'd made sure he knew where she was and who she was with, his attention had been focused elsewhere. A new and extremely uncomfortable feeling colored his thoughts. *Failure.* He sifted through Bengals words. It would take time to digest the rebuke. The reprimand and the emotion behind it were obviously well-intentioned. What Bengal had said about Guardian would also take time to absorb. Guardian was tracking his parents' killers. How had he not known that? The fact that the organization cared enough to devote man-hours and resources to finding their killer said a lot about the integrity of the organization. He glanced at the screen and nodded in silent agreement with Bengal. He had not done as much as he could do to ingratiate himself with this woman. That he would rectify and he would start tomorrow with her doctor's appointments. He glanced at the clock and then outside. Another hour, and it would be dark. He'd accomplish the actions necessary as the world slept.

CHAPTER 5

Eve slammed her car door shut and circled to the front of the vehicle. She wiggled her fingers through the grill of the car and found the latch to release the hood. Using the metal pole to prop the hood up, she glared down at the combustion engine and silently fumed at her lack of knowledge. She had no idea what she was even looking for, let alone be able to identify or diagnose why her vehicle wouldn't start. She glanced at her watch. No, she didn't have time for this. She'd order an Uber and deal with her vehicle after her appointments. Her anxiety and stress levels were already through the roof without having to deal with the nonworking vehicle. She'd purchased this car less than a year ago. It was supposed to be reliable. So much for truth in advertising.

"Are you having car troubles?"

Eve spun at the sound of her neighbor's voice. "So it would seem. I have no idea why I lifted the hood, other than maybe to make sure I still had a motor." She lifted her hands in exasperation and let them drop, slapping her legs. "I'm going to be late for my appointment."

The doctors were not known for their congeniality, especially if she were late, or when she had to change a scheduled an appointment. She wasn't the one paying the bills, and from what she understood, some of the doctors who worked in the clinic gave their time pro bono to help patients like her. She could understand them expecting her to be on time.

"Well then, this may be your lucky day. My work called last night, and it seems that I suddenly have nothing better to do than play chauffeur to a neighbor in distress."

She felt her eyes widen in surprise. "Oh, well, thank you? Ummm... I wouldn't want to bother you. I can grab an Uber."

He lifted the hood of her car, freed the rod propping up the metal, and closed the hood with a loud thump. "It won't be a problem at all. Besides, it's the neighborly thing to do, correct?"

She watched as one of the few smiles she'd yet seen spread across the man's face. He turned and made a motion to a huge SUV parked at the far corner of the parking lot.

She fell into step beside him as they headed toward the vehicle. "Then thank you, yes, I'd appreciate a ride, but I'd also like to reimburse you for the gas. My appointment is on the north side of the city. It'll take at least forty-five minutes to get there."

"Well now, that is fortuitous. I was heading that direction anyway; I have a business concern in that area so I can work on that while you keep your appointments and then we can travel back together. Thank you for the offer to pay for gasoline, but perhaps you could invite me to dinner instead?" Dolan hit the fob and unlocked the doors to his vehicle. He opened the passenger side door for her and waited until she climbed into the SUV.

"Deal. Dinner tonight." Her skin tingled with heat from having Dolan's full attention on her. She felt the blush rise to her cheeks. "Really, you don't have to wait for me." She wasn't sure which battery of tests the doctors would put her through this time. It seemed to vary every time she went in. After so many years, she'd given up trying to anticipate what they would do to her. It sufficed that they kept her healthy, right? So what if she had no control over the appointments.

He smiled at her, shut her door, and walked around in front of the vehicle to climb up into his seat. "We can play it by ear. Here, enter your number and text yourself mine. I'll text you when I'm done with my business. If you're ready, I'll give you a ride. If you're not, well, there is that Uber you were talking about."

She picked up his phone and keyed in her number, sending a text to her phone. It was the first time a man had asked for her number, which was weirdly thrilling and admittedly, just a little sad.

"So, I know you said you don't have any family. How did you come to live here in Rochester?" Dolan stretched his arm over the space between their seats and placed his hand on the back of her chair, as he turned and reversed the large vehicle out of its parking spot.

"I went to college here. I'm a teacher at the elementary school, about six blocks that way. What about you? What brings you to Rochester? Wait, you gave me hints. Let me try to figure this out." She turned in her seat and examined him intently until he glanced at her.

He widened his eyes and lifted his eyebrows several times. "Go ahead. I'd like to hear your guess."

"Well, let's see. You work erratic hours, and you travel a lot." She remembered every word the man had ever said to her, his Irish accent replaying over and over in her mind.

"You are correct on both of those points, but before we get too involved in this guessing game, would it be easier to take North Broadway Avenue or jump onto US 14 and then merge onto US 52?"

"Take North Broadway Avenue. It's just past Forty-Eighth Street Northeast in a new development just west of Buckridge Park."

He nodded and made his way toward North Broadway. "You still haven't guessed what I do. Is it too tough for you?"

She narrowed her eyes at him and shrugged. "Nope. It's easy. You're a DJ for the new FM station that was just built north of the city."

"Woman, you're going to have to tell me how you came to that conclusion." He laughed as he accelerated through an intersection.

"Well, you have a very nice voice and a wonderful accent. You work erratic hours. DJs work some of the most insane hours I've ever heard of. How far off the mark was I?"

His laughter was just as amazing as his smile. It filled

the cab of the vehicle and eased the remaining tension from her shoulders. She hated the fear and anxiety brought on by her appointments. His laughter seemed to wrap itself around her and divert her from that fear.

"You're about as wrong as you can get. I work for Guardian International."

"Guardian? They're an investigative agency that works for the federal government, correct?"

She tried to remember everything she had heard or read about the organization. Guardian had been mentioned in several stories she'd read, although their role was never fully explained. She seemed to recall something about the organization being privately funded. She thought the agency was federally recognized, which was confusing to her, as well as the author of the article she'd been reading.

"I actually work for the international arm of Guardian Security. I'm here on a temporary assignment. My specialty isn't needed overseas at the moment, so I guess you can say that I've been farmed out." He shrugged. "I'm just getting a feel for the assignment I've been handed."

"You're investigating somebody?"

"Meh... more like monitoring a situation and trying to determine if there is an actual need for Guardian's services. Boring stuff, actually."

"Boring compared to your specialty?"

"Absolutely." He nodded and made eye contact, giving her a wink in the process.

"And what is your specialty?" She really liked this man, this version of her neighbor.

"I'm involved in a type of personnel management." He flicked his turn indicator to merge onto the highway.

She blinked at him and then busted out with a laugh. "You think personnel management is exciting?" The poor HR people at her school were overworked, understaffed, underpaid, and underappreciated.

He laughed along with her before he answered. "I guess. There are rare moments of intense personal satisfaction. The actions I take change the... ahhh... I guess you could say current environment for the better. That sustains me during the times when frustration and a lack of movement tie my hands."

"That's a really great way to look at it. So many people don't look for the good in what they do. I mean every job, no matter what it is, can be fulfilling."

She firmly believed that. Watching the medical staff as she grew up, she learned to care about what she did, just as the wonderful nurses, medical technicians, and doctors who had cared for her. Anxiety flared in the pit of her gut once again. The constant living in fear of the next test results was stressful. She tried desperately to live for each day, yet, inevitably the anxiety and fear seem to seep into her day, especially the closer the calendar crept toward her appointments.

"I can tell you're one of those 'the glass is half-full' type people." His comment pulled her away from her thoughts.

"Actually, I'm one of those 'the glass is overflowing' type people. I woke up this morning. I'm alive now. I'll put every bit of my energy into making sure something good happens for someone today. You know that saying, be the reason someone smiles today?"

He looked at her and shook his head as he chuckled, "I can honestly say I've never heard that before."

"Ha, well, I probably saw it on the Internet, but dang it, I thought it was a pretty darn good sentiment." Simple things to make life better. Those were things she concentrated on.

"Saving the world one person at a time?"

"Oh no. Saving the world? That's way too big for me, but sharing a smile? That I can do."

They traveled in silence for several moments before he glanced at her. "Why is a beautiful woman like you single?"

He didn't look at her, instead navigated the traffic on Broadway. If he had looked at her, the heat of the blush currently coloring her cheeks would have been even more embarrassing. She glanced out the window and stared sightlessly at the passing buildings.

"I'm sorry, obviously that was too personal. I've been told I lack tact."

She sent a quick flick of her eyes his direction. His apology seemed sincere. "The appointments you're taking me to are medical. I'm a survivor of a very unique form of cancer. So unique that the doctors haven't named it. It just has an alpha-numeric designation. BSW0237. To the best of their knowledge, my doctors believe I am the only individual to have survived the manifestations of the disease. So, it isn't that I don't want to date. I don't because I don't know when the disease will come back. The only guarantee the doctors have given me is that it *will* come back. Bringing someone into my life only to succumb to my illness again and leave them? It's not fair to them or to me. I live in fear of the day I get the notification that it's back. Some days the anxiety leaves me numb. Even at the best of times, death is front and center in my mind. I've made peace with the fact I'm going to die early. It's the waiting that is almost intolerable. So, that's why I'm not in a relationship." She wiped an errant tear from her cheek and glanced over at him. "Turnabout is fair play. Why aren't you in a relationship?"

He gripped the wheel so tightly his knuckles turned white. Perhaps she, too, had overstepped, but she was curious. He glanced at her. The hardness of his stare momentarily shocked her.

"I had a traumatic experience growing up. My mother and father were murdered in front of me. They were my entire world. I lost everything that night. I lost them and I lost who I was. I vowed I would never allow anyone to become that important again. For different reasons, it would seem, we've both surgically removed emotional attachments from our lives."

She leaned back in her seat and silently agreed with the man beside her. They rode in silence. It wasn't strained, but she appreciated the time to retreat into her own thoughts. When they got closer, she guided him to the newly constructed medical buildings and once again thanked him for a ride.

"I'll be here waiting when you come out. What I have to do won't take long. I can work on emails on my phone until you're done. I'm in no rush. Take your time." Dolan waited for her to close the door before he pulled away, slowly. Her eyes followed the vehicle until it exited the parking lot.

She walked to the double glass doors and drew a deep breath prior to opening them. Nothing she could do would change what happened today. She closed her eyes and said a word of prayer. Not for herself, but for the people who worked in the facility. Wasting prayers on herself seemed selfish. She already knew her fate.

THE PROCESS WAS THE SAME, but the faces changed, occasionally. The medical professionals asked the same questions. She provided them her journals. Her weight, calorie consumption, exercise levels, and daily health assessments like when she had headaches and anxiety attacks or any other of the maladies her physicians required her to annotate. Today, her doctors seemed distant and distracted, which was never a good sign. Her inquiries about last month's tests and blood draws were met with furrowed brows and dire expressions.

After going through her routine exams and providing the technicians with vials upon vials of blood, she sat in the examination room. Unlike past exams, she was told to leave the hospital gown on. Her skin crawled as if a thousand ants were marching over her exposed nerves. She jumped when the door opened and two physicians walked in.

She didn't wait for them to speak. "It's back, isn't it?" Her body shivered so hard her teeth chattered.

Dr. Stephanopoulos, one of the medical researchers

on her team, crossed his arms over his chest and leaned back on his heels. She spared the other doctor a glance, but she didn't recognize him.

"Indications from last month's tests are concerning. To make it simple to understand, I'd like to start combating what we believe is a resurgence."

"When?" Her eyes bounced from one stern face to the other.

"Today. Immediately." He nodded to the physician she didn't recognize. Following his gaze, she studied the man in front of her. Cold, she was so damn cold. The new doctor's clinical study of her chilled her bones further.

"Will I stay here, or will I be hospitalized?"

The new doctor shoved his hands into his lab coat pockets and narrowed his gaze at her. Doctor Stephanopoulos rubbed his jaw as he studied her. "Your benefactor would prefer you stay here. We made arrangements for overnight staff coverage so we can monitor any side effects of the new treatment."

"Can I go home after you give me the treatment?"

"We would prefer you did not. Here you have people to monitor your condition."

This was it, wasn't it? She glanced to the frosted pane of glass and imagined the world outside. It was a magnificent world, even if she wouldn't live in it much longer. She didn't want to be sequestered in a small room. She wouldn't do that again. Not yet.

"No, I'm refusing treatment."

Eve had prepared herself for this day. She wasn't going to go through the pain of the tests and the experimental treatments. This was it. She was going to die, and she was going to die on her terms. She refused to spend one more day in the hospital. When the time came and she could no longer take care of herself, she'd allow the medical institution to consume her. Not a second before.

"Excuse me?" The new doctor snapped his head her direction, biting out the words before he spun on Dr. Stephanopolous. "You said she was under control."

Under whose control? "What do you mean? You know what? Never mind. I don't care. No. I won't submit to any experimental treatment. I refuse to stay here. I refuse to lose another day of my life to this disease. I'll die on my terms, because I've lived on this disease's terms for far too long." She slid off the exam table and reached for her clothes.

"Your benefactor has decreed this line of treatment will be performed." Doctor Stephanopoulos reached for her clothes.

She jerked them back out of his grasp. "I really don't care. This is my life. Mr. Wellington has been kind, however, I say what happens to my body. I am in control of my treatment."

"Ms. Salutem, I do not believe you understand the gravity of the situation. As such, I'm deeming you incompetent of making an informed decision, and I'm afraid I must insist you remain. We'll send in orderlies to get you squared away."

Stupefied, she stared as the doctors walked out of the small exam room. She heard a click and raced to the door, pulling on the handle. Oh God, they'd locked her in the room. She beat on the door. "Help! Someone open the door!" She beat on the door again. No. No, this wasn't happening. She dressed quickly and grabbed her purse, pulling her cell phone out.

Who was she going to call? Lori and Mark had gone to Las Vegas. Her mind raced and then screeched to a halt. Dolan McDade. He was big and scary. Perhaps if he came inside looking for her? God, they couldn't keep her without her permission, could they? Incompetent of making an informed decision? In what universe?

She pulled up her text messages and found Dolan's number. She closed her eyes and hit the telephone icon. She listened to the phone ring.

"So, have you decided to call an Uber?" His voice held a hint of laughter.

"Ummm... no. I'm afraid I am having some difficulty. The doctors believe my cancer is back, but I refused treatment. They won't let me leave. When I tried, they locked me in the exam room and declared me incompetent to make a decision. They have orderlies coming to force me to submit to treatment. Dolan, I'm really scared. I don't want any treatment. If I'm going to die, I want to die on my own terms. I hate to ask you, but could you come in here?"

She could hear him moving in the background and the sounds of wind through the cell phone as he spoke, "Where are you?"

"Go in the big glass double doors. Take the hallway to the right. I'm in the second or third exam room on the right-hand side. No, it is the second exam room."

"I'll be right there."

The connection ended.

She stood with the cell phone in her hand and stared

at the closed door. In all the years she'd endured the countless tests and treatments, she'd never felt violated. She did now. Those doctors had stripped her naked and removed every vestige of humanity from her with their words. She *was* competent. She was in charge of her own treatment. Mr. Wellington had no right to dictate her treatment. There wasn't a judge or psychiatrist in the world who would tell her she was wrong.

When the door slammed open, she jumped and dropped her phone. Dolan reached for her and grabbed her hand.

"We need to move. Now."

Eve swooped down, grabbed her phone, and let Dolan pull her out of the exam room. Within four steps, two bulky men barred their path forward. Dolan stopped and pushed her behind him. He crouched, brought his hands up, and moved his weight over the balls of his feet. Terrified, she placed her hand on the small of his back, trying to keep a connection. His Irish brogue deepened with a threatening growl, "You have a choice here. Move and live, or attack and risk your lives."

It happened so quickly; she wasn't quite sure who moved first. Dolan's body jerked as he punched out a lightning quick strike to his right. A sickening snap and then crunch preceded a pain laced moan. The man dropped to his knees. She stared at the red that oozed from his cupped hands and splatted in massive droplets onto the tile below.

Dolan moved, disconnecting her hand from his body. She glanced from the injured orderly to where Dolan had dropped. Well, dropped wasn't the right description. He'd crouched low as he swept the legs out from underneath the other orderly. She watched as the man fell backwards. His arms flailed and failed to stop his backward momentum. His head hit the tile floor with a sickening thud. Dolan stood and grabbed her hand, pulling her toward the exit. She heard yelling behind them but was too terrified to turn around and look.

"Get in the truck, hurry." Dolan opened the door, lifting her up into the vehicle with a massive heave. She lunged over the center console and opened the driver's side door for him. He hopped into the vehicle, shoved the key in the ignition, turned it, and put the vehicle into gear.

Instinctively, Eve ducked when something hit the windshield. Dolan's hand pushed her further down onto the center console.

"Stay down. They're shooting at us."

The vehicle lurched underneath them, and the motor raced. Several loud claps sounded against the vehicle.

"Why are they shooting at us?" Pulled from the deepest recesses of her soul, her screamed question echoed her terror.

Dolan slammed on the brakes, propelling her onto the floorboards. "Stay down!"

The vehicle lurched forward, accelerating violently. Dolan shoved his phone in front of her. "Press and hold number five. When the operator answers tell her sunset operative five is initiating Saint protocol."

"What?" Eve fumbled with the phone but pressed and held the number as directed.

He looked down at her for a brief moment before he

snapped his eyes back to the road. "Sunset operative five initiating Saint protocol. Repeat what I said."

She didn't get a chance.

"Operator Two Seven Four."

"Ahhh... Yeah, sunset operative five is.... Ahhh... initiating Saint protocol." She listened but there was no response. "Hello?" She pulled the phone from her face and realized the connection had been terminated. "They hung up on me."

"Keep your head down."

"Where are we going?" Eve clutched Dolan's phone to her chest and tried to find a marginally comfortable arrangement of arms and legs.

"First order of business is to get out of sight. Quickly. Second, we contact my people. Third, you disappear." He glanced down at her. "Breathe."

"Breathe?" Eve dropped Dolan's phone into her lap and ran her fingers through her hair, clutching fist-fulls tight against her scalp. She pulled a gasp of air into her lungs. Oh, God. What in the world? Lifting her eyes to the man driving the massive SUV, she stared at his profile. Questions that had no answers bounced through her mind. Who was this man? What was a sunset operative? Saint protocol? How had Dolan been able to fight those two men? What had she fallen into? What was she going to do?

CHAPTER 6

Thanatos slammed the accelerator to the floor and searched his memory. What was the quickest route to the private airfield outside of Minneapolis? He called up and eliminated several of the emergency routes he'd studied when he'd been handed this assignment. Fuck him, implementing emergency protocols and her removal was the last thing he'd anticipated today.

He divided his attention between the road in front of him and the rearview mirror. So far no one had pulled up on their six. He glanced down at the woman huddled on the floor. The men who had blocked their way had been well armed but not trained. He'd snatched the second man's weapon before he extricated Eve from the building. Hell, it was a medical *research* facility. There were too many red flags to ignore. The front doors had been locked. A bullet angled to shatter the plate glass eliminated that obstacle. No staff manned the reception desk. No array of files, no computer system, no patients. The two goons had come from the far hallway near the back of the building. When he'd reentered the parking lot after making sure Eve entered the building, he'd seen two panel vans. The black one was of particular note. The license plates were already logged in the note section of his phone and the partial he'd gotten on the computer screen last night fit. A habit born of a lifetime of suspicion.

"What is that?"

He glanced at Eve. She pointed at the weapon in his hand. "This is a FNX-45 Tactical with an enhanced-capacity magazine."

"It's a... a... gun!" Eve shouted the accusation at him.

"Yes." He palmed the weapon and flipped it. The serial numbers had been removed. Chemically dissolved, not scratched out. Professionally manipulated. He glanced at the road before he thumbed the magazine out of the grip of the weapon. Fuck. Hollow point. The vehicle was armor plated, but those rounds would leave one hell of a hole in the thin outside metal. The bullet-proof windshield had stopped the rounds that had hit it, but any cop worth a damn would pull them over based on that damage alone.

"Where did you get it?"

He shot her a glance. Her stare of complete loathing was locked on the weapon. "From one of the 'orderlies' trying to keep you in the research facility."

Her mouth opened and closed several times before she said, "Research facility? No, it is a medical clinic. Please, you have to call the police. They need to make sure the doctors and technicians are okay."

"No time for that right now."

"You have to make sure they are all right. What if something happens to them? I can't live with that."

"They are fine, I assure you. Where's your phone?"

The woman's head snapped toward him. "How do you know?"

"I know. Your phone?"

God, he seemed so sure, but if anything happened to them, how would she live with the knowledge that she could have helped but didn't?

"Eve, where is your phone?"

His barked question startled her. "It is in my purse."

"May I see it?"

She unzipped the blue leather satchel and pulled out her phone, handing it to him.

"Thank you." He rolled down the driver's side window and pitched the phone out of the car.

"What the hell!"

Her shout turned into a shriek as he hit the brakes and decelerated rapidly, jerking the wheel sharply. Veering in front of a slower moving vehicle, he took the off ramp. He looked up quickly, glancing at the rearview mirror. No one was following them. He pulled into a truck stop parking lot and drove around to the back of the building. *There.* He maneuvered his SUV into a parking slot at the rear of the building. Based on the parking patterns he'd wager the vehicles parked here were the employees'.

She lifted his phone and waved it at him. "I can call 911. Why are we stopping? Where are we?"

"Do not call 911."

"But we need the police! The medical staff could be in danger. Those men were shooting guns at us!"

He glanced at her. There was a limit to what he was supposed to tell her, but fuck it, it was her life. "I'm with Guardian Security. I *am* law enforcement." Kind of. He held up a hand, forestalling whatever she was about to say. He needed a minute to ascertain what kind of surveillance, if any, was in use in the back parking area. "Stay here. Stay down. And whatever you do, do not call anyone. Are we clear?"

The woman stared at him. "What are you going to do?" Her voice was small, but he didn't detect any manic or hysteric edges.

"We need a new vehicle. We're going to borrow one."

"You're going to steal a vehicle? I can't... No, I won't be a party to breaking the law." The hysteria that had been missing before was front and center now. Fuck him.

He turned and bent down, getting in the woman's face. "Unless you'd rather be dead or held against your will for the rest of your life and used as a human lab rat, you'll be a party to whatever I tell you to be a party to. I have been sent here to protect you. I'll explain everything as soon as we're safe, but until that point, you need to listen to me. Otherwise we're both in jeopardy. Do you understand?"

Her head moved from side to side. "No. I don't understand any of this. I don't understand why anyone would shoot at us. I'm not important! I'm a schoolteacher for God's sake!"

"I have no idea if I should hand you an Academy Award for Best Actress or if you are simply the most gullible person on the face of the earth." God's truth. He had no fucking clue.

"What do you mean?" Her eyes rounded and her voice rose, hysteria edging the words.

Fine, he'd lay it out, gauge her reactions, and find a side to land on once and for all. He leaned closer and ground out the information he knew to be gospel. "That cancer those doctors said you have? It's a lie. You've been a lab rat your entire life. They use you and your super immunity to build antidotes for weapons of mass destruction. The only reason you've ever been sick is because those bastards injected you with their newly developed bio-weapons so they could use your blood to make vaccines and antidotes for their fucked up diseases. The parents you think left you? They probably don't exist. You were born as a result of some fucked up in-vitro experiment by a monster. Your blood is valuable to every motherfucking warmonger on this planet."

"No... that... that can't be true."

"Answer this. Have you ever had a cold? Have you ever caught the flu? Sniffles? Allergies? The headaches you get are from stress. Other than that, have you ever been sick except for when you were undergoing *treatments*?"

Her eyes grew large and her head once again moved from side to side. "This can't be real. It can't be."

"It is. Think about it. Think hard. While you do that, I'm going to get us a ride out of here. Stay here, stay quiet, and stay down."

If the woman didn't believe him and decided to bolt, it would only get messier. He opened the door to the SUV and exited the vehicle, scanning the area at the back of the midsized truck stop. There were no cameras except over the employee entrance. Even if the camera had a wide angle lens, the possibility of it picking them up this far away from the door was slim. *Bingo.* He glanced heavenward and chuckled. Fucking perfect. A park and ride lot sat across a small ditch from the truck stop. There was a small overhang for shelter and absolutely nothing else. No cameras, no people and several prime choices of nondescript transportation.

He sauntered across the open expanse while examining each car in the lot. He passed over the new, clean, flashy cars. The pieces of shit were dismissed as well. What was left bore examination. Three crossover SUVs and two sedans were potential targets. The blue and red colors of three of the SUVs excluded them, narrowing his focus to the sedans, one white, the other silver, both too old to have any on board GPS tracking vulnerabilities but new enough that a breakdown wasn't a major concern. He walked around the white car. The tires were almost new. Several pieces of decomposing trash had accumulated around the right front, and based on the fact there was currently no wind, the car had probably been here four days ago when a heavy storm had blown through. This was the car.

He surveyed the area one more time, ensuring he was alone and not being monitored before he got to work. Accessing the car, swapping license plates, and driving it to the rear of the truck stop took less than five minutes. He fingered the fob for the SUV and opened the back hatch. "Let's go."

Eve popped up from the floor. She swiveled around. "Where are we going?"

"To safety. Get in." He heard her scramble out of the vehicle while he unlocked the weapons storage area and pulled three cases out of the hold along with an emergency communications kit, the standard provisions kit, and a backpack full of supplies that each Guardian vehicle held. He secured the SUV and dumped everything into the back seat of the car.

He got behind the wheel and put the car into gear. They had three-quarters of a tank of gas, which would put miles between them and Rochester.

"My phone." He extended his hand to her.

She handed it to him and pulled the seatbelt across her chest, buckling in. He merged back onto the interstate and headed toward Minneapolis before he placed his call.

"Operator Two-Seven-Four."

"Sunset clearance. Fifth Operative."

"Standby." The woman's voice never wavered or changed.

"Authenticate Emerald." Bengal's voice ripped across the connection.

"Isle."

"What the fuck happened?"

"Someone tried to take her today."

"She's safe?"

"She is."

"What's the fallout?"

"Guardian's SUV is sitting behind a truck stop. The transponder is active, so you'll be able to ping it. I have most of the gear. We are in a white Ford Taurus and I'm heading to the Twin Cities for extraction."

"Plates?"

"Exchanged with another sedan in the park-and-ride where I acquired this one. I'll need a plane to take us out."

"We are working on an evacuation plan."

Which meant Guardian had intel the airfields were under surveillance or compromised.

"If we don't go by air, we'll need another vehicle."

"Understood. What is the damage to the asset?"

He glanced over at Eve who was staring holes into him. "She's shaken up but seems to be okay physically. She knows the truth."

"All of it? Does she know about you?"

"In general terms, no specifics, but she knows most of it." He swung his attention from the road to her as he spoke the words.

She mouthed, "most of it" and glared at him.

He nodded.

She closed her eyes and dropped her head into her hand, rubbing her forehead.

"How did it go down?"

"She thought she was going to a routine medical appointment. They forcibly prevented her from leaving after she refused a mandated 'treatment'. She got scared but had the wherewithal to call me. I removed her from the situation."

"Casualties?"

"None that I'm responsible for." Not that he wouldn't have loved to extinguish both of the goons who came at him, but if a death wasn't sanctioned, he wouldn't take a life... save the one bastard who he would kill no matter what. "What is my destination?"

If he wasn't getting an aircraft, he needed a marker to shoot an azimuth toward. Miles between them and the situation was the best course of action no matter the destination, but he needed to go the right direction.

"Head toward Anubis. I'll call as soon as I have specifics. Bengal out."

"Roger that." He hung up and put the phone down. It made sense to get her to the complex in South Dakota, or perhaps further west in Arizona. He had several safe houses in the States, but none in the middle of America.

"What did you mean, most of it? There's more?" The woman's voice was so low he almost didn't hear her.

He nodded his head. "Let's get to safety and then I'll tell you everything I can."

"Everything you can or everything you know?"

He swung his eyes from the road to her. "Everything I can. What I know could get you killed."

"You're not in HR, are you." It was a statement not a question.

He wouldn't confirm or deny that comment.

CHAPTER 7

E ve picked at the cracked pleather wrap on the armrest of the stolen car. "Answer this. Have you ever had a cold? Have you ever caught the flu? Sniffles? Allergies? The headaches you get are from stress. Other than that, have you ever been sick except for when you were undergoing treatments?" Dolan's words sped through her mind on a continuous loop, replaying against her memories. Could any of the atrocious accusations be true? She stared out the car window not seeing the passing landscape.

"This will hurt."

She recalled the nurse's words right before she was hooked up to the IV. She had to have been what, five or maybe six? A swell of bile rose in her throat. She'd been so sick after those treatments. So damn sick.

Then when she was ten—God, the ache in her body even now as she recalled that round of treatments. She'd lost her hair and had broken out in a full body rash of oozing sores. Her gums had bled, and she hadn't been able to eat or drink. She'd begged to know if she was dying. Only one man, the one who'd been drawing her blood every day during that treatment, had answered her. "Eventually but maybe not this time."

That man never came back. Many others did. Year after year, treatment after treatment. The nurses and doctors always wore full body suits with hoods and breathing apparatus. They told her the precautions were taken so they didn't bring any germs in her treatment area.

"I don't feel sick! Please, I don't want it!"

She squeezed her eyes shut tightly, hoping the action could stay the swelling memories. To this day her heart pounded, and her body was crushed by the relentless pressure that bore down on her whenever the doctors had told her she needed more treatment. Her damn thoughts pushed past her weak attempt to block them and focused on that year. The year she turned seventeen.

The doctors told her she would undergo a new therapy. Back-to-back drugs administered in rapid succession. She'd almost died once during the administration of the medication, or at least one of the doctors had told her she had. Crushed by sickness, sometimes she prayed for death, for a release from the agony. That horrific, fragmented nightmare cleared slowly over the course of a few months. It was only a few weeks after her hair had started to grow back when she was notified that she'd been approved to be released. Granted, she would be tied to the doctors by tests and constant monitoring, but she was being allowed to live alone outside a hospital setting as long as she followed the rules dictated by her doctors.

Their speed slowed suddenly. She shot upright in her seat and searched the horizon before whipping her head to the rear, looking for what caused the change in speed.

"We need gas." Dolan nodded his head toward the exit marker and the tall neon sign rising above the trees.

"Where are we?" She looked for a city marker.

"Mankato. We'll gas up here and head to Interstate 90 and go west."

"To where?"

"Not sure right now. My associates will be calling back with our destination."

"I don't understand why we can't just go to the police."

"It is simple really." The man shrugged and pulled into the gas station. "Do you need to use the restroom?"

What? "You'll let me go in, alone?"

"Of course. Look, as I see it, you have two choices, one, you stick with me and you live as a free woman or two, you go find the police; they enter your name into a system, any system, and the target on your back shines like a beacon for the people who want to take you. Will those people kill you?" He shrugged. "I suppose, eventually. I figure some stupid bastard will shoot you up with too many combinations of chemicals or diseases and finally kill you, but until that happens, you'll exist as a lab rat for the worst of humanity to experiment on."

She shivered at his callous, chilling words, so casually thrown out as if to slap her in the face with her past.

He shrugged and opened the driver's side door but didn't get out. "Make a choice. Me or them. It's no skin off my nose if you leave. In fact, it would be easier for me to just drive away and disappear. Chew on that while you go freshen up. Oh, and if you decide to stay with me, grab me a Coke, would you?" He placed a twenty-dollar bill on the seat and got out without a backward glance.

She picked up the money and slid out of the passenger seat, closing the door quietly behind her. Her life had become surreal, as if she was living in a hallucination. Everyone around her scurried and rushed around, but her movements were slow. Her feet felt as if they were moving through wet cement. The fluorescent lights inside the gas station stripped the interior of any warmth, just like the lights in the medical facility used to strip any hope of warmth from the rooms where she'd lived. Antiseptic cleaning solution assaulted her nose when she pushed open the bathroom door. Horrendous in familiarity, the stench threw her back to that facility. Automatic movements sent her toward the sink. She turned on the faucet and held her cold hands under the warm water. She watched the water pour over her hands, the swirling bubbles over her cupped hands and wrists warmed her skin, but the heat could never melt the frozen center of her soul.

"Are you all right, hun?"

"Shit!" Water flew everywhere, some landing on the elderly lady who'd spoken. "Oh, I'm so sorry." Eve grabbed the sink and drew a deep breath. She cringed. Water ran down the woman's cheek and neck and spread in a wet splotch along the neck of her shirt. She spun and cranked the handle on the paper towel dispenser, handing the woman a foot-long piece of white paper.

"I'm so sorry."

"It's quite all right, really. I needed a good spritzing. It's so hot out there today." The woman patted her face with the towel and smiled.

"I was lost in thought. I'm so sorry."

"No need to apologize again. I noticed you weren't with us, but I was more concerned about the tears. Are you okay? Do you need help?"

"Tears?" She whipped her eyes to the mirror. Damn. Her eyes were red and swollen. She swiped her cheeks and tried to laugh. A poor imitation even to her ears. God, she'd been crying? "Ah... no, not tears. This is... allergies."

The woman leaned back and narrowed her eyes. "In the middle of summer?"

"Oh, yeah. Definitely. If you'll excuse me, I need to use the..." She pointed at one of the stalls and spun on her heel. Plausible, right? Allergies in the middle of summer. Hell, who knew?

She used the facilities and waited until she knew she was alone in the restroom before she emerged, rewashed her hands and headed out to the front of the station. The woman who spoke to her was near the drink cooler when she came out. Eve plastered on a smile and grabbed a Coke for Dolan, a bottle of water for her, and because she was starving, she grabbed two protein bars on the way to the register.

She paid and hustled out of the store only to freeze on the sidewalk. The white car wasn't at the gas pump. She twisted to the right and then to the left. Oh, thank god. He'd parked in front of the convenience store. Dolan leaned against the car, his legs crossed as well as his arms. She hurried over to him.

"Was it that difficult of a decision?"

"What? No, there was never any choice. I was always going with you."

"Then why were you in there for over twenty-five minutes?" He took the soda she offered him.

"I... I was working through some things. This old lady asked me if I was in trouble. She told me I was crying. I didn't even realize..." She looked down at the water bottle and protein bars in her hands. They were shaking. "Why me?"

Dolan stood and put a finger under her chin, forcing her to meet his eyes. "Let me give you some words of wisdom, words a friend of mine gave me a long time ago. Bad shit happens to good people. There is no reason for it, no predestination, no fickle finger of fate. You aren't cursed and bad luck doesn't exist. Bad shit happens to good people. It just does. Believe that and all the noise goes away."

She nodded. "Simple in theory."

"It took me a while to internalize it, but it works." He nodded toward the vehicle.

She walked around the car and got in. "Is your friend a shrink?"

He threw back his head and laughed. "He probably should be. He's worked with some pretty damaged people."

"Damaged?"

Dolan's laughter faded. "Yeah."

"You like this guy." She could sense he'd loosened a

bit, softened maybe, when he spoke of the man. "Was he the one you talked to on the phone?"

"Oh, hell no. Demos and I met over twenty years ago. I've seen him three times since then, but he was the one that believed in me when no one else had a reason to." He shrugged. "I guess you could say he made a positive impact on my life. He was the one who recruited me into Guardian."

The car accelerated under them. She felt him turn onto the road. She opened a protein bar and handed it to him before opening the other for herself. "You are not in human resources, are you?"

He took a bite of the bar. "No." He said the word around the food in his mouth.

"What do you do?"

He shook his head. "It's complicated."

She glanced around the little two-lane road. They seemed to be the only car for miles. "We have time. Explain it to me."

He glanced at her and lifted an eyebrow. Those gorgeous blue eyes sent her a sharp look. "Let me rephrase that. It's complicated and classified."

Whoa. She never considered that. He was government, well, sort of... Guardian was federal...ish. She took a bite of her bar. "Classified?"

He nodded and took another huge bite, rolling down the wrapper first. Whoa, almost all of his was gone with that bite.

She chewed her sawdust and peanut butter flavored protein bar before she asked, "Like secret agent classified? X-Files or James Bond-type classified?"

Dolan chuckled and shook his head before he took a drink of his soda. He put the bottle back in the cup holder. "Like, I'm-not-saying-anything-more-about-it classified. The questions you have regarding my employment are irrelevant. Your involvement in this situation, however, bears examination."

"My involvement? You mean being threatened back there?"

"No. Specifically, how much have you profited from your involvement with Wellington? Are you really so damn naïve you had no idea you were being used, or are you part of the organization that manufactured and profited from bio-weapons that could literally wipe humans from the planet?"

"You think I was knowingly involved? You think I made money from... from..." Her shriek was sharp even to her own ears, but how could he believe she'd be a party to hurting anyone? "I couldn't! Life is a sacred gift!"

"Really? Excuse me if I find that hard to believe. You never once wondered why someone would spend millions of dollars to keep you alive?"

"He... they said he was doing it because he lost someone to the disease." Her body was shaking. She hugged herself, looking for warmth.

His eyes narrowed and he threw her a sidelong glance before he shrugged. "As I said, I don't have to decide your guilt or innocence, but I'd be a fool not to ask those questions."

"You think because I didn't ask those questions I'm a fool? Is there no room in your cynical brain for the possibility I'm innocent? That maybe I am the victim in all this? I didn't know. I didn't."

He snorted. "I've thought of little else since I was assigned your case. I'm not sure whether you're an angel or you've aligned yourself with the devil."

She blinked up at him. "What? Why would you say that?"

"Because I'm not afraid to ask the hard questions."

She dropped her head back against the headrest and started to laugh. His comment and the suspicion and mistrust it revealed wasn't funny. God, it so wasn't funny, and she wasn't sure when the laughter turned into tears, but when they came again, she couldn't stop them. She cried to purge the pain, the lies, the loneliness, and the shattered perceptions of what and who she was. If only the trauma his words and accusations had caused could melt into teardrops and be flushed away.

She didn't know he'd pulled over until he unfastened her seatbelt. His arms wrapped around her, and he pulled her into the seat with him. She grabbed his shirt and fisted it tight. It was instinctual to cling to him. Her grasp on the material would keep her grounded, keep her from losing her mind. Wouldn't it?

CHAPTER 8

I dling on the side of the road was exactly where he didn't want to be, it was too precarious. His focus split between the rearview mirror and the stretch of road ahead of them. He'd had to stop. The woman had been losing it. Her misplaced rush of laughter turned hysterical and then she dove over the cliff headfirst into an emotional breakdown. He spared a second to glance down at her. Hell, a leech had nothing on this woman. She'd affixed herself to him and had a death grip on his shirt. Her tears had saturated the material, but at least she'd stopped sobbing. Hiccupping breaths and shivers indicated she was winding down. He stilled the hand that had been rubbing her arm. The need to comfort her grated against his need to remain distant. He patted her arm to get her attention. "We need to get back on the road."

She sniffed and nodded but didn't release the strangle-hold she had on his shirt.

Trying again, he added, "I can't drive with you in my lap."

Other possibilities about what he could do with her in his lap flitted through his mind, but he shut down those inappropriate urges with emphasis. The woman was a hot mess—at least mentally. The physical packaging was perfect but as far as psychologically? Hell, the woman had been devastated. He needed to focus on her extraction and nothing more. He wasn't a total barbarian, although some would argue that point. He rolled his eyes and checked the road again.

He rubbed her arm again and squeezed her bicep. "You okay?"

"Mental breakdown notwithstanding, yeah." She sniffed again and her hands slowly loosened their grip on his shirt.

"Hey, what's a mental breakdown between neighbors?"

She rewarded him with a small chuff of laughter. "I don't suppose you have any tissues?"

"Look in the glovebox. If not, you can use my shirt." It was wet and wrinkled anyway. "I have another in the back." There were clothes in the backpack he'd snagged from Guardian's SUV.

She nodded and moved to her side of the car. Her hair fell in front of her face, but not before he saw the results of her breakdown. She looked at least five years older, but it was her change in personality that worried him the most, although he couldn't say why. She opened the glove box and pulled out some paper napkins.

"I couldn't do that. I... I'm not a monster. I couldn't

hurt anything...a nyone." She lifted her red rimmed eyes. "When you live expecting to die, every breath is precious, every hour numbered. I'd rather take my own life than see someone else hurt. I'm not a monster."

He stared at her and she held his eyes, meeting them with a conviction he'd rarely seen in another. His vacillation between believing she was innocent and wondering if she was connected to Wellington, profiting from the experimentation, ceased. The pieces to the dark side of the puzzle no longer fit. The woman's actions and emotional responses could no longer be molded to fit that picture. "So it would seem. Are you good to go?"

She nodded and closed the glove box.

He pulled onto the road as she blew her nose and mopped up.

This was another reason he didn't like dealing with people. Emotions sucked.

Oh, sometimes he'd let himself pretend he was normal, like when he'd stayed with Bethanie and Ethan. That time he played house with them up there on the mountain had really fucked with him. The long-term effects of that happy hiatus still rolled through him on occasion. The hope that stay had inflated inside, that even Lycos, as bitter and fucked up as he was, had found a way to live with his past and forge a way into the future, free to love and have a family, bounced around inside him like a damn balloon. As much as he pretended indifference, that hope lived on, scratching out a place somewhere near the hole that used to hold his heart.

Lycos could walk away, and he had left Guardian for Bethanie and Ethan. That option was available to Lycos, but not for him. Never for him. He pulled the image of the man who haunted him into his mind. Finding that monster is what drove him, not the distant, anemic hope of something more, of someone... No, what he was sufficed. He existed as a Shadow, a warrior, a person who associated with the unspeakable and did the unthinkable so others could live. He'd buried his soul in the graveyard along with his parents, along with any ability he once had to love. Women like Bethanie and Eve needed and deserved better than an assassin hell bent on revenge.

"I'm sorry." She blew her nose again.

He glanced over at her. "Don't be. Life dealt you a shit hand."

"It's a lot to try to understand." She pushed her hair behind her ears and leaned back against the seat, turning her head to stare out the window.

"Why don't you recline the seat a bit and see if you can rest." She had to be exhausted. Expending that amount of emotional energy would leave her drained.

She didn't say a word but dropped the seat back and curled on her side, turning away from him. He let the miles roll under them. He wasn't sure she slept the first hour, but after that, the small rhythmic puffs of air he could hear confirmed she was out. When his phone vibrated, he answered it in a hushed tone. "Go."

"Authenticate Emerald."

"Isle." He glanced at the woman next to him and switched languages, speaking in a Russian dialect both he and Bengal knew. "I'm getting itchy here. I need a destination."

"Where are you?"

"A couple hundred miles from Sioux Falls, South Dakota. Maybe less."

"Stop there. Get a hotel and get some rest. There are complications we are working."

"Define complications."

"Interested parties are no longer private entities. Several representatives from hostile nation-states, including those backed by our enemies, are actively participating. If we move any asset to your location, the movement will be noted and scrutinized. Remember, Guardian is not in the shadows here in the States. To a degree, personal security officers and investigators can legally be monitored."

"Are our comms suspect?"

"Jewell is scrambling this connection to the moon and back. Do you have the communications kit from the SUV?"

"I do."

"Next time you call in, use the phone in that kit. We've advanced in our technology. We will never again allow anyone to track us using our Sat phones." His friend referred to the way the Morales Cartel's contracted hitman had followed Fury and his woman. It had been a concern for everyone in the field.

"Am I going to the Annex?"

"No. Proceed to the Rose." The Desert Rose, the new complex in Arizona. He had an idea of the general location. Tonight with encryption on both ends of the conversation, he'd get the exact coordinates.

"Are they expecting me?"

"They will be by the time you get there. Get some sleep tonight. We'll keep watch and keep you informed."

"Understood." He made the move to hang up, but his hand stilled at Bengal's voice. "Hey, Thanatos?"

"Yes?"

"How is she?"

He glanced at the woman. She hadn't moved, but he had no doubt she was awake and listening to a conversation she, hopefully, couldn't understand. "She's broken."

"Do me a favor, my friend, show her some compassion."

"Apparently, you've confused me with someone else."

"I haven't. You care deeply."

"It's funny how you sound so sure of yourself."

"You do. I've seen it."

A low evil chuckle rumbled through his chest. "You imagine things. I care about one thing and one thing only."

"I can't believe that's true. I've seen you with Kadey. Lycos said Bethanie and Ethan adored you, and you've saved my ass too many times to count."

"My actions to protect assets contain little emotional depth. As far as Kadey, my empathy does not indicate any lasting emotional attachment, and it doesn't extend to others."

"You really do believe that, don't you?"

"Of course. I do not lie."

"No, you're very concise with your answers."

"My only goal for this mission is for it to be successfully over. I will keep her alive and try to keep her from going insane with questions and worries, but I'm not here to shower her with compassion or sit and hold her hand. I'll take her to the Rose, and I'll drop her off. That's it."

"You're pretty damn adamant and fucking wordy about that." There was a chuckle in Bengal's voice.

The bastard. Thanatos rolled his eyes. Yeah, he had stood on a fucking soap box, hadn't he? "Do you have anything else of value to add to this conversation?"

"Nah. Call me when you're set up, or sooner if you need help with all the handholding going on out there."

"Fucker." Thanatos cut the call before his so-called friend could laugh at him again.

"What language is that?"

He glanced down. "Russian, or a dialect thereof."

She lifted onto her elbow. Her eyes were still swollen from her tears, but she looked much better. "What happened to your Irish accent?"

He lifted an eyebrow. "You mean this one?" He dropped back into the familiar cadence and inflection.

"Yeah, is that accent even real?"

"As real as I am." Which wasn't a lie.

"Are you Irish?"

"Partially." Again, the truth.

"How many languages do you speak?" She sat up and lifted the seat back from its reclined position before grabbing her water bottle and drinking half of it.

He used the time she was busy to think about the question. "Five, depending on whether or not you classify different dialects as different languages, if you do, then nine. How many do you speak?"

"Ahh... one, unless you count medical terminology as another language."

He smiled at her attempt at humor. "Well, it should be one if it isn't."

"I agree. Where are we?"

"East of Sioux Falls, South Dakota. I'm going to get us a room so we can get some sleep. We'll head out again tomorrow."

"To where?"

"West, to Arizona."

"What's in Arizona?"

"A very safe, very secure location where you will be taken care of."

When she didn't say anything, he glanced at her. She seemed to have shrunk. Her eyes were wide and... terrified? He snapped his eyes to the road and cleared the area before he demanded, "What?"

"Taken care of? How are you going to take care of me? With a gun?"

He blew out an exasperated breath. "For fuck's sake, why in the hell would I go to the trouble of getting you away from them if I wanted you dead?"

"I don't know. I know almost nothing about you, and you're very good at answering questions without answering them. Why would Guardian want to protect me? You were speaking Russian, then English with no accent, and then an Irish accent, and how do I even know you're Guardian? How do I know you aren't someone worse than the people who—"

Dolan reached in his back pocket and tossed her his billfold. "Open it." It held his Guardian credentials. The ones that had been delivered to him once he arrived in Rochester. One side displayed the Guardian issued ID with his current name and the other side held a silver shield. He'd never had reason to pull his credentials before, but he was glad to have them right now. The woman was winding up for a total freak out.

"As far as why Guardian wants to protect you, well, that's kind of what we do, you know. Protect the innocent from the bastards of this world."

She met his gaze, still running her finger over the badge. "Yeah, okay. But how did Guardian find out about me? How long have you known the truth about what has been going on? Are you going to give me to the United States government, and are they going to want to experiment on me? What exactly is so special about my blood?" She threw her hands up in the air. "Pick a question, any question. I'll take an answer to any or all of them."

"Guardian found out about you exactly thirty-seven days ago."

"How?"

"You were revealed to an operative who was assigned to neutralize the bastard that was responsible for your birth, the experimentation conducted on you and the deaths of thousands of others. That operative told Guardian about you."

"Neutralized? You mean killed?"

"Yes."

"And this operative, do you know him?"

"Yes, I do." He turned his head and met her gaze. She gulped. He didn't necessarily want to tell her it was him, but he would if she asked. He wouldn't lie.

She pulled her legs up into the seat with her and wrapped her arms around her legs. It was several minutes before she asked another question. "Guardian employs people who kill other people?"

"Do you really think anyone would ever confirm an accusation like that? Besides, I fail to find the shock value in this. Every police agency in the world employs personnel who follow orders and enforce laws."

"Enforcing laws does not include assassination!"

"I disagree."

"How? How can you possibly rationalize killing another person?"

"What about the police officer who kills the madman in a crowded theater, the one who is randomly shooting people who have no way of defending themselves... is this police officer an assassin?"

"No, obviously not, but that's different."

"Really? Please explain to me how it differs?"

"He's responding to the threat, not going out and killing someone."

"The man who was responsible for your upbringing and the experimentation done on you also orchestrated the testing of his chemical weapons on thousands of men, women and children, before he sold those chemicals to people with even less morals and scruples than he had. There are mass graves where that man had the dead concealed without remorse or second thought. How is neutralizing him *not* responding to a threat?"

"A paid killer? I'm sorry... I hate the actions of that man but how is taking his life making anything better? He should be tried for his actions, punished to the full extent of the law."

An evil, bitter laugh escaped before he spat out,

"People like him don't go to court. They buy, bribe or murder their way to freedom, and if that doesn't work, they disappear only to reappear somewhere else. Laws are made and upheld by civilized people who reside in a society that demands structure. People like the man who tortured you do not understand morality or respect the laws of society."

She blinked back at him. "Tortured?"

"What would you call it?" He glanced at her. Her gaze now focused on the dash. She shook her head but didn't respond. He returned his attention to the road and let the car devour the miles.

They drove in silence for almost an hour before she cleared her throat and whispered, "Am I responsible for the deaths of all those people?"

He snapped his gaze to her. "What? Fuck, no. The man who ordered, developed and tested the biological weapons is responsible. The only thing you are responsible for is your actions. You'd never hurt anyone."

"How do you know that?" She rolled her head, her eyes meeting his.

"Because if you were different, you'd have been applauding that monster's demise rather than defending his rights. You asked me to call 911 to make sure the doctors and workers at that research facility, the same ones who wanted to conduct more experimentation on you, were all right. I bet you don't kill spiders or bugs you find in your apartment, do you? You catch them and put them outside." He'd seen her do it as he'd watched over her this last month. No, she was a good, kind-hearted, person stuck smack dab in the middle of a fucking shit-show. His belief in that had solidified as they talked.

"I couldn't hurt anyone. Ever. Life is so finite and precious. Taking a life, there is nothing, absolutely nothing that could condone that. Don't you see? I'd never... Please, you have to believe me. I didn't know."

Every instinct he'd honed over the course of his life-time fell into complete alignment. He nodded. "I believe you didn't know what was happening, but I disagree with your statement. There are horrible people in this world. People who don't deserve to draw another breath. Monsters that should be put down."

"I don't know how you can possibly think that." Her whisper floated to him.

"I know." He drew a breath and hated the truth of her statement.

CHAPTER 9

Eve stood on the balcony of the room Dolan had acquired for the night. The Sioux River gurgled and rushed past the hotel and under a brick bridge. Dolan had escorted her to the room, swept it and told her not to open the exterior door or leave until he returned. The time alone had been a godsend. She needed to sort through the wreckage the day had left in her mind and not have anyone around to witness the emotional toll the events had taken. She swiped at the tears that fell down her cheeks, tears she didn't try to stop because the attempt would be useless.

Everything she knew about her life had been a lie. With that fact placed against her past, her entire world lay in a ruined mess. If she believed Dolan, she'd never been sick. She leaned against the metal railing and stared sightlessly at the river below. Deliberately, she recalled her illnesses, starting with the last time she'd been given drugs and working, as best as she could, backwards. Just like this occasion, she'd never felt ill before the doctors determined she needed treatment. Shaking, she pushed away from the railing and went back into the hotel room, almost falling onto the small couch in the tiny living area. She held her head in her hands and forced herself to remember things she'd tried to bury. Were they injecting her with chemicals or diseases to see what her blood was doing to combat it? Had she been a living petri dish? Was she an incubator, a millennial's version of Typhoid Mary?

The radical shift made her stomach roll with waves of nausea. How could she know for sure? Had her entire life been based on lies and deception? She threaded her hands through her hair and clenched it tightly in an attempt to stop the scream that threatened to rip through every cell in her body. Her present had been violated, and her past stolen. Her future? Who knew? She'd lost her sense of direction. There was no way forward because she didn't know where she was now.

Where would she go? Would Guardian let her go? What was so special about her? Why had the doctors suddenly wanted to do more experiments? Dolan said the guy who was running the show had been eliminated. Eliminated? Try killed. Assassinated. Murdered.

She couldn't refute what Dolan had said about the man. How could she? But she didn't buy the parallel between assassination and law enforcement. She knew with every fiber of her being that killing was wrong. There was a difference between responding to a threat and seeking out a person and killing them. She'd never, ever accept that there was a reason to kill another human. Life was too precious. So very, very precious. Those who never faced their mortality probably wouldn't agree, but she knew. She understood. Taking a life was unforgivable, no matter the justification. A huff escaped at the thought. There was *no* justification for taking a life.

And yet, thousands of people had died. The man who'd manipulated her, who'd used her, had died for his sins. What about hers? What role had she played in all those deaths? If that man didn't have her, if her body hadn't adapted to the drugs so they could use that information to create newer biological agents... would thousands of innocent people still be alive?

She groaned and leaned back on the couch. Realistically, did she kill those people? No, she didn't, but would they be alive today if she hadn't existed? The quiet room provided no help in answering her question. She chewed on her thumbnail and bounced her leg, staring at the dark blue accent wall.

Removing all else, every other factor, the one thing she did know was that those people were dead because she'd lived. Even if she didn't expose those people to the poisons those monsters created, she'd been the linchpin to their death. How could she live with that knowledge?

Her head snapped to the front door. Someone had slid a card in the slot disengaging the lock. She jumped to her feet, rushed across the small room and crouched down behind the television stand.

"Eve?" Dolan called out after the door clanged shut.

"Here." She stood up in the corner of the room.

"Why were you hiding?"

Well, duh. "Because people are after me?"

He held up several bags. "I don't believe we were followed. I didn't mean to scare you by asking you not to leave. Dinner and a change of clothes for you." His accent was decidedly American now.

The thought of food made her stomach roll. She'd been too preoccupied with the questions she had about him and Guardian, and what would happen to her... no, food wasn't an option. "Thank you, I'll think I'll pass on dinner."

He set the bags down on the coffee table and crossed his arms over his chest, staring at her. "Why?"

She crossed her own arms and glared up at him. "Do I have to have a reason?"

"Yes."

"That's unreasonable."

A flash of a smile split his lips. "That's me. Unreasonable could be my middle name."

"I have no doubt. Absolutely none."

He cocked his head. "Why?"

"Why? Because you're *being* unreasonable. From the first moment I met you, you've behaved unreasonably. Is that even your real voice?" What part of this conversation wasn't he following, and why did he sound like that?

He waved one of those big hands dismissively. "All the accents are my real voice. I didn't want to attract attention, so I slipped into this one."

Wait, what? All the accents? She'd heard two.

"Now stop diverting the conversation. Why are you passing on dinner?"

She answered honestly. "Oh, because I'd be sick if I ate. How many accents do you have?" He probably wouldn't enjoy wearing her dinner.

"As many as I need, and why?"

"Why *what*?"

"Why would you be sick?"

Tenacious much? Seriously what was so important about food? "What are you, two? Is *why* the only question you know?"

"At the moment, yes."

"Infuriating. Try that for a middle name."

"I think I prefer unreasonable."

She narrowed her eyes. "I'm. Not. Hungry."

He mimicked her squint and shot back, "That's. A. Lie."

"Excuse me? I told you, I'd be sick."

"No. Tell me *why* you won't eat."

"No?" *He* wouldn't excuse *her*? What?

"Yes, no."

Aggravating, obnoxious.... Exasperated, she threw up her hands. "You're... unbelievable."

"No, unreasonable."

"For the love of... I don't want anything to eat!"

"Why?"

"Because I'll throw up!"

"Why?"

"You don't want to know why!"

"I asked you, didn't I? Tell. Me. Why." His voice elevated.

"They're all dead because of me!" She yelled, punching herself in the chest when she enunciated each word. She spun and looked up at the roof. "I'm sickened by guilt. I lived, and they died." She wrapped her arms around herself and collapsed onto the couch. She whispered those words because the weight of them was crushing her, cell-by-cell, destroying her. Oh God, her body shook, and she tried to turn away from him.

Warm, strong arms surrounded her and pulled her close. She buried her face into his chest, and for the second time today, she used him to anchor her as her thoughts constructed obscene images and screamed horrendous condemnations.

Wrapped in his warmth she pushed closer to him, closer to the strength of the man holding her. Dolan rocked slowly as he held her. She shifted, realizing she was sitting on his lap with no recollection of how she'd gotten there. She was so tired. So incredibly tired. She closed her eyes and let oblivion consume her.

THANATOS HELD Eve long after she'd fallen asleep. The sun had set, and the room slipped into darkness. She'd assumed all the weight of Wellington's sins. It was a responsibility she didn't own and yet, she grieved for the people who'd been killed. He removed his HK .45 from the holster at the small of his back and set it on the couch next to him. Shifting slightly, he pulled the leg of his jeans up over the hilt of his knife so he'd have access if needed. His fallback weapon was in the other boot. His brass knuckles were in his back pocket, a simple sweep and catch maneuver away from breaking a jaw, nose or rupturing a kidney. The room was at the end of the corridor, near the emergency exit, and if unable to leave through that door, he'd drop her to the balcony below or they'd jump into the Sioux River, although the injuries that could be sustained with that maneuver made it the absolute last choice in any scenario. He closed his eyes and let his head fall back against the wall, listening to the noises of the hotel.

Eve's hand twitched on his chest. The woman felt every emotion so deeply. When she was happy her eyes danced. Fear, regret, remorse, confusion, uncertainty; he'd seen every emotion she'd felt. Allowing her feelings to overwhelm her was reckless and costly.

She'd broken down twice today, a luxury he would never permit himself. He knew the exact day and hour he'd stopped allowing himself to genuinely feel... anything. He wouldn't have a clue how to grieve like she just had.

He wasn't defective. He *could* feel. He chose not to care when he eliminated a cancer from civil society. He chose not to feel when he memorized the horrendous crimes, learned of the atrocities inflicted on the innocent. He chose not to care when the monsters begged, bargained and cried. His lack of feeling was deliberate and necessary. If he opened himself to those emotions, others would follow, and emotions were a gateway to weaknesses he couldn't allow.

Guardian's shrinks had tested him, repeatedly. The words "sociopathic tendencies" got tossed around and then dismissed because none of the other markers were present. He was self-reflective, and meditative, and empathetic. He wasn't egocentric, nor did he fail to learn from life. Shame and remorse? If he allowed himself to feel any emotion, shame and remorse would engulf and consume him.

Eve mumbled something in her sleep but quieted. Her sleep wasn't restful or restorative. She twitched and moaned again. Her horrific day plaguing her dreams, no doubt. While he murmured quiet shushing sounds, he drew his hand up and down her back as his other arm pulled her a bit tighter. Her body stilled, slender and soft against him. She murmured something unintelligible and settled again. Once she fell back into slumber, he forced himself to stop the caress. Guardian's Sat phone vibrated beside him. He'd disposed of his phone when he'd been out earlier. The silenced device still rent the quiet with its activation. His internal debate whether or not to answer the call from his superiors lasted five seconds, and that was six seconds longer than it should have. Wasn't that a red flag of warning in and of itself? Admittedly, it was one he wasn't going to address anytime soon.

He lifted it and swiped the face. "Sunset Operative Five."

"Authenticate Emerald."

"Isle." He switched back into the Russian Dialect they'd used earlier.

Eve lifted her head from his chest. Her heavy-lidded eyes opened to slits. He wasn't sure she was actually awake. She blinked at him. "What?"

"Go back to sleep," he said, low and quiet.

"Are we okay?"

"Yes. I promise."

"Okay."

He waited for her to settle again. "Proceed." He once again spoke to Bengal in Russian.

"Did I interrupt something?"

Thanatos closed his eyes and dropped his head back again, running his hand up and down Eve's back. "No," he snapped flatly.

"Riiight. Okay, we have a clean vehicle on its way along with cover identities, credit cards and cash. The Rose has been apprised of your pending arrival. We don't know about the extent of resources the people who are after her have so we've assumed the worst. Her photo is available."

"Understood." He needed to avoid any municipality, county or state-owned traffic camera system. They were supposed to be secure, but any hacker worth their salt would be able to access the camera system and implant a program to find them. He'd watched Lycos do something similar several times. Quick and effective.

"You arrive at the Rose in three weeks."

"I only need two days." He was going to drive straight through and catch a nap if he needed one. He knew his limitations.

"We need three weeks, minimum. We'd prefer more."

"Why?"

"There are now interested parties within our own government. Our patron saint is working on defusing the chum in the waters."

"Explain."

"Documents on the DarkNet were intercepted by the CIA, who turned it over to the FBI."

Fuck him, Guardian was concealing her from the US government as well as rogue nation-states. What the hell?

"Her identity has been contained as far as we can

determine. She is being referred to as Exhibit Zero on the DarkNet."

"May I ask why she is of so much interest?"

"The white hats want to use her for medical research."

"So, she'd be a lab specimen again. The black hats?"

"Want her dead."

"Explain. The bad guys continue to make money on bio-terrorism and weapons of mass destruction. Wellington said vaccines had been made and stored, so this is a non-player."

"Unfortunately, no. Reliable information indicates the vaults storing the vaccines had been rigged to explode if opened without proper protocol. They were breached and blew, taking everyone and everything with them. According to the chatter we've intercepted, there are no copies of the documentation indicating how the vaccines were made."

He swallowed and shook his head even though Bengal couldn't see him. "She's paid enough."

"Which is why Archangel has asked the Saint to intervene. He's engaged and working the situation."

Thanatos didn't know the identity of the patron saint Bengal kept mentioning, but his best guess was the man whom the current Archangel replaced. Honestly, he didn't care who the fuck the guy was as long as he found a way to stop the feeding frenzy.

"I'm assuming you have a safe house or know of one."

"You would assume correctly." He'd head south. He had a small place in Alabama, close enough to access a city if required, far enough away to stay out of technology's electronic bull's-eye.

"Your contact will be at your current location at 0400 hours. Give him the Sat phone you're using now. Even though we are confident in our abilities with the new scrambling and encryption software, we aren't taking chances. The vehicle will have a replacement phone in the glove box. Don't activate it unless there is an emergency. Be at the Rose three weeks from today.

"What are my limitations?"

"Protecting Eve? None."

"Repeat?"

"There are no limitations. You have been coded and authorized to perform duties on American soil."

"Unusual." He'd never heard of authority being given to a Shadow operative to perform duties inside the United States.

"At this time, she is considered a priority resource. Use all means and measures to ensure her safety. Access and utilize the dead drop for updates or orders after your contact leaves."

"Affirmative."

"So, did I interrupt anything?" The laughter in the man's voice was contagious.

"Be well, my friend." He terminated the call, and after checking the time, turned his phone off. Six hours until his contact arrived. He shifted Eve slightly and waited for her to settle before he closed his eyes. Sleep was an asset at this point. One he would utilize.

CHAPTER 10

The immediate realization of an out-of-place sound woke Thanatos. His hand covered his weapon and brought it to bear on the front door of the hotel room. The door opened slowly, spreading a cascading light from the illuminated hallway.

"Well, at least you put a suppressor on the damn thing."

Thanatos eased the trigger back down and lifted his weapon from the man's chest where he had targeted it. "So, I see you're still not dead."

Eve mumbled and rolled, plastering herself against his torso.

"Did I interrupt something?" Fury shut the door behind him.

"I am fully dressed, sitting on a sofa, holding a sleeping woman who is fully dressed. Does it look like you've interrupted something?" He gathered Eve and stood. When she stirred, he shushed her and headed into the bedroom. Carefully, he lowered her onto the bed and flicked the corner of the bedspread over her. She snuggled with a pillow as he turned and exited the bedroom. He pulled the door shut behind himself.

"It has been a long time."

"Since DC."

"I understand you have a new brother-in-law." Thanatos chuckled when Fury growled.

"At least I don't have to worry about anyone messing with Jewell." Fury shrugged, dropping a backpack onto his arm. He grabbed the strap and extended it to Thanatos. "Credit cards, cash, driver's license, Social Security card, the usual things. Jewell wanted me to remind you to conceal her identity around any cameras, traffic, ATMs, even large stores. Any place that stores security footage in a cloud can be accessed."

"I have a place I can take her off the beaten path." He wasn't going to say where that place was and knew Fury wasn't going to ask.

"Did you take care of the vehicle you used to get here?"

He cast Fury an eat-shit-and-die look. "I sanitized the interior and exterior. That thing is cleaner than it was the day it rolled off the lot. It's parked in a relatively secure location where somebody will find it eventually. What am I driving now?"

"Four-wheel-drive truck. The silver three-quarter ton parked behind the building at the end by the dumpsters. It's registered in South Dakota. Behind the seat in the locked compartment, you have four other sets of license plates. There is a small armory behind the passenger seat. It has dual tanks, so stopping for gas will be at a minimum.

"You and the woman need to fall off the face of the earth. At present, the powers that be are denying any knowledge of her whereabouts. Even if they have you on camera, they won't be able to match your identity. So, ghost it, and stay that way. A minimum of two weeks, but bank on a hell of a lot longer." Fury crossed his arms over his chest and leaned back against the wall.

"Why are you involved?"

"I was available. Actually, I'm in transition. I'm moving my family to the Rose and taking over the facility."

"I thought the Shadow facility was at the Annex. That's where Anubis works. Asp is based out of that locale also."

"Don't forget Moriah. The Annex has always been intended as a training facility for normal operations, the teams, and the Personal Security Officers. We have based some Shadow operations from that location and have provided secure quarters where our kind can lie low and ensure they're not seen, but the intent of that facility was never training for Shadows. It is more or less a bunker in case a mass recall of all Shadows and executives is required."

Holy fuck, the thought of Guardian having to recall its assets and shield them... fuck, it was unthinkable. There would have to be one hell of a volatile situation in order for that to happen. Scattering to the ends of the earth would be his first instinct, not sheltering all assets together.

As far as Arizona... "The Rose will be utilized as a training facility for Shadows? Since when do we have a formalized training program?" Killing people the way they did wasn't actually a skill one sat down in a classroom to learn.

Fury shrugged. "Our former status quo is no longer. With the Fates and Stratus pushing their international agendas and our old enemies not backing down, Guardian is changing how it does business. All Shadows will be rated. Those who can, will work with teams. They'll be integrated so the teams won't know they are Shadows, but with the access they acquire as team members, they will be in a unique position, should we need to utilize their skill set."

Thanatos crossed his arms and leaned back, staring at the man he'd known for over twenty years. It was probably the most he'd ever heard come out of the man's mouth in one sitting. "Why are you telling me this? This shit's on a need-to-know basis. For the life of me, I can't think of a reason I need to know."

"I was given carte blanche to set up the Rose. Consider this an invitation to interview for a position."

"Doing what exactly? Fuck, never mind. I'm not a paper pusher, and I don't play well with others."

"Exactly why I want you." Fury lifted off the wall and palmed the doorknob. "I've taken care of the camera system for this hotel. The wires were exposed, and it's been awhile since I fucked with anything, so I did you a solid. Jewell has scrubbed the storage in the cloud. I'll see you in three weeks."

"We'll be there, and for your information, I was going to take care of that after you left and use the dead drop to ask Bengal's woman to remove us from this city. I didn't know it was you who'd be showing up."

"Keep your ass down and your eyes open. That factions within our own government want her for the same reason Wellington did is concerning—not surprising, but concerning." Fury tossed a set of keys toward him.

Thanatos snagged the keys out of the air, and the man walked out the door. He would have wiped down the doorknob, but Fury had worn leather gloves.

"What did he mean factions inside our government want me?" Eve stood in the doorway.

He'd heard her approach and knew she'd overheard Fury. Hell, he figured Fury had meant to be overheard so the woman would be aware of her situation. Just like the bastard to stir the pot and leave.

He rolled his shoulders and pocketed the keys. It took two strides to cross the room to pick up his weapon. He unscrewed the suppressor and holstered the gun. "The CIA knows of your existence. They have shared that intelligence with the FBI, which is unique and rather unbelievable. Normally, those two organizations don't communicate. Agencies within the government have decided you are a person of interest."

"A person of interest, how?" She wrapped her arms around herself. Her eyes were huge and luminous in the low light of the room.

"Well, I could sugarcoat this and tell you lies, but I won't. The foreign and domestic intelligence branches of US government want to use you. The bio-weapons developed by your benefactor Wellington, all documentation about their creation, and everyone who might have been able to recreate them, were destroyed in an explosion. Your body—specifically your blood—has become a unique resource." He grabbed the backpack and opened the top zipper.

"No. I can't do that again. The government can't make me, can they?"

"Not as long as you're in Guardian's custody. We've been ordered to disappear for a while. We'll get ready and head out."

"Where? Where can we go where the government can't track us?" Her whispered question cracked toward the end.

He removed the distance between them and placed his index finger under her chin until she looked up at him. "I know everything there is to know about disappearing. I'm damn good at it."

"Where will we go? How will we survive? I don't have any money that isn't tied to my benefactor. I even deposited my paychecks into the account he opened. God, I was so naïve." Eve lifted her chin away from his hand. "How could I have been so damn naïve?"

"Naïve? Personally, I think they preyed upon your innocence. You could only know what they told you."

"Why do you think they let me out of the hospital? Why did they let me go to college? I mean, I was thinking about that. Why didn't they just keep me locked away? I never tried to leave. I never asked to leave. Why didn't I?" She sat down on the couch they had slept on. "Shouldn't I have questioned them?" She looked up at him.

He placed his hands on his hips. "Again, they preyed

on your innocence. You accepted them as the authority figures in your life. I can understand why you never questioned them. As far as why they let you leave, I have a theory."

"And what is that?"

"I believe Wellington was impressed."

She scrubbed her face with her hands. "Why was he impressed?"

"I think he was rewarding you for not dying during the last battery of experimentation. Of course, that's only a guess and based on a lot of presumption." That, and the fact the man had indicated he was impressed with her strength. Based on what Jewell was able to obtain and the information Eve had given him, he'd bet anything Eve was rewarded for surviving with her freedom.

Not that she had actually been free. She still submitted to tests, but Wellington hadn't directed any more experimentation. Why the doctors monitoring her tried to seize her yesterday was a question that needed to be answered. He'd get that query to Bengal. If Guardian didn't have the answer, they'd find out. Leaving any stone unturned at this point would be a grievous mistake. Eve deserved to live free. That included living free from the constraints of her own government or the likes of Wellington.

Wellington's death had been too good for him. Eve's eyes widened as she stared at him unblinkingly. It was a lot to take in. Hopefully, though, they could get through the day without her breaking down again. He nodded toward the bathroom. "Go get ready for the day. There's a

change of clothes in that bag. Put your hair up and wear
the cap in the bag, please."

FLICKING the damp towel she had used to dry off around
her and tucking it in so it wouldn't slip, Eve reached into
the bag Dolan had given her, pulling out several hangers
with new underwear dangling from them. A quick scan
of the tags tinged her cheeks with a blush. He'd gotten
the sizes right. She reached back into the bag and pulled
out a large-toothed comb, several packages of hair ties,
deodorant, toothpaste, and a toothbrush. At the bottom
of the bag were two pairs of shorts, a pair of jeans, and
three shirts–two tank tops and one soft pink T-shirt. The
sizes were correct. How?

She dropped the towel and made quick time getting
ready. She gathered Dolan's purchases and carefully
stowed the hygiene items he'd been thoughtful enough to
acquire for her. She glanced at the mirror. The tan cap
with a dark brown bill concealed portions of her face.
She turned this way and that. She'd never worn a baseball cap before. Hell, there was so much she hadn't done.
So much those doctors told her she couldn't do. What she
had given up, not experienced, feared to do, all because of
the lies. Tears formed in her eyes again. No, damn it, no.
She wasn't going to be the victim any longer. She wasn't
going to be afraid to live her life. She wasn't going to let
anyone use her for any reason. She'd had enough of
people telling her what she could do, what she could eat,
how to exercise, how to live, how to fucking breathe... No,

she was done. It was time for her to take control of her life. Once and for all. She squared her shoulders and nodded at the reflection staring back at her. It was time to become a different woman. One who didn't live in fear. Before her resolve crumbled, she opened the bathroom door and stepped out into the bedroom.

Oh. My. God. Dolan stood shirtless in the small front room. He leaned over the small sink and washed his face and upper body. He glanced over his shoulder. "I'll be ready in just a second. Your new identification is over there." He turned back to his morning ablutions, ignoring her. She pulled her attention from the rippling muscles of his back to glance where he had indicated.

She sat down in the seat which would give her the best view of her neighbor turned savior. He grabbed a small hand towel and started to dry himself as she watched. The muscles of his back played underneath his skin. She could plainly see the cording ropes at his neck and the flat wide striations over his shoulders. His waist was narrow and there was a divot on each side of his spine that undulated with each movement. His arms bulked and stretched as a towel made its way across his skin. He turned sideways, revealing glimpses of his chest. She swallowed quickly and averted her eyes to the table in front of her before she got caught ogling the man.

A Georgia driver's license with her picture on it immediately piqued her interest. Evelyn Larson. Her birthdate was wrong, although her height, weight, hair color, and eye color were correct. She set the driver's license down and picked up the rest of the items. Two credit cards in Evelyn's name and a wallet with... one hundred and fifty dollars in cash. "Guardian has made us a couple."

She glanced up and nearly swallowed her tongue.

Dolan leaned against the counter by the sink. The small hand towel lay around his neck. A smattering of brown hair dusted his chest. There was a tattoo, words she couldn't distinguish, over his heart. His thick bulging arms crossed over his chest. "It'll make traveling easier."

Oh. "Okay." She licked her suddenly dry lips. "Where are we going?"

"I have a place south of here. I'll take you there." He lifted off of the counter and grabbed a plain, white t-shirt. He tossed the hand towel on the counter and pulled the t-shirt over his head. "If you're ready to go, we can head out."

"Isn't it awful early?" The clock beside the television indicated it was barely four thirty in the morning.

"Early bird gets the worm and all that shit." He laughed as he moved to his right. It was then that she noticed what was on the counter. Fear once again coiled around her stomach and tightened forming an icy knot. She watched as he clipped a holster at the small of his back, and then shoved a nasty looking handgun into it. He pulled his t-shirt over what protruded from his jeans and made his way to the couch beside her. He lifted his jeans and pulled on a pair of boots. Before he pulled his jeans down over the top of his boot, he stuck a sheathed knife down the outside of the left boot, and a smaller gun, clipped in a holster, at the top of the right.

Standing up, he stopped and ensured his jeans had dropped over his boots and the weapons before he swiped up the identification sitting next to hers. "We'll keep it simple. If anyone has any reason to ask, we were up here for a small vacation. We're heading back home."

"Who would ask?" She shivered, but not from the cold. The sight of his weapons opened the floodgates of yesterday's events.

He shoved his identification into his wallet. "Things like that come up in casual conversation. If we stop to have lunch the waitress may ask. It's good to have a few facts, otherwise, you could look suspicious. Are you ready to go?"

With the firm handhold on her bag containing her clothes, she stood and followed him across the room. "What's your name?"

"John D. Larson. That way if you slip and called me Dolan, it could be explained away as my middle name."

"Oh, the same way if you call me Eve, it's a short form of Evelyn. That makes sense." They walked down the hall together and waited for the elevator. She chewed on her bottom lip as she tried to process what had happened yesterday and anticipate what would happen today. Hopefully, she could pull herself together enough not to have another emotional breakdown. She glanced at Dolan. No, his name is John. She said the name to herself over and over again, trying to get it to take root. It was impossible. He didn't look like John. Not that she knew what a 'John' looked like. A small inappropriate laugh struggled in her throat. A John. Like she was a hooker. Good Lord, she'd watched too much television since she'd been released from the hospital, but she loved the old cop dramas. Colombo, Kojak, Beretta, Starsky and

Hutch... She was a closet retro junkie. It was her one guilty pleasure. Well, that and books.

"What's so funny?" Dolan allowed her to enter the elevator first before he got in and punched the ground floor button.

"Seriously, nothing. I think my brain may have fried a little yesterday from all the crying." She chuckled and shook her head. "I'm really sorry about all that, and I apologize for putting you through it. I'm not usually so emotional."

The door opened and Dolan dropped his arm over her shoulder. She snapped her attention up to him. The unexpected contact startled her. He leaned down and whispered in her ear, "We are a couple." He moved forward, his arm bringing her with him. They strolled across the small lobby where Dolan laid two keycards down on the counter. "Checking out of room 304."

The clerk stifled a yawn and reached for the keycards. "Was your stay okay?" The question was asked with complete and utter disinterest.

"Perfect, man. Later." Dolan started across the lobby and she fell into step with him. With his arm still over her shoulder, they walked to the back of the building and the far end of the parking lot. Dolan opened the door of a massive, silver, four-wheel-drive pickup and helped her clamber up into the cab.

She looked down at him from her unbelievably high perch. "Are we expecting a snowstorm?"

He laughed and shut the door, circling the vehicle before he got in.

He started the vehicle and it rumbled underneath

them. The headlights cut a swath into the early morning darkness. He reached over the center console to the glove box and popped it open. "Perfect." Sitting beside a phone was a leather-bound book. He grabbed both but handed the book to her before he shut the glove box and sat back up.

"What's this? Oh my god! Is this an atlas?" Opening the book, she laughed at the pages and pages of maps.

"Old school, baby. When people are tracking you with electronic devices, you go old school." He grinned at her, stretched his arm over her seat, and backed out of the parking slot.

She glanced around the cab of the vehicle. It was basic, no bells or whistles. No power windows, no electronics installed in the dash that she could see. Just an AM/FM radio. She was used to backup cameras, GPS systems, and linking her car to her phone. This was almost... stone age. "What am I supposed to do with this?" Dolan threw back his head and laughed. "You're the copilot. Navigate."

"Navigate? What? I have never been out of Rochester. While I was in Rochester, I relied on the GPS in my car. I have no idea how to read a map." She made a point of fanning through the hundreds of pages of maps. "I wouldn't even know where to start."

"Lucky for you, I know to get on I-29 south. We'll stop when we find someplace to have breakfast and I'll show you how to read a map." He reached over and patted her hand with his. "By the time we get to Auburn, you'll be an expert."

"Auburn? As in the color?" She vaguely recalled

mention of a town named Auburn, but why? Where had she heard it?

"Auburn as in Alabama. War-damn-Eagle." He glanced over at her and winked.

"I realize you're no longer speaking with an accent, but would you mind speaking English? What the hell is a war damn eagle?"

"College football? Roll Tide? Hottie toddy? Go blue? Any of those ring a bell?"

"No. I didn't go to college football games when I attended school." The humor of the moment drained quickly. "The doctors told me that my immunities may have been compromised and directed me to maintain as much distance between myself and the school population as possible.

"So you didn't go to any games? No social events? Dances, concerts?" Dolan glanced at her as he drove.

"No. I was terrified to go to classes. Those I could take online, I did." She shook her head and stared sightlessly out the passenger side window again. "There's a lot I haven't done or experienced."

"Well, hell. As long as it doesn't compromise our safety, I'll do my best to make sure you get to experience the things you haven't."

She twisted quickly in her seat. "Yeah? You'd do that for me?"

"Sure. As long as it doesn't compromise our safety or security, we can do whatever you'd like." He nodded toward the glove box. "There should be a pad of paper and a pen in there. Make a list."

"Really?"

Dolan looked at her. "I can't take you to populated areas, but within the confines and restrictions needed to make sure that you're safe, I'd be honored to help you experience some of the things you've missed. Make your list, and when we get to the diner for breakfast, you can share it with me."

She pulled out a small pad and a pen and closed the glove box. Slipping off the flip-flops Dolan had purchased her, she pulled her legs up onto the seat and tapped the pad as she thought. What did she want to do that the doctors had forbidden her to do? Well, a road trip, but that was covered. Oh! She scribbled the word on her pad of paper. As soon as the first word flowed from the pen to the page, a smile spread across her face. The ideas flourished as she listed absolutely everything she'd ever wanted to do but couldn't. She knew some were out of the question, but she wasn't going to restrict the list. Some people had a bucket list, things they wanted to do before they died. She had a life list. Things she wanted to do while she lived. The doubts and fears of yesterday rolled away like a mist. In its place, the sunrise of her life dawned.

CHAPTER 11

Thanatos pulled off the interstate. Usually, a truck stop was the best place to find a good breakfast, but truck stops had camera systems monitoring the interior and exterior. Instead, he headed in toward the small town and searched for a place to stop. At a little café, he drove around the block twice looking for any indication of a camera system, but the small Nebraska town was quaint and, from what he could see, without traffic cameras or surveillance systems.

"Oh, thank goodness. I'm starving." Eve swung a smile his direction and grabbed the road atlas and her small tablet. He watched as she shoved her feet into the leather flip-flops he had purchased for her. It was encouraging to see her so animated, especially after the events of the last twenty-four hours. Getting out of the truck, he went around to her side to help her down. She handed him the book and tablet, which he set on the running board before he reached up and grabbed her at her waist. Her hands found his shoulders. He lifted her down, slowly, her body skimming his as her toes found the ground. With a breathless voice, she asked, "Because we're a couple?"

Dolan blinked. Yeah, sure, let's go with that. "We have to keep up appearances."

He busied himself closing the truck door and handing her the items from the running board. His momentary lapse irritated the fuck out of him. Eve deserved better. She was innocent in so many ways. Innocence, integrity, truthfulness... traits his targets didn't have. Perhaps that was why he was drawn to the woman.

They walked into the diner and seated themselves. A harried waitress swung by with two coffee cups and plunked them down. "Coffee?" She held up an insulated container and looked back and forth between them.

Dolan nodded, but Eve shook her head, "May I have water, please."

"Sure, hon. Would you like some juice or milk?"

"Orange juice, please?" The woman nodded and filled his cup. She gestured with a tip of her chin. "The menus are over there with the salt and pepper shakers. Only breakfast is served now. You'll find that menu on the back page. I'll be right back with your juice and water, and grab your order."

He reached for the plastic-covered menus and handed one to Eve. It took two seconds to find what he wanted. He put his menu back. Her head popped up from behind her menu, and she bounced her eyes between him and the discarded menu. "Aren't you getting anything?"

"I'm getting a short stack of chocolate chip pancakes,

four eggs over easy, and two orders of bacon. What about you?"

She blinked at him repeatedly. "Do you know how many calories, nitrates, and cholesterol are in that meal?"

He narrowed his eyes at her. "No, and the question should be, why do you?"

She leaned back and crossed her arms over her chest. "What are you trying to say?"

"Maybe it's time to start living a little? Have you ever had chocolate chip pancakes?"

Her eyes grew huge. She shook her head. "That would be my calorie limit for the day."

"Do you like pancakes? Do you like chocolate chips?"

"Yes, but I've never had them together."

"Then you're in for a treat."

"I can't eat that."

"You can if you want to. The question is do you want to?" Watching the array of emotions flit across her expressive eyes was quite interesting. If the woman ever broke out of the confines that had been placed around her, she would be... exquisite. And there he was back in inappropriate territory.

The waitress appeared at their table again. She placed the orange juice and water down in front of Eve and pulled her order pad out of her apron. "What can I get for you?"

Thanatos gave her his order and they both looked at Eve.

Eve glanced at the waitress and shrugged. "One poached egg on dry toast. Plain yogurt, and any fresh fruit that you may have, please."

It was disappointing that she was still so cautious and refused to take the plunge, but he understood a lifetime of conditioning probably better than most would. His conditioning was self-inflicted. She had no choice. When she refused to look at him after the waitress left, he assumed it was a self-defense mechanism. She was embarrassed or afraid of what his reaction would be. So, he grabbed the atlas and opened it up to the map showing Nebraska. Together they huddled at the corner of the table as he explained how to utilize a paper map. It definitely showed the generation gap between Eve and himself. He wasn't that much older than she was. She was twenty-seven he was forty-five. He mentally rolled his eyes. He was a damn lifetime older than she was. Eighteen years difference, not to mention several lifetimes worth of experience. Hell, he could actually be her father. Didn't that just set a man on his ass?

"Oh my God, would you look at that?"

His eyes snapped toward the door. His hand grabbed the butt of his weapon, scanning for whatever threat she'd seen. It took half a second to realize that she was referring to the arrival of his breakfast. The waitress flicked a tray stand with one hand and dropped her serving tray from her shoulder onto the stand. The descriptor 'small stack' was a complete misnomer. The pancakes were the size of hubcaps and stacked five tall. There was easily a rasher of bacon on his plate along with a side of toast he didn't recall ordering. When the waitress set down Eve's plate in front of her, he'd have to admit, he felt rather gluttonous, for about two seconds... maybe. He hadn't eaten since, hell, well over twenty-four hours. He glanced at his watch. No, it was actually pushing thirty hours. He was fucking hungry, and he wasn't going to apologize for it.

"I can roll you to the truck, but fair warning, there is no way I'm going to be able to lift you into it." Eve stabbed a piece of melon with her fork and waved it at him.

He may have moaned when he called it quits on the food in front of him. He'd eaten most of it, managing one final sip of his coffee before he flagged down the waitress and paid for their meal in cash. He suggested they both use the facilities before they leave and wandered out of the small café as he waited for Eve. By his calculations, it would take another sixteen to eighteen hours to make it to his safe house. He sauntered to the ancient-looking payphone outside the café and dropped three dollars of change into the machine.

He punched the numbers into the phone. He needed to notify the elderly couple he employed to maintain his house and work its acreage of his imminent arrival. They lived in a small house at the back of the property that he provided them rent-free. Charlie and Joanne Hunt no longer did the manual labor around the property as they had once done almost twenty years ago. As they aged, he ensured they had access to enough money to make their lives easy and allow them to hire any maintenance that was required. The phone clicked several times before he heard ringing at the other end. "Hello?"

"Hi, Joanne. I'm on my way home."

"Oh! Dolan! When will you be here?" She covered the

phone with her hand but he could still hear her muffled excitement as she spoke to her husband.

"We'll be pulling in tomorrow, probably early afternoon."

"We? Did you say, we?"

"Yes, ma'am, I'll be bringing a friend with me. If you could get the guest room ready for her, I would appreciate it. Also, if you wouldn't mind making a run to town to get some food for us, I'd be grateful."

"Oh, absolutely. We needed to go into the Walmart anyway. Muffy had herself a litter of pups a couple weeks ago, and we need to get different colored collars for them so we can distinguish who gets which pup. They are all spoken for, well, except for the runt."

"Muffy is the new bitch you got a couple of years back?" Joanne raised champion bloodline German Shepherds.

"Yes, Her Royal Majesty Fredricka Von Maxwell. This is her second and probably last litter. She had problems with this one. She's a sweetheart and throws beautiful pups, but I'm not going to put her through that again. There is no reason for that type of nonsense. But anyway, I got carried away. We'll pick up groceries. How long will you be here?" The hopeful anticipation in her voice made him smile.

"Will be there at least two weeks, but plan on three."

"Oh, excellent! I can't wait to hug your face. Is there anything else you need us to do? The house is just waiting for you. I go down occasionally and dust, open the doors and let in the fresh air."

"No, ma'am. Thank you."

"Well, then we will see you tomorrow afternoon. You'll be having dinner with Charlie and me. Fried chicken, mashed potatoes, homemade bread, and butter. I'll slap a vegetable on the table because it'll make me feel better."

Her rumbling laughter forced a chuckle from him. Eve walked out of the diner and he lifted his hand at her asking for a minute. She nodded and lifted her hands into the air, stretching. God help him, his eyes devoured her. He squeezed his eyes shut and tried to tune into what Joanne was saying. "... The county is going to fix that."

"I'm sorry, I didn't catch that. What exactly is the county going to fix?" He didn't want anyone around the property.

"The access road. Remember I told you about that the last time you were here? It's taken over eighteen months, but the county has finally started out this way. They are going to grade the access road. Should be starting in about two weeks."

"Right. Yeah, I remember. Okay, look we should get back on the road. Tell Charlie I said hey and that I will see you tomorrow."

"Sure thing. Drive safely."

"Was that... ah... work?" Eve looked up at him from where she was sitting on the running board of the truck.

"No, actually I called ahead to make sure my property managers knew we would be arriving." He opened the side door and once again helped her up into the cab of the truck. And no, he didn't notice how enticing her backside was as she got in. Nor did he pause when she flashed him a megawatt smile. He didn't even think about adjusting himself when he walked around the back of the truck. Nope, none of that happened. He opened the driver's side door and hauled himself up into the cab.

"So how long until we get to where we're going? Auburn." She reached back and pulled her seatbelt across, clicking it in.

"It'll be a solid two days. We'll stop off somewhere, grab a hotel room tonight to sleep." He backed out into the street and headed to the interstate. "Okay, navigator, where we heading?"

Eve opened the atlas. She had put her pad and pen on the page where they currently were located. She glanced at the map and then at the legend at the bottom. "We're on Interstate 29 until Kansas City, then we take Interstate 70 eastbound toward St. Louis." She flipped the page and examined the map. "St. Louis is about the halfway point. Do you want to get a hotel room, there?"

He shook his head. "No, somewhere between Kansas City and St. Louis or someplace after St. Louis. My intent is to drive straight through the city as quickly as possible. While there's no reason for anyone to suspect we're in this vehicle, stopping in the city and making ourselves visible would be a mistake."

He glanced over and noticed her staring at the list she had written. "We didn't talk about the things that you'd like to do. That's quite a list you've got." The ink stretched down the page and formed three columns.

She gave a rueful laugh. "Yeah, I started just listing the things I'd like to do in the next three weeks, but I figured why limit myself, you know? So I put down everything I could think of that I would like to do. I mean I know I'll never get to do some of them because I'm not rich, and I'd have to have a lot of money to do these things, but still, the idea that if I saved I could actually do them? That's wild." Her flushed cheeks seemed to get redder as her smile widened. Her eyes danced as she lifted the notepad. "Want to hear it?"

"Absolutely. Every one of them."

She threw back her head and laughed. "Not all of them. Some of them aren't fit for members of the opposite sex."

Say what now? He pried his attention from the road and stared at her. Not the sweeping glances he had been giving her, rather his full attention. Was she talking about sex? She gave him a saucy wink and then waved a hand at him. "Watch the road, I need to live long enough to do all this stuff."

He glanced at the road ahead of him before he looked back at her. "Well then share what you feel you can."

"Okay. Well, first I want a drink." She reached over and slapped her hand on his arm. "I want a martini. No, wait, champagne. I want a glass of champagne. Does it really tickle your nose?"

"You've never had alcohol?"

She shook her head. "Nope. On the forbidden list. But not anymore!"

"Well, that's a simple one. We can do that. What else?"

"I want to go on a picnic. I want to ride a horse. When I finally get my own place, I want a cat or dog or maybe both. I want to travel, too, so maybe I'll get my pets after I travel? I don't know." Her nose scrunched as she frowned at the list in front of her.

"Where do you want to travel?"

"Oh man, where don't I want to go? Let's see..." she flipped the paper over, and he laughed when he saw another list. "Okay, the obvious places, of course."

"What are the obvious places?"

"Well, duh... Paris in the spring. Washington DC when the cherry blossoms are blooming. The East Coast during the fall. I want to see the covered bridges when the trees are turning colors. I want to see the Grand Canyon, the Great Wall of China, watch the changing of the guards at Buckingham Palace, a bullfight in Madrid, cruise the Mediterranean. Oh, wait! What about a cruise through the Panama Canal? Yeah. I want to do that too. Oh, and Alaska! I want to see Alaska and a bear, and a moose, and reindeer. I want to go to Australia, Tasmania, and New Zealand. Oh! Africa!" She jotted down another word to her paper.

"That's a hefty list." He chuckled as she hummed an agreement, still writing on the small square.

"Have you been to any of these places?" She flipped the page back to her list of things she wanted to do.

"Well, I've been to Paris in the summer and in the winter, never in the spring. I tried to avoid Washington DC at all costs, but yes, I've been there. And no, I've never looked at the cherry blossoms. I have walked on the Great Wall of China, been past Buckingham Palace, and although I've been to Spain several times, I've never been to a bullfight." He glanced at her. "You're going to have to refresh my memory on the rest of it."

She laughed and swatted at his arm. "Alaska, Australia and Africa. Oh, and the Mediterranean."

"I actually have a cabin in Alaska."

"No way! Is it like the reality TV shows? Do you have a bathroom? You know they don't on the shows, right? They have outhouses." Her eyes got huge and she shook her head. "I couldn't imagine getting out of a warm bed and walking three hundred feet in fifty below to go to the bathroom. Could you?"

Well, no. That's what chamber pots were for, but no, he wasn't going to bring that subject up either. So instead he shook his head. "Sounds very austere." And yes, he was laughing hysterically beneath the serious façade he presented her. The woman was a fucking riot.

"Yeah, that's what I thought too. What about the other places? Australia?"

He nodded his head and spoke as he passed an eighteen-wheeler that was barely going the minimum speed limit. "I've traveled extensively in Australia."

"That's so cool. Where was your favorite place? Sydney? Perth?"

"Actually, my favorite part of the country is closer to Alice Springs."

She twisted in her seat, bringing her leg up underneath her. "Where's Alice Springs? Why do you like it?"

"It's halfway between Darwin and Adelaide. It's in the middle of Australia's desert. Nothing but red dirt and blue skies. The climate is as harsh as the landscape is beautiful. The vast expanses of absolutely nothing are mesmerizing." He loved that territory. Most people didn't. They couldn't see the beauty in the barrenness. "If you've never seen the sunrise or the sunset over that majestic expanse of red dirt, then you've never seen true beauty."

"Dang it. Now I have another place I have to see." She turned the paper over and scratched the words in the very corner. "Of all the places you've traveled, which one did you like the most, and why?"

"What is this, twenty questions?" He glanced her direction and lifted an eyebrow.

"Only twenty?" She laughed and practically bounced in her seat. "Let's do a hundred, at least."

"What are the rules?"

"Ummm… If the questions are too embarrassing we can pass. That being said, no embarrassing questions. We can each decline to answer five questions. Does that sound fair?"

"With the exception of my job, I'll answer any question you ask. My job and my work for Guardian are completely off-limits."

"That's understandable. I don't believe I have anything that would be considered off-limits, but I reserve the right to use that tag."

"Fair enough. You start." He glanced up at the rearview mirror, making a mental note of the vehicles behind him.

"Okay. Favorite color and why?" She turned, so her back was leaning against the passenger side door.

He nodded at the door. "Do me a favor and make sure that door's locked." He waited until she clicked the lock down before he answered. "I've never really thought about it, but I like purple. I have no idea why, I just do. What about you? Same question."

"Gray."

He sent a quick glance in her direction. "Why gray?"

She shrugged and bit her bottom lip. "Because they told me I'd never live long enough for my hair to turn gray. Stupid, but it's the truth."

"It's not stupid, but I don't see you with gray hair. Silver, perhaps. Gray... nah."

"Why do you talk with so many accents?" She held up her hand. "Not in regards to your job, so maybe I should rephrase the question. How do you have so many accents you can call up? Oh, and which one is your real accent?"

"I learned accents when I studied people, learning their mannerisms, their inflections. The quality and measure of the words they use, and the way they use them, was a requirement for me when I was younger. Once you understand the basic manipulations of diction and have immersed yourself in the culture, it isn't difficult to pick up."

"Okay. Which one is your real one? I've heard four so far."

"Four?"

"Yes. The first was the Irish brogue. The second was the Russian dialect, although that wasn't really an accent, was it? That was a language. Then there was the way you spoke to the man in our room this morning. That accent had almost a singsong quality to it. And then the fourth is the one you're using now. Almost a southern accent, but not quite."

The woman was sharp. He'd slipped into the modulated pattern of his childhood, the same tone he used while speaking to Fury this morning. "My father was born and raised in Egypt, although not Egyptian in nationality. My grandfather was an American diplomat and raised my father and his sister in Egypt. My mother was poor and from Louisiana. We spoke a blended language of Cajun, modern standard Arabic, and English. The way I'm speaking to you now is without pretense. My turn. How old were you when you were first kissed?"

She didn't answer right away. He glanced at her. She was looking at him with her eyes narrowed as if she was thinking. Finally, she shrugged. "Well, I said nothing was off-limits. I've never been kissed. The only man who ever held my hand, is you. You're the only man who's ever held me, actually. So, that's kind of pathetic. What about you? When was your first kiss?"

He took a deep breath and let it out. "I believe I was nineteen?"

"Nineteen? Is that late for boys?"

"Probably. After my parents were killed, I retreated from the world. My interests were solely academic. I wanted to learn as much as I could in order to go after the man who killed them. Friends or lovers weren't a priority. What is your degree in?"

"Early childhood education. I love kids. They are so honest and real. They have their lives ahead of them and nobody to tell them they can't live it. Is that why you learned different accents?"

"Next question." He vetoed. It would brush up against what he did for Guardian.

"Oh, snap, that has something to do with work too, huh. Okay... How old are you?"

"I just turned forty-five."

"Shut the front door!" She gaped at him. "No way. There's no way you're that old."

He lifted an eyebrow and turned his head slowly toward her. *Really? That old?* She seemed to realize what she had said as he stared at her.

Her hands slapped over her mouth and a high-pitched squeak escaped. "Oh my God, I'm so sorry. That was so rude. You're not that old. It's just that, I wouldn't think you were forty-five, looking at you. I mean, you're hot. Oh, shit. You're not hot. I mean... Yes, you are, but oh, shit. I just need to shut up."

She lurched toward him and grabbed his arm. "Can we just forget I ever said that?"

"Which part specifically? The part where I'm old? Or the part where I'm hot?" He laughed at her face-palm and groan.

"All of it, please. I am such a dweeb." She scrubbed her face, knocking her baseball cap back. With a huff, she straightened it and squared off in her seat. "Can a person die of embarrassment?"

"It's been my experience that's one of the few ways people cannot die. Why be embarrassed? We're both adults. I know forty-five may seem old to you, but I can live with your opinion. As far as you thinking I'm hot? I'll take it as a compliment. What forty-year-old man wouldn't want an attractive twenty-something woman to think he's hot?" She had to know by now he wasn't the type of person to play games. Why would he front like he was?

"You think I'm attractive?" Her cheeks tinged with a rose color. A shy smile spread across her face.

"I do. But I'm sure you get that all the time." He checked the rearview mirror before he clicked on his turn indicator to switch lanes and pass a slower vehicle.

"I don't, not really. Lori keeps telling me I'm attractive, and there have been a couple of guys, but it always felt like they were telling me I was pretty as a means to an end. I wasn't interested enough in any of them to even think about that. You know what I mean?"

He hummed an agreement. Indeed, he did know. He had a healthy sex life. Well, if you considered never fucking anyone twice, or not bothering to know anything about them healthy, then yeah, he had a robust sex life. So, his little assignment had never been kissed, and she'd rarely been complemented. That was a volatile combination. She was like tinder, dry, brittle and unassuming. Apply a modicum of heat and she'd explode into a flame so brilliant the person who set it off would be blinded. Was it ludicrous that he wanted to be the person to apply that flame? Lord, he was screwed six ways to Sunday... he wanted her. Not just physically, but damn it, there was emotion involved. Getting involved with her would obliterate her innocence. He was filth and death and she was pure innocence and light. Every instinct he'd honed over the last twenty-five years urged him to contact Guardian and have them send somebody else to watch over her. Every. Instinct. She was young, innocent, pure, and he could do nothing but tarnish her life.

"What is your happiest memory?" She glanced at him, no doubt gauging whether or not he would answer her question.

"Christmas, when I was nine. It was a big family affair.

My aunt, uncle and grandparents were able to come for Christmas. My father was so happy. I think he missed living close to his family more than he let on." His father had given up everything to be with his mother. His grandparents didn't approve of her. She wasn't the same religion, from the same background, or the same socioeconomic status. But that one Christmas, they seemed to set aside their differences. He'd probably embellished that memory, but it was one he treasured. "What about you?"

"That's a tossup. The day they told me I could leave the hospital was amazing, and terrifying. It took about a year of them working with me to transition out of the hospital and to be able to live on my own. I had counselors who taught me how to cook, clean, take care of myself. When you're institutionalized, those things aren't taught or expected, but the absolute best memory, was my first day alone. The magnitude of total quiet in my apartment when the counselor left? That moment, well, it was perfect. Soon after, reality intruded. You know, the worries, concerns, frantic days of studying, decisions to be made on my own, all those things followed, and they were amazing, too. But when the front door closed on my first apartment, leaving me alone? I think that is my best memory to date. Probably because it represented so much I thought I'd never have."

"Do you miss any of the people who took care of you?" She had to have had somebody who actually cared about her.

"Oh, well, yes? There were a few people who were

very kind, but they never stayed long." She turned away and stared out the window.

His hands tightened on the wheel. How could those motherfuckers live with the knowledge they were experimenting on a child?

"Do you remember the names of the people who cared for you?" Tortured you? Experimented on you? His mind snapped accusations he refused to let past his lips.

"There were so many. I remember a few, but now I ask myself if those names were even real. I mean, they lied to me about everything else. Why would they tell me their real names?"

Because they didn't expect her to live. He doubted anyone would have guessed Wellington would allow her to leave. He knew how the minds of the sick, twisted, individuals in this world worked. He'd used their fucked-up mentality against them too many times not to be able to anticipate their moves, reactions, and countermeasures. Perhaps Bengal's woman would be able to find identities. After all, he'd been given carte blanche to protect Eve. Protecting her from the monsters of her past fell into that realm.

"How did we get on such a maudlin topic? Let's change the channel. What's your favorite animal?" She swiped at her cheek to remove a stray tear.

"That's a tough one. Either the three-toed sloth or the Sabretooth tiger."

Her laugh filled the cab, delightful and refreshing. He smiled at her and vowed to make her laugh more than cry today.

CHAPTER 12

As the sun set, a comfortable silence lingered in the cab of the truck. The one hundred questions game seemed to have broken the ice this morning, and they had visited aimlessly about so many things. She knew far more details about the man called Dolan than she did this morning, but sifting through the conversation, he'd provided nothing of substance. Well, he loved his family until they were taken from him. She knew his favorite color and the fact he'd eat just about anything and had on a dare. But she knew nothing of his life now. The glimpses he'd shown her were poignant and reflective of the love he had for his family. In reality, they were opposites. She knew everything about his past and nothing about his present. He knew everything about her present, but nothing about the hell she'd lived through in the past. She didn't purposely keep that away from him, but he seemed inclined to keep the conversation light today, which she appreciated.

They'd stopped for a quick lunch and then later for

dinner and gas. Traffic snarled and slowed to almost a standstill in St. Louis. They pushed through, heading south while looking for a place to stop for the night, although what specifically Dolan was looking for, she couldn't say. They'd passed numerous signs indicating hotels, but he didn't slow the vehicle. She'd given up trying to figure out his criteria. Another yawn stretched her jaw. Man, she was exhausted, even though she hadn't moved from the truck except to eat. She closed her eyes and leaned her head back on the headrest. The vibration and rumble of the road droned like white noise, stilling the thoughts that continued to swirl through her mind.

The vehicle slowed, waking her. She snapped upright with a jerk.

"It's okay, we are pulling off the interstate. There's a small hotel." He pointed to the right.

She blinked trying to focus.

"Stay in the truck, I'll check us in." He pulled into the parking lot and disappeared into the office of the hotel after ensuring she locked the cab of the vehicle.

She yawned hard, surprised she'd fallen asleep so completely.

He returned to the truck and helped her down. She grabbed her shopping bag from him as he unloaded the truck. The bags he had brought with them from Rochester were awkward and looked heavy, yet he carried them as if they were nothing.

He allowed her to open the door to the room but was the first inside. He searched the entire room, well, what little there was of it. Separated no more than two feet, a queen-size bed and two nightstands occupied the wall across from a dresser that held a box-style TV. A small door off to the right led to the bathroom. It was quite possible she could sit on the toilet, wash her hands in the sink, and take a shower at the same time. After the luxury of the Sioux Falls hotel the night before, this room screamed economy.

"If you needed more money, I have some in my wallet." She placed her bag on the dresser beside the television.

His rumbling laughter filled the room. "I don't need money, thank you. We rented this room because it is not a chain connected by a common computer system, doesn't have camera surveillance, and we can pay in cash. Granted, if this motel were in the city, it would probably host working ladies and their clientele by the hour. However, it'll do for us. Go ahead and grab a shower, I'll go after you." He busied himself with several of the cases, totally dismissing her.

Although the shower stall was small, the water pressure was excellent, and the hot water felt amazing. She jumped at a sharp knock on the bathroom door. "I'm leaving a T-shirt for you to sleep in." She felt a cool draft and heard the door snap shut. Peeking out from behind the white plastic shower curtain, she wiped the water from her eyes and blinked the room into focus. A folded T-shirt sat on the side of the sink. He was a wonderful person. Not many people would've thought about her comfort. Or at least she assumed they wouldn't. She really didn't have anything against which to compare the experiences of the last two days. She dried off quickly, brushed her teeth and shrugged on the dress-length T-shirt before she wrapped her towel around her wet hair.

Cool air hit her when she opened the door and slipped out into the room. Dolan reclined against the headboard with the TV on but turned down low.

"Please don't leave the room, and don't open the door for any reason." He grabbed a stack of clothes and disappeared into the bathroom.

She arranged her new possessions in her bag and dropped the towel to comb through the tangles. As she pulled the plastic teeth through her hair, she glanced at the bathroom door. The oddest sensation trickled down her spine. Dolan was acting... distant. Was he upset? Had she done something? She combed through her hair as she worked through their conversation today. No, there hadn't been any awkward moments since this morning. It was probably her imagining things.

She was tired. Tired with a capital T. She couldn't wait to drop onto the bed. The bed. Singular. *Oh shit*. She glanced around the room. The carpet on the floor was less than appealing, but she could put the bedspread down and sleep on that. It would give him the bed. He needed it more than she did since he was the one driving tomorrow.

She grabbed the synthetic gold and brown material when the bathroom door opened and she glanced at him. *Dear God in heaven*. She froze with the slippery bedspread clutched in her hands. His jeans hung low from his narrow hips. The button fly was open, exposing his black boxers. His bare chest glistened with a few errant drops of water the towel had missed. He looked from her to the bedspread. "What are you doing?"

"I was going to sleep on the floor so you could have the bed." She lifted the bedspread as evidence.

"That's not necessary. There's more than enough room on the bed. We're both adults and perfectly capable of sleeping in the same bed. Unless you don't trust me."

She looked at the bed and then looked at him. Did she trust him? Yes. She did. Whenever she was close to Dolan, she wanted to cling to him. Rationally, she knew it was because he signified safety to her. Last night when he held her, when she fell asleep against him, it was the safest she'd ever felt. So, yeah, she probably had a little hero worship going on, but she did trust him. Implicitly. She nodded. "Yeah, I trust you."

He grunted in response, turned off the television, and the overhead light, leaving only a small lamp in the corner illuminated. He flicked down the sheet and blanket and sat on the bed. She quickly flipped the bedspread back onto the bed and slid between the sheets. The small lamp clicked off and darkness consumed the room. She heard the flutter of material and then felt the bed depress beside her. Had he taken off his jeans? She squeezed her eyes shut and drew a deep breath. Why would she think he was sleeping in his clothes? They were adults. She could do this.

"Goodnight, Eve." Dolan's tired words reached her in a soft whisper.

"Goodnight." She whispered in return. She turned on her side facing the man who was not only her protector but quickly becoming her friend. She could see the outline of his broad shoulders in the faint light broadcast throughout the room by the alarm clock on his night-stand. What would it be like to have someone as wonderful as Dolan in her life? A protector, a friend, a lover. Someone to grow old beside. That dream was once an impossibility. Now? Well, now she needed to survive this transition, and then maybe, just maybe, she could work on obtaining that dream.

She woke slowly. Like a feather drifting softly on a current of air, she slowly landed in the realm of reality. Half-awake, and half-asleep, she was at that comfortable place where you could rest forever. The warm arms that cradled her... *Holy shit!* She popped her eyes open and stared directly at Dolan's chest. The hair that dusted over his pecs was soft under her cheek.

Carefully she arched her back, peeling away, only to have his arms tighten around her. Dolan pulled her back into him and covered her legs with one of his. His hard body pressed up against her from toe to shoulder. She relaxed against him until she realized his hard body was hard everywhere. The feel of his large, hard, penis against her stomach was... terrifyingly exciting. She'd studied human anatomy and physiology. She knew about procreation. She understood the mechanics of sexual inter-course, but being held against a man's sex for the first time? It was... hard. Literally. Dolan's breath exhaled against her cheek in a steady rhythm. She waited for several minutes to make sure he was asleep before she dared to move. Finally, she steeled her resolve and did what any woman in her position would do. She moved far enough to look down.

His boxers tented away from his body. His hard shaft pushed against the cotton material. She froze, not blinking, as if her eye movement would wake the man she was examining. Carefully and slowly she visually mapped the long and incredibly thick outline, burning the visual into her memory. The sculptures she'd seen hadn't looked anything like the man who lay next to her. She felt warm and tingly, and yet incredibly guilty at the same time. It was probably a huge social faux pas to ogle the sex organ of the man who was trying to protect you, but hey, she had tried to move. Right? No. Hell, who was she kidding? Her curiosity was piqued, and she wanted to see what was behind the cotton. She had an incredible desire to run her finger up the outline. What would it feel like without the cotton? It was hot against her stomach. Would it be hot against her hand? She felt her cheeks warm as the thoughts of touching this man seemed to obliterate any other thoughts.

As if by its own volition, her finger extended. She stopped just short of touching the tip, pausing to make sure his breathing hadn't changed. Slowly she allowed her fingertip to touch the mushroom cap outlined by the black cotton. Dragging her finger across the top, she could feel slight moisture. It twitched under her hand and pushed harder against the cotton. Dolan moaned and rolled his hips, trapping her hand against his cock between their stomachs. She knew the second he woke. His body went from relaxed to tight in less than a second.

It took just a moment more before his hips retracted away from her.

"Fuck." His sleepy exclamation was low, but she heard it.

She lifted her head as he rolled onto his back and scrubbed his face with one hand. "Good morning."

He glanced over. "Good morning." He withdrew his arm from under her head and rolled off the bed, going straight into the bathroom, closing the door behind him. Even with the direct route, she was able to ogle his thick, muscled legs, tight ass, and that beautiful chiseled back. She should probably feel guilty right now, but she didn't. It was part of her new resolve to live her life the way she wanted. She wanted to experience sex. She wanted to experience it with a partner who could teach her what she needed to know. Eve lifted onto her elbows and stared at the door. Dolan was older and experienced, or at least she assumed at forty-five he'd had lovers. She wanted to see his body *without* those ass-hugging black briefs, and she wanted to know what it was like to make love. The question was how in the heck was she going to ask Dolan to show her?

The water stopped suddenly, propelling her into action. She was dressed and had her hair pulled into a ponytail before he exited the bathroom. She turned to talk to him and once again froze like a stop-action photograph. He held a tiny white towel around his waist. His skin glistened with moisture. The dark hair on his chest was even darker and the thin trail of hair down to the edge of the towel seemed to demand all of her attention.

"Forgot my clothes." Dolan snatched his jeans and a

small backpack before he spun and closed the bathroom door behind him again. Holy snips and snails and puppy dog tails, that was so not a little boy. She spun and fell onto the bed. She drew a deep breath and exhaled it whispering, "Thou shalt not mack on your protector." She rolled her head and looked at the bathroom door. *Right. Too late.*

Dolan was noticeably quiet today. They stopped at a small diner for breakfast. The conversation was polite and extremely distant. The only thing she could think of that would make him feel so uncomfortable was the fact she had touched his penis this morning. Her face flamed with heat each time she thought of what she'd done. Dolan paid for the breakfast neither one of them ate much of, and they walked out of the small mom-and-pop establishment. He opened the truck door and as she started to climb up, he put his hand on her arm, stilling her.

"Look, I think we need to talk." He glanced down at her and then shifted his eyes away quickly as a car passed.

She gulped a lungful of air and agreed, "I know. I think we need to talk about it too. I want to apologize."

"Wait, what? Apologize? Why?"

"Why? I was the one who touched it, of course. I'd never seen one before. It was hot and big. I didn't mean to wake you up."

For the first time since she'd met the man, he looked completely flummoxed. "What?"

"Well, I woke up first. I tried to move but you hugged me tighter. Then I felt... you know... *it*. I couldn't move, and I'd never seen one before, except in art or textbooks, and the outline didn't look like any of the Grecian statues I've seen. I touched it. I mean, you." She buried her hands in her face and blurted out, "I don't know why! I'm sorry. I know it was wrong, and the only thing I can say is I'm sorry. I'm really, really sorry." Her shoulders rose up until they almost touched her ears. Finally, she managed enough strength to glance up at him quickly. "Please don't be mad."

His mouth was slack and slightly open. He blinked and snapped his mouth shut. "Wait. What exactly are you talking about?"

Oh shit. Her head popped up and her shoulders fell at his question. "Why? What are you talking about?"

"How we should present ourselves to my property managers when we arrive this afternoon." His eyebrows had risen to his hairline.

She gulped and swallowed hard. The morbid embarrassment at her words and actions nuked her from the inside out. If her face wasn't as red as a cooked lobster, she'd eat the baseball cap she was wearing. "Okay. Let's talk about that." *Please, dear God, let's talk about that.*

"Joanne and Charlie are my oldest employees. I don't lie to them, but I don't necessarily tell them the entire truth either. So, telling them about the circumstances of how you came to be with me should be left vague." He swung open the passenger door and motioned for her to get in. She didn't wait for any assistance but clambered into the vehicle and shut the door. Good Lord if she could imitate a piece of the upholstery she would. For the love of Pete, when had her mouth taken over her life? Obviously about forty-eight hours ago.

He opened the driver's side door and climbed into the truck. They were silent until he drove onto the interstate and headed south. He looked over at her and smiled. "So, it was hot and big, huh?"

She dropped her head into her hands and groaned, "Please, just kill me now." His laughter filled the cab of the truck. What were the chances of the earth opening up and swallowing her?

THANATOS TRIED and failed to suppress his humor at the situation. He liked this woman. She had zero pretenses and even fewer defenses. So, she had touched him this morning. He had awakened with a raging hard on. Not that that was uncommon. The fact that he rubbed one out in the shower with her right next-door, that, was uncommon. "So, it was hot and big, huh?"

She pushed back into the truck seat and mumbled something like, *just kill me now*. She was so easy to embarrass. And what guy didn't enjoy having a woman tell him he was well endowed. He knew he wasn't lacking in that department, but having it validated, even by a novice, was a stroke to the ego. His laugh was probably louder than it needed to be.

"Yeah, okay, make fun of me, but you were pressing into me." She crossed her arms over her chest with a huff and glared at him.

Busted. "Completely natural, I assure you. I slept with

a beautiful woman in my arms all night long. I'm not going to apologize for the biological result." There was no way anything this woman said would embarrass him. Being hardened and jaded as fuck, embarrassing moments didn't mean shit. However, he would apologize if it would make the situation between them easier for her.

They rode in silence for almost one hundred miles before she turned in her seat to face him. He glanced over. The woman was working up the courage to say something. The question was, what could possibly come out of her mouth now? God knows the last revelation had been interesting. She faced forward again but kept glancing his direction. Sooner or later she'd gather enough intestinal fortitude to say what was on her mind. He reached forward and flicked on the truck's radio, finding an old classic rock channel to listen to.

"Do you find me attractive? I mean attractive enough to make love to me?" She twisted in her seat and stared at him.

Damn, well... all right, that wasn't expected.

"I've never made love to anyone."

"You're a virgin, too?" Her voice raised reaching glass-shattering octaves and then she squeaked at the end of the question.

"What? Hell, no!" Where the fuck had she gotten *that* idea?

"But you just said you've never made love to anyone..." She stared at him like he had three heads.

"There is a very real difference between fucking and making love. You asked me if I found you attractive enough to make love to you. I have never made love, and I probably never will."

"Why?" She cocked her head at him, studying him far closer than he cared to let her.

"Don't ask questions you really don't want the answer to. Do I find you attractive? Yes. I've already told you that."

"When we get to your home in Auburn, will you fuck me?"

He jerked and the vehicle swerved to the right. His eyes slammed back to the road, correcting the truck before the tires caught on the shoulder and flipped them. "What the actual fuck? Why would you say something like that?"

"Never mind," she mumbled and turned toward the window.

The remaining eight and a half hours passed by at a snail's pace. Her polite yes and no answers shut down any conversation he attempted. He had no conceivable idea how to fix whatever the fuck had broken between them, and in all honesty, he wasn't sure he wanted to fix it. He didn't think he could handle anymore of her surprise questions. Distance was an absolute requirement in this situation.

Hell no, he wouldn't fuck her. She was a job. She was his mission. Sure, the woman was hot and sexy. Sure, he'd sure as fuck rub one out thinking of her, but he wasn't a training aid for a curious virgin who no longer wanted to be one. Hell, he'd never *been* with a virgin. They were as rare as rainbow shitting unicorns and world peace. They didn't exist in the real world. She needed to save that for the man she married. Yeah, that was his father's heritage talking, but damn it, any man who was worth his fucking salt would be over the moon receiving a precious gift like that. He wouldn't sully her or stain her in that fashion.

When he turned onto Interstate 85, he drew a long breath. He was almost home. Well, as close to home as he could get as an adult. Fifty minutes later, he turned down the long winding county road that led to the small white house with a wraparound porch. The barns and outbuildings were several miles further down the road. It was one of the reasons he purchased this home. The activities of the small farm wouldn't interfere with his solitude. He could tell Joanne had been to the house. The fans on the porch had been turned on, and the front door was open with only the screen door keeping the summer-time bugs outside.

Putting the truck into park, he scanned the old house. When he first saw it, his mother's words whispered across his thoughts. When he was a child, they'd often sat drawing pictures of houses they someday wanted to live in. He'd drawn skyscrapers or massive homes. She had always drawn the same house, a small, white, house with a wraparound porch. She added rocking chairs and hanging plants, and she told stories of how she would have a garden and grow fresh vegetables and fruit. When he saw this house, he saw his mother.

"It's beautiful." Her first unsolicited words since this morning.

"It's your home for the next three weeks." He opened his door and dropped down to the gravel before he reached back for his gear. "Do you need help?"

"No, thank you."

Annnd... they were back to awkward.

He made his way into the house, listening to her as she entered behind him. He nodded down the hallway on the right with the tip of his head. "Your room is the first one on the right." She nodded and headed that direction. He waited until she opened the door and disappeared inside before he headed to his office. It was the one room in the house Joanne and Charlie had been forbidden to enter. He placed his thumb on the pad outside the door and entered his six-digit code. The locks sprang and he pushed the door open. To the untrained eye, the small office was much like any other. However, Lycos had hooked him up.

The old-fashioned desk telephone had rotating encryption keys he could activate by punching any of the buttons on the bottom of the phone. His computer system, likewise, was state-of-the-art. Guardian's encryption and security software were uploaded and protected his privacy. He left the door ajar and deposited Guardian's gear beside his desk. He dropped into his chair and groaned.

What a fucking zoo of an assignment. He had zero problem tracking monsters across the globe. It didn't faze him. He had no problem watching those bastards take their last breath. He tracked and killed at his country's behest. Put a horny, sexy, twenty-seven-year-old, virgin next to him and ka-boom, he loses his fucking mind. Hell, for the last eight hours they'd both been acting like they'd had a lobotomy.

She was embarrassed and wouldn't talk to him, and

he was trying to be a gentleman by ignoring the problem, tippy-toeing around and choosing his words carefully so as not to offend. Holy hell, when had he fallen into a Victorian era novel? He leaned forward and dropped his head into his hands. Yeah, this shit was stopping now. He scrubbed his face and stood, only to find Eve standing just outside his door.

"I wanted to apologize for what I said this morning." She pulled her bottom lip into her mouth and bit it as she looked at him and waited for an answer.

"Come in and sit down." He lowered himself back into his chair and waited for her to come into the office. When she was seated, he cleared his throat and leaned forward, placing his forearms on his desk. "I want you to understand that while I find you very attractive, my job is to protect you, not to teach you about sex." He lifted a hand as she started to speak. "I'm flattered and honored that you asked me, but I will not cross that line."

She leaned back in her chair and stared at him. It wasn't the reaction he expected. "We're here for the next three weeks, alone. I'm not asking you to marry me. I'm not asking for commitment or a relationship. Put yourself in my position. You're twenty-seven years old and have done absolutely nothing your entire life. Soon, hopefully, your world will explode into a myriad of possibilities. I don't want to be taken advantage of by some asshole."

"Your virginity is —"

"Is mine to do with as I choose." She leveled a determined stare in his direction.

"Granted." The absolute truth of that slapped him in the face.

She shrugged. "Okay. I get it."

She stood, but before she could leave, Joanne called from the front room, "Dolan, where are you?" Joanne walked into the office wearing blue jeans, a T-shirt and tennis shoes. Even at sixty-five, the woman exuded boundless energy. "They are you are! Come give me a hug!" She held her arms out, and he found himself crossing the room to enfold the woman. "It's been too long. Far, far too long." When she released him from the hug, she zeroed in on Eve. "Oh, and who do we have here?"

"Joanne, this is my friend Evelyn. Evelyn, Joanne and her husband Charlie manage this property for me."

Eve smiled shyly and extended a hand. Joanne made a sound in her throat and reached past the extended hand to pull her in for a hug. "Welcome to the south, darlin'. We're huggers down here." Eve's eyes widened to the point of saucers over the older woman's shoulder, as Joanne hugged her.

Joanne finally released Eve and swung her attention back to him. "Charlie and Chase are over at the barn puttering with that old tractor. I just wanted to pop down and tell you dinner would be at six sharp. Bring your appetites and nothing else. It was good to meet you Miss Evelyn; I look forward to getting to know you." She leaned in for one more hug before she power-walked out of the house.

"Wow."

He chuckled at Eve's response. Joanne had a way of making the world seem like it was standing still while she alone was spinning. "Yeah, I agree."

"You mentioned Charlie was her husband, but who is Chase?"

"He's their son. He's a lawyer." A successful one who practiced in Montgomery.

"Oh. Okay. What is our story? You said to keep it vague, but we never discussed..." She looked at the floor and shrugged.

"We keep it vague and based in truth. You and I met during a work assignment and are working a joint project but have a three-week layover before we can complete it."

"Just that simple?"

"The truth, yet not."

"You're very good at that, aren't you?"

"I don't lie."

"Ever?"

"I refuse."

"So you tell shades of the truth instead?"

"Nothing I said was a lie."

"Semantics."

"To you."

"To everyone."

"I disagree."

"I noticed. Anyway, I'm going to get cleaned up and changed. I don't want to be the reason we're late. I think that lady meant business. I'll see you in a few."

The sound of her footsteps over the hardwood floors faded until he heard the bedroom door click shut. He powered up his computer and checked his Guardian dead drop email account. There was nothing waiting for him. The question as to why the medical staff would try to hold Eve the day before yesterday still niggled at the back of his mind. It didn't fit. He opened a draft message and typed:

> Arrived at destination. Query: Why was staff instructed to hold asset? Who gave orders? Head of the viper removed. Another party involved? <

He saved the message as a draft and signed out. He checked his other dead drops, the ones the Shadows used to communicate with each other and the ones he used privately with each of the original Shadows. He opened a specific account and added a new draft.

Tempest's disappearance a couple years ago hadn't been a surprise. He'd dropped off the face of the planet, either by design or because he was dead or captured. He understood what it was like to need backup and think there was none. He'd systematically left breadcrumbs for Tempest to follow—nothing a stranger could find, nothing that would raise suspicion. He realized while he was riding in silence today, that he'd never actually reached out in a way that would allow Tempest to ask for help. What if the man was incapacitated, or needed assistance and couldn't access the resources they all knew of and utilized? It would suck to be lost in that storm. Like Eve. No support, no way out, just riding the waves of what life was bringing her way. So, against protocols, he accessed Tempest's dead drop and left a plain, un-coded, message. If people were watching Tempest, he'd given away one of the most sacrosanct communication methods utilized by the Shadow structure.

He closed down the system, wiping his computer with Guardian's software. He closed his eyes. They burned, road-weary, but not tired. Eve was a resilient woman.

She'd been handed a hell of a revelation and was trying to make the best of it, although her fixation on sex was... interesting. If he pushed away the thoughts of duty, and the misogynistic teachings he'd been raised to believe about a woman saving herself for marriage, he could see her point. Learning about sex with someone you trusted made sense.

He shook his head. That was the problem, however. She shouldn't trust him. She didn't know him. She knew the window dressing, nothing real. Nothing solid. Just shadows that danced in the mist created by a smoke-screen that was reflected by mirrors. He was a hired killer. Eve's opinion of him was sealed. He harbored no hope for a future once she realized what service he performed for Guardian. Her abiding and unquestioning belief that all life was sacred was engrained and unshakable. Even the filth and abominations he eliminated were, in her eyes, sacrosanct. She would regret having him in her bed and for some reason, he didn't want her to regret him, not when her life was filled with so many betrayals already.

He heard her bedroom door open and stood to stretch out the kinks. Thankfully, Charlie stocked some damn good scotch. He could use a drink tonight.

OR TEN. He filled his tumbler for the second time as he watched Chase and Eve visit on the front porch. From time to time, the sweet sound of her laughter would filter back to him. His jaw tightened just before he slugged down half the tumbler. Charlie ambled up and stood shoulder to shoulder with him. "That boy stepping on your toes?"

He glowered at his old friend. "No."

The old man chuckled. "Right."

Thanatos took another slug from his drink. "It's complicated."

"It always is, son."

"No, I mean, this is a work thing."

"Uh-huh. I get that. Can't mix business with pleasure."

"Right." He agreed. He'd go with that.

"You know that's bullshit, too, right?" Joanne said as she poured herself a scotch.

"Ma, stay out of the boy's business."

"Pfft... since when have I stayed out of anyone's business? That girl out there stared holes through this one all dinner long. Chase ain't got a chance in hell with her." She snorted a laugh before she threw back her drink. "I need to check on them pups." She smacked her tumbler down on the counter. "Don't wash that. I'll want a nightcap."

They watched her bound out of the house and stop at the rocking chairs. Eve smiled and practically jumped out of the chair. Chase laughed and followed the ladies down the steps and out toward the kennels.

"She hasn't changed." Thanatos shook his head and finished his second drink, pouring a third.

"What would make you think she would? That woman is my life, but she is a busybody." Charlie poured himself a second drink, and they both ambled out to the porch and the rocking chairs. The large outdoor ceiling fans rotated slowly, stirring the thick, humid air. The night crickets began their song. They could hear the instant Joanne opened the kennel doors. The sharp yips and barks carried in the night air. "Ma just has Muffy now. This will be the last litter. When that dog whelped, it tore her up. That woman was frantic. She can't lose that dog. Attached to it. Hell, I had to air condition the kennel for the darn thing. That dog slept at the foot of our bed until she whelped. I'll be damned if I'm going to have seven German shepherds push me out of my bed. I drew the line and then installed an air conditioner." Charlie rocked back and lifted his scotch glass. "Here's to being the king of your castle."

"Especially when Ma lets you." Chase laughed as he approached the porch. He hung over the rail and smiled. "Dolan, I think you're in trouble. Evelyn grabbed hold of two of those pups and I'm not sure she's gonna let go."

"Now, she's going to have to let go of all but one. Every pup except the runt is spoken for, but hell, if that girl wants a pup, she can have that runt. Don't need two of those dogs shedding all over." Charlie chuckled. "I'd caution her, though. Those shepherds need exercise and constant companionship. They wouldn't do well being left alone all day."

"I'm not sure what Evelyn's future holds. I don't think she is sure either." Thanatos glanced over at the kennels. That wasn't his decision to make. He saw her the second she walked out of the kennel. Her smile lit up the darkening summer sky. Joanne was laughing loudly at something Eve had said as they approached.

"The puppies are adorable! Joanne said all but one

has been claimed. The littlest one, he has such an attitude. He thinks he's bigger than he is." She smiled directly at him.

Thanatos was immediately engaged by her exuberance, but he couldn't help noticing the way Chase's eyes followed her as she started an animated conversation with Joanne. A wisp of anger curled around his gut with disturbing efficiency. The sensation perched like acid, burning somewhere down low and deep inside. He didn't like Chase's attention toward Eve. Didn't like it... no that was bullshit. He outright railed against it and that shit ate at him like acid. Eve said she wanted sex with him so why was he being such a goddamn hero and "saving her"? Fuck it. He was getting off *that* white horse.

CHAPTER 13

The walk back to Dolan's house was quiet. She stopped as they cleared the tree-lined drive. The multitude of stars expanding across the heavens was awe-inspiring. The light pollution from even the small city of Rochester had dimmed the spectacular view of the heavens. Here, in the middle of nowhere, the stars twinkled and illuminated the sky with a thousand pinpricks of light. It was phenomenal.

She realized Dolan was still walking and scurried to catch up. He turned as she slowed to a walk beside him. The awkward silence from the truck today had never really seemed to dissipate, even though she'd tried to explain her point of view. Oh, she knew the mechanics of sex. She'd read sweet romances on her Kindle. She also had a folder for books that were more... tantalizing. Perhaps she was wrapping her attraction to Dolan in a rose-colored book cover. The heroes in the books she'd read always wanted the heroine. There was always an attraction, lust or desire. She had that in spades for this man. Yeah, the fact that he rescued her and was keeping her safe probably played a huge part in that attraction. Yet, Joanne's son was a very attractive man, and she felt absolutely nothing sexual when they talked. When she talked to Dolan or hell, was even near the man, she... tingled. That wasn't exactly the sensation, but it was close. It was like something vibrated under her skin, pulling her toward the man. What concerned her, however, was he obviously didn't share the attraction. She'd thought he did. He admitted he found her attractive.

Oh shit. He must not like her. She stumbled, and he reached out a hand to stabilize her. Only she hadn't tripped over anything physical. He thought she was attractive, but he didn't like her. *Wow*. That had to be the explanation. He didn't like her as a person. She shoved her hands into the pockets of her shorts and curled in on herself, fighting the shaft of ice-cold realization. Okay, as difficult as it was to accept, she'd have to acknowledge the fact he didn't like her. Perhaps after everything settled down, she'd ask him what specifically he didn't like. She sure as heck wasn't going to do that now. Rejection on any level hurt. Rejection on such a personal level, it was going to take a while for her to gain distance and perspective.

"Goodnight." She tossed the words over her shoulder as she bolted up the steps and through the front door of his house.

"Eve. Can I have a moment?"

She stopped halfway to her room and slowly turned around. "Look, I already apologized. I'm not going to bring it up again. Let's just get through the next three weeks." She turned and headed down the hallway to her room.

"Eve."

With her hand on the cool doorknob, she dropped her head forward with a thunk against the wood door. *Dear God, please let me escape this morbid embarrassment.* She rolled her head against the door and looked at him as he walked down the hall toward her.

He didn't say anything as he slipped his arm around her waist and twisted her gently away from the door. He didn't speak a word when he pulled her close against his body. Their communication wasn't verbal. It was in the look he gave her before he lowered his lips to hers. The soft brush of skin against skin. The delicious warmth that carried his aura around her, wrapping her in nothing but him. The deep rumbling groan inside his chest when she sighed and leaned into him. Volumes of literature had been written on the body's reaction to a specific stimulus, but there were no words to describe the way she felt when held in his arms.

She gasped when he licked her lips. The kiss deepened and she pulled away. "I've never..."

"I know. I know." He lowered his head again, kissing her and licking his way into her mouth. He pulled away, bringing his fingertips to her face. "Kiss me back." He lowered again and repeated the sensual actions. Tentatively, she stroked her tongue against his. He tightened his hold on her and moaned in response. She lifted hands that had been dangling lifelessly and mapped the muscles of his arms before she twisted her arms around his neck.

Dolan slowed his assault on her mouth, dropping several light kisses on her lips. She opened her eyes and stared up at him. "Why did you change your mind?"

He shook his head. "This shouldn't be a decision you rush into. I want you to be sure." He pushed her hair back from her cheek and cupped her neck in one of his strong hands.

She trembled and untwisted her arms from around his neck to cup his face with her hands. "Before yesterday, I thought I was going to die. I was protecting myself by not getting involved with the men who were interested in me. But I'm going to live. I *want* to live. I want to know what it is to have the expectation of a future, to become somebody who doesn't have an expiration date, to make love. Don't you see? I've been living under a death sentence, but not any longer. I want to live. I want this. I want you." She stared straight at him so he could see this wasn't a rash decision.

He straightened, stretched around her and opened her bedroom door. He turned her and with gently placed hands, nudged her into her room. She glanced over her shoulder, surprised at his rejection. He braced himself with his hands against the doorjamb and leaned forward.

Before she could say anything, he spoke, "I believe you want this. I understand why you would, but before this can go any further, certain precautions need to be taken. Unfortunately, I am ill-prepared to go further. Believe me, it is the only thing that is stopping me." His fingers curled on the wood of the doorjamb, white from the grip he maintained on the wood.

"Precautions?" She leaned against the door not trusting her legs to support her.

"Condoms."

Oh. "I can't get pregnant."

He moved away from the door slightly and lifted his hand to cup her neck. "How can you be sure? All the lies..."

She closed her eyes because she couldn't meet his eyes and speak. "Before the last treatment, the doctors told me that they wanted to harvest eggs, the treatments were expected to make me infertile." She shook her head. "At the time I thought maybe someday I'd be whole, you know? But after the procedure, the doctors said the disease had compromised my reproductive system. They said the previous treatments had left me infertile. I haven't had a menses since before the last treatment, so yeah, I believe them."

"I'm sorry."

"It is something else they've stolen from me." She slid her cheek against his palm, wanting to push past the memories. They weren't welcome here. Not now. "As far as I know, I don't have any transmittable diseases. Do you?"

Dolan leaned forward and stepped into her bedroom. "None." His arms wrapped around her waist and his lips found hers. The sweet press of flesh against flesh scrambled her brain. She knew he was guiding them toward the bed but trusted him to lead the way. When the mattress hit the back of her legs, he lowered her carefully onto the soft queen-size bed.

He lifted away and waited until she opened her eyes

to speak. "I'm going to go slow. You can stop this at any time."

"I know." And she did know. She knew down to the deepest recesses of her soul that the man with her now would never willingly hurt her. It wasn't a trust born of years of familiarity, rather an innate knowledge blossoming from extreme circumstances. Stripped away from the clutter of day-to-day life, her knowledge of his character was resolute.

Kneeling, Dolan straddled her on the bed. He reached behind him and stripped off his shirt. The muscles of his chest and arms rippled in the low light of the bedroom. The hallway light emptied into her room, illuminating him from behind. The shadows that enfolded him only added to his masculine beauty. "Touch me." His words rumbled in the silence.

Pushing up and moving to her knees, she lifted a hand and trailed a fingertip up his arm. Under her touch, his body shuddered. Emboldened by his reaction, she allowed herself to feel the soft hair on his chest. She continued on, trailing a finger over the flat copper disc of his nipple. His head dropped back, and he stifled a moan.

"You like that." She said the words more to herself than to him.

"I like your touch, yes."

She glanced up at him when he spoke. Lifting her other hand, she allowed herself to map the planes and valleys of his muscled chest and arms. "Can I see more of you?"

"Only if I can see more of you."

"I have scars." She ran her fingers across his chest

again, watching as they trailed through the dark brown hair. Her fingers found a scar on his chest. They had deep wounds in common it would seem, but she didn't want to disappoint him. "Biopsies, surgeries, treatments."

"A person who would focus on your scars and not on the beauty of your soul isn't worthy of being with you." He slowly reached for the bottom of her T-shirt. "May I?"

"Yes." The word came out as a whisper. She lifted her arms as he pulled the shirt over her head. He mimicked her actions, tracing a finger up her arms to her shoulder. She shivered at the sensation of the callused pad of his finger trailing over her skin. So warm and yet she shivered? The contradicting sensations pooled and spread. His exploration continued as he trailed his finger along the lace scallop of her bra. She reached behind her and unclasped the hooks. He ran his fingers under the straps and pushed them off her shoulders. She closed her eyes as his hands traveled to her breasts. His finger now rasped across her pebbled nipples.

Her words reflected back at her as he said, "You like that."

"I do."

He leaned forward and kissed her, pushing her onto her back. Her legs opened, cradling him as he rested on his elbows and stole her breath with his kiss. One kiss turned into a multitude. His hands, teeth, lips, and even the stubble of his five o'clock shadow, ignited every nerve ending of her upper torso. He explored her body and showed her how to discover his. He stood and removed his jeans and briefs. His cock protruded straight away from his groin, hard and rigid. His hand cupped around his shaft and pumped slowly up the length several times. Tight full orbs underneath his hand moved as he stroked.

She lifted onto her knees again and reached out. "I want to touch you."

"Take off your shorts." He continued that slow, languid stroke as she stood and removed her shorts and panties. "Lie down."

She slid back onto the bed, only then noticing the warmth and wetness between her legs. She gasped as her hand trailed up her inner thigh. "Oh." Her eyes slammed in his direction.

He lowered onto the bed and crawled over her. "Are you wet for me, baby? Did that surprise you? It shouldn't. That's what your body is supposed to do. Everything is exactly how it's supposed to be." He lowered over her and rolled her to her side so they were looking at each other. "Touch me and let me touch you." His fingertips trailed from her waist to her hip. "May I?"

She nodded, mimicking his actions until her hand rested on his hip. She glanced up at him momentarily before her attention returned to his lower extremities. She dropped her finger and trailed it against the muscle that formed a groove from his hip to his sex. His hips moved forward slightly. She used two fingers, running them from the base of his cock to the tip. "Your skin is so soft on the outside, but so hard underneath." She recoiled at her own words before she glanced up at him.

His eyes were hooded, and his breath came in harsh pants. He moved his fingers slowly toward her core. "Don't ever let yourself be embarrassed when you're inti-mate with someone. Always be truthful, tell your partner what you need or want." He leaned down and kissed her until she couldn't breathe and then rasped, "Open your legs for me."

She complied, lifting her leg to allow him access.

He cupped her sex with his hand, and his fingers slipped through the wetness. The intense sensations that radiated from her sex deepened, and then fisted tightly inside her body. His fingers moved with a rhythm that her hips mimicked. As he stroked, her hips lifted. Her hand clenched around his heavily muscled bicep. A silent cry parted her lips as she teetered on the verge of something cataclysmic. His lips found hers again as his stroking intensified and quickened. When his fingers split and caught the top of her sex, she gasped and arched off the bed.

The bed dipped as he rolled them and placed her on her back. "Don't stop. Please don't stop." She chanted the words over and over.

"I'm not stopping." He lifted her legs to make room for himself. The head of his shaft nudged her sex. "Kiss me." His words penetrated the swirling sensations.

She wrapped her arms around his neck and pulled him down as he entered her.

His kiss muffled her cry. The pain of his entrance obliterated all the wonderful sensations that had filled her body. He withdrew and forced himself into her again. His hand traveled to her breast and gently flicked the nipple. She tried to stop the kiss, to move away, but he refused to let her go. His hips continued their forward and back motion. His hands traveled over her body, calming the fear and pain. "That's it. Come back to me.

The pain will fade." His words were spoken in between kisses and caresses. Slowly the sensations that had fled in a wave of panic started to return.

Dolan lifted to his elbows and rolled his hips. She gasped as the pressure of his body ground against the top of her sex. The warm, pulsing thrum that had enveloped her before flowed around the sensation of his sex entering and exiting hers. Dolan lifted her leg placing it over his shoulder. The change in position intensified the pressure and the pleasure. That imminent feeling of something huge grabbed her again. She had no idea how to ask for what she needed. Instead, she begged for more. Relentless pleas became demands. Whatever he was doing to her body, she needed more.

He lifted to his knees and pulled her up his thighs, his hands grasping her legs, keeping her where he wanted her. She didn't care. She needed so desperately. When his fingers found her sex and rapidly stroked the top she shattered. Her body clenched. Every muscle tightened, forcing an explosion inside her. She screamed his name and bucked wildly against him. His hoarse cry echoed after hers, and his thrusts became erratic and if possible, deeper. He dropped her legs and fell over her, catching himself on his elbows.

Breathing once again became a priority. She lifted her hips and pushed up against him. Delicious tendrils echoed through her. "Oh, god. That was... amazing," she whispered against the side of his neck.

He moved and rolled to his side, still inside her. His big hands pushed her hair away from her face. "I hurt you."

She nodded. "Yeah. Totally worth it." She smiled at him and leaned forward to kiss him. "Thank you."

"For having sex with you?" Humor laced his question. "You don't have to thank me for that."

"No. Thank you for understanding why I asked. Thank you for treating me as a person who can and will control her own destiny. It's a big new world for me. Thank you for giving it to me."

He stared at her for several long seconds. "I wish I could give you the world. You deserve to have it served to you on a silver platter."

"I'd take it on a paper plate."

"Like a picnic?"

"Exactly." She laughed at herself when he mentioned one of the things she'd placed on her life list.

"Perhaps we could do that someday."

"I'd love that." She yawned and settled against his arm. He moved, pulling out of her and they both groaned.

"Let me get us cleaned up."

She smiled sleepily as he headed to the en suite bathroom. The world on a platter. Wouldn't that be amazing?

CHAPTER 14

The sun was starting to crest on the eastern horizon. Through the window, Thanatos had watched the night pass by as he held the sleeping woman in his arms. He'd left the bathroom light on when he'd returned with a warm washcloth to take care of her. There was a small amount of blood that he'd wiped away as she smiled softly and drifted to sleep. The scars on her body, hidden for the most part when they made love, were illuminated in the bathroom light. His heart thundered in his chest; his fist tightened around the washcloth and he choked back the white hot rage that lived just under his civilized veneer. The sight of those scars drove any thoughts of sleep straight to hell and parked them there.

Through the night he plotted many different assassinations. In those plans he counted the doctors who had performed the operations, and the people who'd assisted. He added all those who knew they experimented on a human and looked the other way.

She shifted against him, and he lowered his gaze to her. He felt drawn to her and, in large part, that draw was because of her past and his, though the trauma they'd endured was different. He tracked one man responsible for his pain; she had a legion she could blame. But for whatever reason, being with this woman felt... right, at least for now.

He scrubbed his face and once again stared out the window. Maybe he was finally fucking losing it. He didn't do motherfucking emotions, and yet last night, what happened between them? Son of a bitch. That was an emotional nuclear bomb and the fall out was all over him. He was screwed. Hard. He should have gone back to his room. He never should have kissed her last night. Shouldn't have followed her into the bedroom. Shouldn't have taken her virginity, but he had, and for too many hours last night he searched for any regret, or shame or doubt over his actions. He had none. Pure, unadulterated, possessiveness had bitch-slapped him last night when he watched her interacting with Chase. All those hours watching her, coupled with the intensity of the last two days, had fucking tripped him up in a spectacular fashion. Wanting her was the last thing he'd expected or needed. Jealousy? Who'd have seen that bitch coming? That motherfucker was a red-eyed monster, and that ugly bastard had caught him. Sharp teeth and claws engaged, the motherfucker had hooked in and growled to add emphasis.

No matter. His night spent searching for answers was for nothing. Despite all the puffed-up chest bullshit running around in his head, she was a mission. He'd deliver her to the Rose and leave her there. Life would go on. His hunt for the bastard who'd killed his family would resume. He'd slip into yet another mission and lose more of who he was in order to protect those who had no clue he existed. He should stop this physicality between them, but he wasn't going to.

He had three weeks—twenty-one days—to play the role of lover and protector, then he'd return to his world where he lurked among the damned and the dead. The prospect of having warm memories pulled at him, and this woman beckoned to him as irresistible as a siren's call to a lost seaman. He wanted that magical interlude even though he knew their time together would be nothing but an illusion.

She rolled away from him, and he followed her, fitting his chest against her back. He propped his head up and watched her as she slept. Her small frame fit perfectly against him. He slipped his free arm around her and found her breast, stroking the nipple to tighten the skin. Her body reacted to his touch. He smiled when her forehead furrowed in her sleep. He slid his hand down her flat stomach to her sex and started a soft, circular massage.

He knew the second she woke. Her hand clenched his arm and her eyes flew open. The wild, startled look faded within seconds. He leaned down and kissed her behind the ear. A shiver cascaded through her and goose flesh rose along her neck. She smiled and stretched against him, stilling when her pert ass brushed up against his morning wood.

"Good Morning." Dark, sleepy tones laced her voice. Sexy as hell.

"How do you feel?" His hands traveled her skin. He made a point not to stop over the puckered scars that punctuated the soft smooth skin under his hand.

"Feel? Ummm... a little sore and a lot awkward."

Ah. Second thoughts. Well, that was to be expected, wasn't it? Why hadn't he expected that? He lifted his hand away from her and scooted back, making sure there was no contact between them. "Awkward, how so?"

"Well, yeah, I mean, I've never done this, so... do we pretend it never happened? Or are we going to continue to have sex? Am I allowed to tell you I want that? Oh, and I had a really, really good time last night. That was..." She blew all the air out of her lungs and lifted a hand. "Ah-maz-ing... and wow... and... now I understand the words in the books. Annnd... now I'm rambling and being awkward, and I'm sorry. I'll shut up now."

He chuckled and reached out, turning her to face him and pulling her back into his chest. "A nice hot bath might help the soreness. Let's talk about the next three weeks. You're leading the show on this thing that is happening between us. If you want me in your bed every night, I'll be here, but I won't cross that threshold without an invitation."

"I'd like that. Not the invitation part. The you in bed with me every night part." She ran her hands over the hair on his chest, sending rivulets of sensation straight to his balls. His cock flexed against her. She jumped ever so slightly. "I think you like that idea, too."

"I do..." Hell yeah, he did, and he was damn glad she wasn't having second thoughts, however...

"I sense a 'but' coming." She arched her back to look up at him.

"But we only have three weeks. When I deliver you to Arizona, you and I will be over. I have obligations."

Her eyes widened. "Wife and family-type obligations?"

"What? No. I'm not married."

"Did you tell me that?" Her brow scrunched. "Did I ask that? Man, I can't believe I didn't ask that and then I slept with you. I would never be the 'other' woman. Never."

He thought back over their hundred question game. Maybe she hadn't asked. But as high-minded as she was, he couldn't see her ever as the other woman. "No, my obligations are to my past."

And if Bengal's last update was correct, he'd have a place to start fresh with the search. It was more than he'd had in years. The genetic testing kits had been a godsend for police agencies working cold cases and obviously Guardian had not been left in the dust.

"So, what you're saying is we can do this for three weeks, and then like the adults we are, we say thank you for the wonderful time, goodbye, and have a great life?" She gave him a cheeky smile and lifted her big, green-rimmed, hazel eyes to meet his gaze.

"Yes, that's what I'm saying."

Last night had been transformative for him, but based on Eve's light-hearted, hell, logical, response, maybe what they shared last night wasn't as much of a thing for her as it had been for him. And fuck him very much, wasn't that a knee straight to the balls? She pricked his inflated sense of importance and the sucker just flitted away like a balloon farting out air. Okay. Three weeks of no strings, no emotions sex. If she could do it, he sure as fuck could.

"Okay. Do we need to do a secret handshake or is there something else we can do to seal the deal?" She slipped closer to him and pushed her flat belly against his cock, trapping it between them.

"Oh, I think there is something else."

"Yeah? Well why don't you show me?"

"Game on." He rolled her and pounced. She let out a shrill squeal and then a throaty laugh when he growled and attacked her neck.

All playfulness ebbed with the first kiss. He would spend at least the next twenty-one days showing this woman the way she should be treated, cherished and revered.

Her hands found purchase in his hair as he slowly moved down her body. He found the areas that made her shiver. The small spot by her hip that curved ever so slightly and was incredibly ticklish. The dip of her thigh in the crease that led to her sex. He mapped her body with his tongue and lips. As he explored, she came alive. He settled between her legs and kissed her inner thighs. Against her soft, hot flesh, he whispered, "I want to kiss you. Here." His finger lightly touched her outer lips.

She lifted onto her elbows. Her eyelids were heavy with desire. She licked her bottom lip before she nodded. He kept eye contact with her as he lowered. Her teeth raked in that lush bottom lip. He split her open with his fingers before he lowered to take a taste. She bucked against his mouth and flopped back down onto the bed. He braced her hips against the bed as he feasted on the beautiful woman beneath him.

"Oh, God, it's happening again!" Her legs quivered and her hips moved in rhythm with his fingers, tongue, and lips. He felt the bow tighten until she snapped, and that was his reward. He lapped at her honey and slowly ended his kiss. Her legs and arms snaked around him as he moved up her body.

"Is it always like that?"

"If it's done right, yes." He lowered his weight on top of her, snaking his arms under her body and cradling her head as he devoured her mouth with a kiss. As tentative as she was last night, this morning, Eve's tongue danced with his. He delighted in the small yet bold attempts she made to not only accept, but return, some of the pleasure he was giving her.

He entered her carefully, watching for any signs of discomfort. She closed her eyes as a rose blush spread from her chest to her cheeks. Her hands grasped his shoulders pulling him back down to her. Her body welcomed him. The woman was an inferno and a haven. Her innocence and hesitance only fueled the raging need he barely controlled, but this wasn't about him.

He lifted away and changed their position, rolling her on top. She pushed up and sat back carefully. She shifted her hips and her low moan sounded in the quiet room.

"Oh my god, you fill me up."

She moved her hips forward again and slowly repeated the motion. She moaned again and dropped her hands to his chest, using him as a prop so she could move her hips more freely.

"Oh, yes."

She started chanting the words.

Fuck, the woman's sounds alone were enough to make him come like a horny teenager. His hands found her hips and lifted her slightly. He thrust up into her and was rewarded with her sound of complete and total bliss. She gasped when he did it again and when he sped up, she threw back her head and cried. Fuck, his balls ached.

He flipped them again and encouraged by her pleas, buried himself into her. She tightened and clenched around him. He grabbed her shoulders and pressed into her as deep as he could and held himself there as he exploded. White and red bloomed behind his closed eyes as the wonderful friction forced heat to race from his balls and explode inside her.

He dropped onto his elbows.

Breathing. Breathing would be good now.

He chuckled at his internal coaching.

"Was that funny?" Her panted question forced more laughter.

"No." He dropped to his side and pulled her with him. "No, that was great. I was reminding myself to breathe."

"Oh, yeah. I think I forgot to do that, too." She shivered a bit.

He fished around for the sheets and pulled them up over her.

She snuggled closer, releasing a contented sigh. "You know if I wasn't being hunted by bad guys and wanted for experimentation by the US government, this would be kind of nice."

He ran his hand up and down her arm. "This is nice, and as far as the other matters are concerned, Guardian will never let anything bad happen to you."

Hell, Guardian would have to get in line to protect her. He would be at the front and no one would need to clean up after him. There wouldn't be enough left to fill a dustbin.

"It does seem rather anticlimactic. I mean, we had men shooting at us two days ago."

He lifted onto his elbow. "Wait, this... what we just did, you call that anticlimactic?"

She laughed, shaking her head. "No, this was extra climactic. It just seems like all that other is so far removed from us now. You know what I mean?"

"I do, and for what it's worth, that is what is supposed to happen. That means I've done my job well. We'll lie low until it's time to head to Arizona. The drive will be a little harder. We'll have to be on guard for any tails, but by not being on anyone's scope for three weeks, we should be able to throw everyone off our tracks."

"How long is the drive to Arizona?"

"I'm not sure, probably three, maybe four days, depending on how hard we push it."

"Wouldn't it be easier to fly?"

"It may be a possibility." He'd have to check with Bengal. A three-day drive or four hours in the air. Guardian had private aircraft. He'd never needed to employ that type of asset, but there were several small airports in the area. It was definitely a possibility he and

Guardian would look into before their time here was up. The biggest obstacle now was keeping Eve out of sight, but tucked away here in the Alabama countryside, that wasn't much of a concern. He needed to check his dead drop. Guardian was doing what it did best, gathering intel and working solutions. He'd do the same while protecting her. He'd work on her past as well as his own. He wasn't her future, but he could sure as hell avenge her past.

CHAPTER 15

Eve glanced down at her watch and hurried her steps. She hoped she hadn't ruined Dolan's dinner plans. A laugh filled her throat and bubbled out. But, puppies! They were adorable and a handful, and she loved each one of the little guys. They all had their own personalities. Jogging the last hundred feet to the house, she ran up the steps and pulled open the front door.

"Wow, what's all this?"

Candles lit up the living room. The furniture had been pushed to the walls and a small table with two chairs occupied the center. A white tablecloth and one slender red rose lay across a plate setting. The splash of red on the white drew and held her attention.

"This is you and me on a date. Or as close to it as we can get without leaving this place." Dolan strolled into the living room. His dark blue suit, crisp white shirt, and grey and blue striped tie made her blink. He was absolutely breathtaking.

"Oh." The word escaped her as he wrapped his arms around her.

"You're late."

She nodded. "I ahh... the puppies."

He chuckled and bent down to brush his warm lips against hers. She sighed into his kiss, melting into his embrace. He ended the kiss with several feather light passes of his lips against hers. "I have a present for you."

"You do?" She pressed her hips against him, smiled, and then wiggled her eyebrows. Sex with Dolan was a present she wanted to open over and over again.

"You'll get that gift later. Go into the bedroom. It's waiting for you on the bed."

Out of his arms in a flash, she jogged to his bedroom where they'd both been sleeping since that wonderful night a week ago. She stopped at the doorway. "Oh my."

Red silk draped over the side of the bed. She walked closer and reached down to trace the material of the sleeve. The gown's bodice was embroidered with small crystals that danced and played with the light in the room when she shifted the fabric.

"I thought since we were having a date, you'd want to dress up. Charlie went into Atlanta today and picked up some things for us."

"How did you know my size?" She picked up the dress and held it in front of her. She shifted her gaze to him and smiled.

"Educated guess and I asked Joanne if she thought I was close. The clothes I got you in South Dakota weren't exactly designer labels, but hopefully I got close with this."

"It's the most beautiful thing I've ever seen." She had to blink hard to keep tears at bay. No one had ever given her such an over the top gift. "Thank you."

"Get dressed. There are a couple more surprises in store for you tonight." He winked at her and started to pull the door shut behind him.

"You are such a good man. Thank you."

He paused for a moment before he spoke softly. "I'm as far from good as you can get, but you are most welcome."

Eve closed her eyes and hugged the material she was holding. "Dear lord, how am I ever going to be able to say goodbye to him?"

THANATOS PULLED the door shut and made his way to the kitchen. Good? Had he ever been a good man? No... but he would be what he believed a good man was, tonight.

He pulled the champagne bottle out of the chiller and settled it in a bucket of ice that he then placed by the small table. The meal tonight was simple, but elegant. Beluga caviar in a chilled crystal serving cup. He set the mother of pearl spoon down beside the small slices of boiled potato. Each one had a small dab of sour cream on top, the perfect accompaniment to the fresh beautiful taste of the caviar. After he placed the appetizer on a chilled plate, he checked the oven and turned it off. The Beef Wellington was ready, as was the dessert, strawberries dipped in the finest chocolate imported from

Switzerland. He owed Charlie for his part in getting everything ready for tonight.

He checked dinner one last time before he leaned against the doorjamb and stared into the front room. He was a fucking sap, but damn it, Eve deserved wonderful things. The flame of the candle flickered, drawing his attention. The flame consumed the wax and wick, much as Eve consumed his time. He wanted each day to count, to be days she would cherish for the rest of her life. It was selfish of him, granted, but he needed to know she wouldn't forget him when they parted.

The door to his bedroom opened and he held his breath. The delicate click of heels against the hardwood floor announced her arrival.

"It's beautiful." He extended his hand to her and then lifted it, allowing her to twirl for him. "You are magnificent." And she was.

The red silk draped her body and accentuated her curves. The bodice snugged against her breasts and nipped her waist. The Swarovski crystals winked seductively in the candlelight. Her beautiful brown hair swept her bare back and the fall of the skirt brushed her beautiful legs. The size six Louboutin's made her almost as tall as him. The effect was stunning.

"Thank you. I feel like a princess." A blush colored her cheeks. Natural beauty, no makeup, just Eve.

"You deserve to be treated like one." He led her to the table and pulled out the chair for her.

"Is that caviar?" She leaned over and looked at the plate he'd placed on the table.

"And champagne." He pulled out the chilled bottle

and unwrapped the foil around the wire nest that held the cork.

"You remembered." Her smile was brighter than the candles that illuminated the room.

"I remembered." And he prayed he'd never forget.

THREE DAYS LATER:

"Seriously, where are we going?" Her hands drifted up to pat the blindfold again. The truck trundled down a really bad road. She dropped her hands and held onto the seat when the truck hit a rut.

"You'll know in a minute."

"Kidnapping me is redundant, you know. I'm here willingly." She patted to the right and found the door handle, keeping a grip on it in case they hit another unexpected bump. "It's a good thing I don't get car sick or have vertigo."

"Stop whining."

She whipped her head toward him even though she couldn't see him. "Whining? I'm not whining, I'm complaining."

"And pouting." His deep laugh filled her with warmth.

"*So* not pouting. I'm curious." The truck slowed to a stop.

"Stay there. I've got to do something, and then I'll be back for you."

"How long?" She shouted the words and jumped

when his low laugh sounded right in front of her. She felt his lips touch hers. "Not long. Trust me."

"I do." The admission was so easy to make. Dolan had won her trust with his small gestures, his kind touches, and the man he revealed himself to be since the day he'd rescued her from the people at the clinic.

She listened as he got out of the truck. Her sense searched for a clue about what he was doing, yet she had nothing. "Dang it!" She jumped when her door opened. "Don't do that! Warn a lady, will you?"

"So sorry. I can close the door, and we can wait."

"Oh no you don't. Now can I take off the blindfold?"

"Not yet. Turn in your seat and reach down to me."

She patted around and found the doorjamb. Twisting in her seat, she extended her hands and felt him immediately.

"I've got you."

She slid into his arms, and he lowered her to the ground. He briefly kissed her upturned lips. "Hold my hand. The ground is flat. We are going about a hundred feet straight ahead."

"What are we doing?"

"You'll see."

"Obviously not. I'm blindfolded, or did you forget that?"

"How could I? You haven't stopped mentioning it."

"Because it's a pretty big thing in my life at the moment."

"Understandable. How about we fix that?" He stopped, and she followed suit.

She blinked as he lifted the blindfold, and then she turned and hugged him. "Thank you." She kissed him soundly before she turned again. In front of her was a small lake. The blue water was a beautiful backdrop for the red and white checked cloth that had been unfolded on freshly cut patch of grass. Next to it sat a picnic basket. She squeezed his hand and smiled up at him. "You remembered."

"I remembered."

And she'd never forget.

～

Five days later:

"Stop laughing at me!" Eve rubbed her butt with both hands. "Trotting is horrible. How did you make it look so easy?"

"I've ridden horses my entire life. I told you to stand in your stirrups and showed you how to post." He sat down on the bed and pulled off his boots before he moved over to her.

"Right. That's like showing someone a YouTube video of brain surgery and then letting them loose with a scalpel. Not helpful." She groaned when he pulled off her boots. "That feels wonderful."

"So, you didn't enjoy riding?"

She struggled to sit up; her eyes huge. "No, I loved it! But next time we are walking or what did you call it, ahhh... loping. No trotting. Trotting is banned. It is like being spanked without the fun of being chased."

Say what? He lifted his head from his task of removing her socks. She smiled at him and winked. *Holy shit.* "So you want to be chased and then spanked?"

She cocked her head and narrowed her eyes at him. "Maybe someday, but not today. My backside has had enough punishment."

"Maybe I should give you a massage?"

"Oh, yes, please. A naked massage?" She sat up and pulled her t-shirt off in one fluid movement.

"That can be arranged."

He pulled her up off the bed and she wrapped her arms around his neck. "In case I haven't told you yet, you're pretty damn close to perfect."

"Right back at you." He kissed her when she raised up to her toes. Perfect and temporary. He pushed the thought aside. Memories lasted forever.

Ten days later:

"I have never been so full." Eve held Dolan's hand as they walked the starlit gravel road from Joanne and Charlie's back to their little house. No, *Dolan's* little house. She corrected herself for the ninety-four millionth time.

"Not so full that you couldn't play with the puppies afterward."

"Oh, come on, nobody could be that full." She chuckled and leaned into him. He lifted his arm and tucked her next to him. She glanced up at the multitude of stars. "It makes me feel so insignificant."

He glanced down at her. "What does?"

She pointed up at the stars. "That."

He stopped walking and stared up at the heavens. "Even in all that beauty, you would never be insignificant."

She turned and snaked her arms around his neck. "You say the most romantic things."

He gave a small chuff and shook his head. "I'm the least romantic person on the face of the earth."

"Take the compliment and kiss me." She lifted her eyebrows and waited. But not for long.

TWELVE DAYS LATER:

Waking up was an instant event in Thanatos' life. The fact he could linger in bed with Eve beside him was a treat he'd treasure. He snaked his arms around her and found her neck with his lips, all without opening his eyes.

She melted into him and her hand stroked his cheek. "Morning." Her sleepy word was a whisper on the morning air.

"Mmm..." It wasn't yet, but it soon would be. He tilted his pelvis and introduced his morning wood to his woman's delightful backside. He tightened his closed lids at the thought. Not his.

Eve moaned and lifted her leg. He kissed her shoulder and aligned his shaft with her core. Soft, warm, morning sex would be one of the indelible memories he'd take away with him when this assignment was done.

He worked his cock into her, slowly moving forward and sliding back. His hands traveled her skin. The slight puckers from her scars had become a part of her, as much as her laugh and smile. He teased her nipples with soft caresses. He'd learned her body. Learned that she enjoyed stronger stimulation in the evenings, but mornings? They were all about soft, languid touches and a slow build up. He shifted her top leg and slid deeper. He dropped his head to hers and breathed against her hair as he pushed into her and pulled out. Her heat grabbed at him, her body ignited a sensory trail that pooled sparks of white-hot energy at the base of his spine. He found her earlobe and sucked it into his mouth. She gasped and pushed back against him and he noted the reaction. Her sensuous sounds agitated those sparks, exciting them into lightning bolts. He slipped his hand down and caressed her clit. The little pearl peeked out of its hood. He used two fingers and stroked both sides at once, mimicking the thrust of his cock. Eve moaned and then gasped. His thrusts, no longer languid, surged into her warmth. Eve's hand clutched his arm, and her nails bit into his skin as she shouted his name. He slammed into her, feeling her body clench around him. He followed her over the edge. He pulled her tighter against him and thrust through his release. He pulled her back into him so there was no space between them. He burrowed his face into her long brown hair and for the first time since his parents died, he prayed. He prayed for a chance. Just one. A chance to be with this woman, forever.

CHAPTER 16

Thanatos checked the surveillance system for the farm one more time. While he trusted their position hadn't been compromised, he wasn't going to get slack. Trust but verify. A motto that kept you alive. He lowered the lid to his computer as he listened to Eve humming in the living room. She knocked on the door. "Okay, I'm out of here. I'll see you when we get done!"

He lifted from his chair, met her halfway, and dropped a kiss on her upturned lips. "Is Joanne waiting for you?"

"Yep. We are putting up dill pickles today."

"You mean she's making the pickles and you're playing with the puppies."

"Well, I will play with them, but I do want to learn how to make pickles. When we canned all those tomatoes, I managed to last the whole day without going out and being mauled by those precious angels." She wrapped her arms around his neck. "What are you going to do while I'm busy?"

"I need to do some work, and then I'm going to town to pick up a few things for us. Is your list on the fridge?"

"It is. I better go. Joanne said we'd start at eight sharp. Come down to their house when you get back?" She lifted onto her toes and swept her tongue over his lips. The woman had blossomed since they'd been on the small farm. She was turning into a little tigress in the bedroom, and she was enchanting.

He slowed the kiss, or they'd never leave the house. She sighed and leaned into him. That small move was his fucking kryptonite, that small sway and happy sigh, as if the world was better when she was in his arms and held tightly. Yeah, when she did that he was made of steel, ten feet tall, and fucking bulletproof. Hell, not only was he hooked, but she had Joanne wrapped around her finger and Charlie would do anything for her. Thankfully, Chase hadn't come back to the farm since that first night, so his initial plans to take out the competition didn't need to be implemented. Besides, permanently removing Joanne and Charlie's kid might cause a rift. He turned her around and swatted her ass when she wiggled it on her way out the door.

The screen door slammed shut, and he listened to the sound of her shoes crunching against the gravel. He flipped his computer open and hit up his dead drops. There was a draft waiting in Guardian's account.

Call.

Well that was easy enough. He pulled the desk-top phone to him and pushed the last button, activating the newest encryption software before he dialed the number he knew by heart.

"Operator Two Seven Four."

"Sunset Clearance, Fifth Operative."

"Stand by Fifth Operative." The woman's voice was a steady balm. She'd never changed. Not in the twenty-five years he'd worked for Guardian. Rationally, he knew it was a computer or some sort of artificial intelligence, yet he still had a picture in his head of Operator Two Seven Four. In his mind she wore a dress like those 1950s telephone operators, and had blonde hair, blue eyes, and bright red lipstick, and rolled her eyes at the type-A operatives who called at all hours of the night. If Guardian's shrinks ever got ahold of that bit of mental imagery for a computer system, he'd probably be pulled from the field.

"Authenticate Emerald." Bengal's voice snapped him back to the present.

"Isle. What do you have for me?"

"Too much to put in the dead drop, that's for fucking sure. What we do know is that Wellington's second in command ordered your asset's intake. As far as we can ascertain, all Wellington's assets, less those destroyed in the vault explosion, were assumed by a P. Negron who is a known associate and long thought to be second in command under Wellington, although Jewell suspects Negron may actually have been pulling Wellington's strings. She's following a money trail now because it has an eerily familiar feel to it. We've seen assets being absorbed without rhyme or reason like this before. Assets that we believe are tied to Stratus."

"Makes sense. So, Negron ordered the medical personnel to bring Eve in."

"It would seem. We were able to track down Dr. Stephanopoulos. He was the only doctor Eve named who we could find. The man had flown to Malta under an assumed identity. Since Asp was in the general vicinity, we had him check in on the good doctor."

"And?"

"Before the man could say much, a hit squad, not ours, paid him a visit."

"Asp?"

"He made it out. Took seven down before he found safe haven. The doctor indicated Negron wanted Eve alive and wanted a new vaccine tested on her. Radiological."

"What the fuck? You mean they are looking for a vaccine for radiation poisoning? Is that possible?"

"No, which is why this is so bizarre. Radiation destroys cells in a way a biological agent couldn't. We have sent queries to researchers in both fields asking questions. Nothing that should be traceable to Eve, but even if they could put two and two together, we need the information to try to figure out what this Negron is trying to do."

"Do you think Stephanopoulos was lying?"

"Asp said the man was dying and knew it. No reason to lie."

"Fuck. All right. What about our government?"

"That is a fucking nightmare, but it is being worked. Somehow, the national news got wind of Eve's supposed abduction. Some woman named Lori Hutchinson is all

over the news sobbing about her friend who's gone missing. An elementary school teacher, loved by the public,
blah, blah, blah... Anyway, there's a picture of Eve on the
news. Every channel, every hour. It's gone viral online,
too."

"All right. So, we need to change her appearance
before we head to the Rose."

"Yeah, don't bother. We'll find an airstrip near you
and fly in for an extraction, but not until we know for a
fact our government's interest has shut down."

"I could take her out of the country."

"That's been discussed, but even if we flew you out on
a private aircraft, you would have less assets available to
assist, more unknowns, and a greater response time
should shit go downhill. Fury and Anubis agree. You stay
put right where you are and keep a low profile."

"I can do that. Are you telling me the three-week
timetable could be extended?"

"I'd be lying if I told you it won't be. All I know is your
lady is wanted by too many people. It's highly publicized,
and her face is all over the news. I'm assuming you knew
that?"

"No. I haven't turned on a television." He flicked his
eyes toward Charlie and Joanne's house. He'd need to
make sure they understood Eve was in protective custody,
not being held against her will.

"How are things going with her?"

"Meaning?"

"Meaning she's been given a shit hand. How's she
coping?"

"Pretty damn well, actually." He chuckled. "She's

supposed to be with one of my property managers making pickles, but I'd lay you even odds, she's in the kennel playing with the puppies instead."

The silence on the other end of the line drew his attention to the phone. "Bengal?"

"I'm here. I'm just... stupefied."

He frowned at the phone. "Repeat?"

"Stupefied, rendered stupid. You actually like this woman."

A bitter laugh pushed out. "And exactly what good would it do to admit an attraction? I am doing a job. I'll deliver her to the Rose and then be back to doing what I do best. What about the lead you've been working for me?"

"Ah, I copy, closed subject. Before I allow you to direct the conversation away from her, I'm going to remind you to keep an open mind. You have a job offer on the table. You wouldn't need to continue in your current role at Guardian."

"Fury has a big mouth."

"Bullshit, but he does have staff meetings, and as Anubis and I are his staff, we know what the fuck is going on. Don't be stupid, Thanatos. Take a chance. Getting long in the tooth in this profession isn't a given. Let the kids with the stamina and more guts than brains take on the world. We've done our time."

He snorted and shook his head. "Thanks for the counseling session, Doctor Bengal, but I'm pretty fucking positive Eve would never be able to excuse my past."

Bengal's voice softened, "Does she have to know?"

"Would you lie to keep your woman?"

"If it meant having her with me? I don't know, man. I'd consider it."

"I couldn't."

"I know, but that doesn't mean I'm not going to tell you what I think."

"You've told me, now do you have any movement on the lead?"

"We've got a possible trail. Jared is sending an investigator to San Francisco to the genetics lab. We want to have the DNA run by an accredited lab and make sure there isn't a mistake. Before you go off half-cocked, this isn't a made for television crime drama. DNA results aren't an overnight process, and we are in a queue behind a fuck-ton of Federal cases. We aren't rocking the boat and getting our inquiry stalled or pushed back. As soon as we know for sure there is something there, I'll let you know. Remember, the DNA hit might not be legit, and this could be a total mind fuck."

Which was what he kept telling himself. The slightest possibility of a lead after all these years played hell with his internal desire to keep hope at bay. "All right, I need to go talk to my property managers about what's been in the news. I'm going to flash that fancy fucking badge you gave me to ensure they know I haven't kidnapped her."

"What kind of place do you have? Never mind, I don't want to know. I trust you to run your own house. Just make sure your position isn't compromised."

"Gee, thanks. I never thought to do that."

"Fuck you, my friend."

"Yeah, not in this lifetime." He chuckled as he disconnected the line and deactivated the encryption devices.

He leaned forward and scrubbed his face. He had a couple dead drops to check before he faced the exposure issue with Joanne, Charlie, and Chase.

He reopened the browser and logged into the communal Shadow account. He chuckled at Moriah's response to Lycos' single word status query from last week. The two-word response that started with "fuck" and ended with "you" was her standard reply to almost every comment. Good to know she was alive and well. The line below was Asp. It simply stated "on-target". Anubis added the word "almonds". Bengal replied "furball" and Thanatos added to the thread with a single word, "Armani". His counterparts had a great time with his fondness for designer clothes. God, if they could see him now. Smoke hadn't logged on yet and Tempest, well, it had been forever since they'd seen the word "teapot" on the check-in list. Fury hadn't responded as he'd been reported dead years ago. The quarterly "are you alive" post was hit and miss, but usually they'd all check in during the year. Usually.

He left the draft in the drop box and exited that account only to enter another. He clicked on the draft and froze. The fragmented words seared against the white digital backdrop.

College Park Atlanta stratus caution situation crimson

The next line gave the address. Holy fuck. He read the words again as he hit the line to Guardian.

"Operator Two–"

"Put me through to Bengal immediately. Sunset Clearance Fifth Operative."

"Standby." The word was clipped and immediate.

"Authenticate Emerald."

"Isle. It's Tempest. I found him."

"What the fuck are you talking about?"

He relayed the information about his dead drop contact, that he'd violated protocol, but he'd found Tempest.

"So, it could have been compromised."

"Fuck, yes it could have, but if it wasn't? If this is him? He's asking for help. He's calling for the cavalry with that crimson code."

"We have personal security teams and investigators in Atlanta. Let me get them moving."

"You know he'll ghost if someone he doesn't know shows up."

"Fuck. Moriah's in Arizona. Anubis is in South Dakota. Asp is making his way back from Malta. I can get Lycos down from the mountain top..."

"I'll go. I'm two hours away."

"No. You have a mission."

"She's safe here."

"And if you don't come back?"

"I'll let her know to contact you if I don't come back by tomorrow morning. You can trace the call and send a team in for her."

"I can't compromise her security. She's too damn important."

"Believe me, I don't want to leave her, and fuck you before you make any wise ass comment about emotional involvement, but this is Tempest. He's been silent for years. Years!"

"Which leads me back to my initial point. This could be a trap; he could have been compromised. I'll fly down from DC. You stay put."

"If you're flying down from DC, fly into Montgomery. I'll have someone from here meet you at the airport. You take custody of Eve until I get back with Tempest."

"What if you're followed?"

"What if the fucking moon is purple, Bengal? Are you going to sit there and second guess this until next year or are you going to get me authorization to retrieve one of our brothers?"

"Fuck. I'll brief it up the chain, but you do not move from where you are without specific authorization from me. Do you understand?"

"Understood."

He disconnected the encryption, shoved his desk chair out of the way, and flipped up the rug underneath. He depressed the floorboard and slid it back, revealing a control panel. Twelve digits and a thumbprint scan later he lifted the portion of the floor that concealed his weapons vault.

He grabbed several duffle bags and started filling them up. God only knew what he'd find going after Tempest, but he'd be ready to either start a war or finish one. He emptied his vault into the two bags and hung a fucking armory off his body. He fished out another bulletproof vest and then darted across the room to the equipment he'd brought from Guardian's SUV, tossing through bags until he found what he was looking for— the compact medical kit. He grabbed all three bags and hauled them to the truck Fury had given them to drive in

South Dakota. He'd already changed the plates so it showed a Georgia registration. The phone rang in his office as he shut the truck's tailgate. Sprinting through the house, he slid to a stop in front of his desk and grabbed the receiver, pushing the encryption button.

"Go."

"You've been given clearance to attempt a retrieval. I'll need the events and when and how you accessed dead drop email."

He rattled off the information.

"Cyber will respond to the email and hopefully Tempest will come back online to receive it. If he does, we'll be able to talk real time. Archangel has ordered a team from Atlanta to assist you. I'll send rendezvous directions to your phone. Dom Ops will bring the mission online. It is the only way we can authorize an armed response in College Park."

"I'll be clear of here in less than ten minutes. Are you flying down?"

Bengal covered the receiver on his end. He could hear him talking to someone. "Yeah, I'm heading to the airstrip as soon as I tie up loose ends here."

"I'll send my property manager. Where are you flying into?"

"Maxwell Air Force Base. Have whoever is coming for me meet me at the Day Street gate at 1800 hours."

"Copy."

"Do you have the Guardian communications kit?"

He glanced at the kits he'd tossed around looking for the medical kit. "Yeah." Pulling the cord on the phone to its fullest extent, he grabbed it. "Got it."

"There is an earwig and small transmitter that clips to your collar. It's inside the top of the hardened plastic kit. Take it out and push the blue button. It will pair with your cell. Depress the red button and it goes into talk-to-activate mode. Depress the white button and you're muted. The phone only has to be within one hundred feet of the device you're wearing, so you can go hands free to take care of business."

"Copy. I'll connect as soon as I get Eve settled."

"You'll be connected to the Ops Center. I'm heading your way."

"Understood." He hung up the phone and hit the encryption button to sever the communication. With a last glance around the office to make sure he hadn't forgotten anything that could help him retrieve Tempest, he locked up his office and headed out of the house at a dead run.

The big truck spit gravel when he gunned the accelerator. He'd just pulled onto the access road heading to Charlie and Joanne's house when he saw Charlie's truck coming at him like a bat out of hell, the old man's arm waving like crazy flagging him down. They both slammed on the brakes and he cranked down his window.

"Chase saw the damn news reports. He called the cops because he recognized Evelyn. He called us to warn us about you being a kidnapper. I told that boy he was full of shit."

"Fuck!" He grabbed his credential holder off the seat and tossed it into Charlie's truck. "I'm Guardian. She's in protective custody. Some fucking nasty people, including our own government, are hunting for her. Your son just blew her cover."

"Knew you weren't a damn kidnapper. That boy of mine. Damn it!"

"I need to get to Eve. Where is she?"

"Ma is keeping her at the house. They are both fit to be tied. The cops will be coming hot and heavy. What do you need me to do?"

His hand pushed his hair back. Think, damn it. Son of a bitch, he was wedged between a rock and a fucking hard place. He couldn't let the fucking local cops get involved in this. They couldn't see Eve, confirm she was there. She needed to leave and so did he, so damn it, she was going with him to Atlanta. He slammed his hand against the steering wheel before he turned his attention to Charlie. "Okay. This is what's going to happen. I need you to be at the Day Street Gate for Maxwell Air Force Base. Be there at six o'clock tonight. You need to pick someone up for me. Just go to the gate and wait. He'll find you. I'll give him your truck's description. I'm going to grab Eve, and we are going to get the hell out of here." Hopefully before the fucking county mounties showed up.

"I can do that. What do you want me to say to the cops when they get here?"

"Nothing. I'll handle that end of it. If they give you any grief, tell them you want a lawyer. My people should be able to handle everything. I've got to go before we're trapped here."

"Go get her, then drive through the orchard behind the house. You'll see a small access road that runs parallel to the McKenzie's peanut field. Take that to your right. Ride it down to where the fence takes a sharp left and then just plow through the soybean field. On the other side you can pop onto Mac's driveway. The soybeans are your crop. It's a level field with no drainage ditch before the road. Go, get her, and get the hell out of here."

His badge and identification came flying back at him through his open window. He snagged it and slammed on the accelerator. The entire conversation lasted no more than thirty seconds, but he fucking felt like a barrel of a loaded weapon was planted firmly against his temple.

The truck slid to a stop in front of the small white house, and Eve flew out. She grabbed at the passenger side door and clambered up. He gunned the accelerator as soon as her ass hit leather. The passenger side door slammed shut from the vehicle's lurch forward.

"Tell me why he'd report me!" Eve pulled the seatbelt over her shoulder as she yelled the question.

"You've been splashed all over the news as a kidnap victim."

"You've got to be kidding me? Who is even missing me?"

"Lori."

"Fuck, she should be in Vegas."

He snapped his eyes her direction. "Just how well do you know that woman?"

"What? Watch out!" She pointed as she screamed. He swerved, clipping the low hanging branches of a peach tree. "For God's sake, drive, don't look at me!"

He floored the vehicle and flew through the rows of trees. A set of tractor ruts sent them airborne. He fought against the pull of the tires and kept them from slamming into a tree. Braking sharply, he cranked the wheel to the right and slid onto the access road, tilting up onto two tires before the truck slapped the ground, forcefully bouncing both of them against their seatbelts. He stomped on the gas and flew down the trail.

"How well do you know Lori?" He shouted but focused on the road.

"I don't know? She's my friend."

"How did you meet her?"

"We started teaching at the same time. We were new so we hung out. Slow down! You have to turn!"

He saw the road veer left and the soybean field directly in front of them. Thank god the vehicle was a four-wheel drive, and it wasn't later in the year. The damn things could grow six feet tall. They flew from the track into the field. The grown swell along the rows of soybeans jolted them like a gunner on a fifty-caliber machine gun. The field seemed to go on forever. Eve braced one hand against the dash and held the oh-shit handle at the front right corner of the cab with the other. Finally, he saw the road and decelerated only enough to swing the vehicle onto the gravel before he punched the gas again. Flashes of blue lights streaked by ahead of them. The main road and the county sheriff, no doubt.

"Get down." He growled and without hesitation Eve bent down, hugging her legs, disappearing from sight. He slowed the truck and stopped at the end of the road. A highway patrol vehicle approached with its lights blazing. One flew by, the siren screaming as it passed. Another, not more than a car length behind the first, gunned its motor and passed the emergency vehicle in front of him. The slower vehicle hit its breaks and barely made the turn into his driveway. The other vehicle flew to a lesser known access point to his property located further down the road. Fuck, Chase had told them everything.

"Stay down." He watched the vehicle fly by before he hit the turn signal and pulled sedately onto the county road.

CHAPTER 17

A cell phone appeared in front of her face.

"Stay down. Get down on the floor so you're more comfortable." She unfastened her seatbelt and slid to the floorboard. With care she sat up, making sure she wasn't visible.

"Sunset Clearance, Fifth Operative."

She snapped her attention to Dolan. "What?"

"Our cover has been blown."

"I know that. What the hell happened?"

He slashed his hand toward her to silence her.

"Rude, much?"

He pointed to his ear. "Affirmative, primary is secure. We were reported by a tertiary contact. County police and highway patrols have responded... Negative, property owners will not talk... I'm taking her with me to College Park... I copy... Standing by."

He glanced down at her and nodded.

"Who were you talking to just now?"

"Guardian."

"What is College Park?"

"A suburb of Atlanta. I have a friend who is in trouble. We're going to go get him and then get the hell out."

"What kind of trouble?"

"I have no idea. I was coming down to tell you I'd be leaving for a day or two and that another person from Guardian would come to watch over you when Charlie stopped me. Why would Lori launch a media campaign about you being missing?"

"I don't know. She and her husband go away for three weeks every year. They should be in Vegas. We usually check in with each other, but... I don't know."

"What's Lori's last name?"

"Hutchinson."

He flicked his finger up again. "Isle... Yes, sir."

He glanced at her and his jaw tightened.

"No sir, I won't be doing that. I can protect her and get to Tempest."

She watched as he shook his head, but he didn't say anything.

"We can't stay where we were, not until Cyber does its magic. We are less than two hours away, and no offense, sir, but I won't leave Tempest out in the cold any longer. He coded his request for help at crimson."

A slight sneer spread across his face, and he looked down and winked at her.

"Affirmative, we are en route."

"They don't want you to take me with you? What was I supposed to do? Stay there for the cops to come take me and then let *them* decide what to do with me? No, thank you. Some shrink would show up, say I'm insane, and then I'd be a lab rat again. They can go fuck themselves if they think I'm not going with you. Just let them try to keep me away. Idiots"

He chuckled and reached for his shirt collar. "Affirmative, Guardian. She was unaware you could hear her."

"They can hear me?" *Holy shit.* She'd just told off Dolan's bosses.

He nodded and flicked his collar over showing her a small box. He mouthed 'microphone'.

"Well, good." She crossed her arms over her chest and leaned back against the door of the truck, facing him. Looking up at him, the sky and trees flying past the windows provided a dizzying backdrop, so she dropped her eyes to her knees and took a deep breath. And then another. Holy crap, they'd just run from the police. A real Bonnie and Clyde maneuver.

She snorted and shot a glance up at Dolan.

He lifted an eyebrow, but she waved him off.

That was all she needed the people at Guardian to hear. *'I was laughing at the thought of us being a Dukes of Hazzard version of Bonnie and Clyde.' Yeah. No.*

Speeding through orchards and fields of... whatever it was they destroyed, aside, running from the police was so not good, even if she was with a federal police officer. Wait, was he a police officer? Agent? Special Agent... no he said operative. Like CIA clandestine type stuff?

His voice sliced through her musings. "I copy. I've arranged for transport to my last location for Bengal. What is the rendezvous location? Copy... Zero hour? Roger... Affirm, I'll have you on, but I'm muting." He chuckled. "Damage control is an affirmative."

He reached to his collar and messed with it for a bit before he extended his hand to her. "You can sit up here in the seat, now."

She grasped the hand extended to her and used it as an anchor to un-wedge herself from where she sat, stuck between the seat and the dash.

"I'm not going to apologize for what I said." She meant that. She wasn't going anywhere that Dolan wasn't.

"From what Guardian told me, College Park is a rough area. I wouldn't ever consider taking you with me on a retrieval operation of this nature."

He lifted a hand stopping her automatic words of objection.

"I would never willingly put you in danger. This operation is dangerous."

"Are we going to do the 'retrieval' that you talked about? Is it like when you got me out of the medical facility? That kind of retrieval?" She pulled the seatbelt over her shoulder, secured it and snugged it tight.

"No, not necessarily. The individual we are going to attempt to find hasn't been heard from in, literally, years. Some believed he was dead."

His jaw clenched and his hands tightened on the wheel.

She understood. "You didn't believe he was gone." It was a statement. Not a question.

"No, I didn't. The way he fell off the map was wrong. He wasn't on an assignment. Our profession is solitary. Sometimes we go years without seeing others who do what we do, but there are mechanisms. We communicate. Check-in. He would have let us know he was walking away." He shook his head. "He would have let us know. I couldn't let it go. So, I reached out in a completely unauthorized way and, quite frankly, it was a last attempt. I kept thinking he could be in a similar position as you. No way out. No help because you didn't know how to get to it. Or you could get to it, but were being monitored. I don't know, something told me to reach out. So, I went against all standard operating procedures."

"And it worked. I'm glad you went against procedures. This man? He's your friend?"

"He's a colleague. One of the few I associate with."

"But you don't associate with them like, hanging out, right?"

He chuckled and shook his head. "No. Two or more of us in the same location tends to be combustible."

"How?"

"That's one of the questions you don't want me to answer."

He glanced at her and his level stare told her he was correct. Still... he was one of the good guys. Yes, they had divergent ideas as to what 'good' was. Many previous conversations had emphasized that, but they'd grown close. He held her at night like she was priceless. He made her feel like a princess. He was kind, considerate, but so damn complex. Each time she thought she understood him, a new facet emerged.

She leaned back in her seat and watched as the trees lining the side of the road flew past. The time with him had been an awakening. Growing up institutionalized, she'd led a sheltered life, but she understood the difference between good people and bad people. The man beside her was good. True, there was a darkness inside him, and it probably stemmed from the murder of his parents. She could understand that. Since finding out about the manipulation of her past, she could understand why there was a darkness. When she was alone, hatred and rage threatened to consume her. She hated the fact that her past had been stolen from her. Rage swirled like a cyclone wrapping around her heart. The pressure, pain, and utter helplessness the past conjured up could be overwhelming. Except. Except for the fact she was free now. Except for the fact she had a chance at a new life. Except for the fact she could go forward and leave the pain and suffering and helplessness behind her. It was that sunshine, that ray of light, that pulled her forward and away from the darkness that threatened to consume her. She rolled her head on the seat and stared at Dolan as he drove. Did he have that hope, that ray of light? Did he have that sunrise in his future? What weapon did he have to fight the darkness inside him?

"What are we going to do when we get to Atlanta?"

"We're going to rendezvous with a team of Guardian personnel. We'll determine at that point the safest measures for your protection." He glanced at her and smiled. "Specific facts about location, personnel, and threats in the area, will determine the course of action we take."

"The safest measure for me is to be with you." In that, she had complete confidence. He made a noncommittal sound. He didn't necessarily agree with her, but then again, he hadn't disagreed. She would take that as a win. They fell into silence as roadside signs started to appear along with billboards advertising companies in Atlanta. Traffic entered the highway and the road snarled and congested.

"There should be a tactical vest and ball cap in the largest green bag. Shove your hair up under the hat. We still need to disguise your face from any camera systems that may be monitored."

"Do you honestly think my face on a traffic camera in Atlanta would be recognized?" She took off her seatbelt and leaned over the seat, rummaging around in the largest bag looking for the hat.

"Ordinarily, I'd say no, but the forces we're dealing with aren't ordinary. There's chatter on the DarkNet about you and, if you believe my handlers, which I do, the FBI and CIA are also very interested in your where-abouts. So, is it a stretch of the imagination to believe someone has implemented a computer program that would sift through facial recognition points such as traffic cameras, ATMs, or shopping centers? No, it's not outside the realm of possibility."

"Shopping centers?"

"Absolutely. Think about it. National brands have national connections and normally have a centralized cloud system. Their security, whether provided locally or through a national brand, uploads surveillance tape to the home headquarters. All it would take is for some-body to come in through a backdoor. One of my contemporaries is a whiz with computers. He does things that would leave you dumbfounded. People have no idea how many times a day their images are recorded and placed in servers or in a cloud. Even in the privacy of their own home, images and voice recordings can happen without their knowledge or permission."

"How?"

"Smart TVs are access points into any home. Any laptop computer, a desktop that has a camera is an access point. Laptops have built-in microphones that are easy to activate without the individual knowing. The same goes for any of the home assist AIs currently on the market. Companies mine for information. How do you think advertisements show up in your feed when you go online?" He glanced over his shoulder before he merged traffic lanes.

She pulled a battered black hat out of the bag. The thing had been crushed at the very bottom of the bag and was smashed. She punched the cardboard at the front of the thing to remove some of the creases. It still looked deformed, but she pulled her hair up into a high ponytail, twisted it tightly, and slammed the hat down on her head. "The government has regulations against people listening through those devices, though, right?"

"For the most part, yes. Have you ever read a terms of service agreement in its entirety? You know, those twenty-five-page documents that nobody understands and nobody bothers to read? Undoubtedly, there is a line or two in there that indicates the company, in its best interests, may monitor conversations after transmission. Of course, that is legal for that company. You agree to use their product under their terms. The unethical hackers don't bother with vague information in terms of service agreements. They will use any weakness in any firewall or system to exploit or utilize the information in a way that would benefit them."

She put her seatbelt back on while his words settled. "I didn't realize the invasion of privacy was so pervasive."

"I'm not saying it is. I am saying there is potential for that happening. For the most part, companies are ethical. For the most part, hackers target systems that contain mass amounts of information. For the most part, people as individuals aren't targeted. However, when you have a powerful entity without scruples looking for an individual, all these points of weakness can be exploited. What we're trying to do is ensure you don't come up on any of the points."

"So that's why being at your farm was safe. But, you have Wi-Fi and computers. So do Joanne and Charlie." She examined her thumbnail as she spoke. Could it be she was never truly safe?

"My computer systems are on a secure, encrypted connection. Charlie and Joanne have a normal system, but the likelihood that anyone would connect them with me or them with you is slim to none. Or rather *was* slim to none. Thanks to Chase calling the cops, we can assume the farm will now be under surveillance."

"So, we're not going back there?" Damn it. She really liked Joanne. She liked his little house and the solitude. She'd miss the animals, the farm, the stars at night. Somehow in time they'd been here, she had come to think of the place as home.

"I don't know. Guardian will work to contain the situation. If they feel it's safe, we'll go back. If they don't, I suspect we will be relocated or sent to the safe house I mentioned before."

"You said until the government bought off on the fact that I wasn't important, we wouldn't be allowed to go to the safe house."

He lifted a finger and cocked his head. The people from Guardian must be talking in his ear again. He reached to his collar and messed with the microphone before he spoke, "Affirmative."

He grabbed his cell phone and perched it on top of the center console.

The phone lit up and a woman's face filled the screen. Her voice was small and tinny sounding in the large noisy cab of the truck, but she could hear the woman distinctly. "In two point four miles, exit right and hang an immediate left at the stop sign."

She whispered, "Who is she?"

The woman looked up and smiled. "Hey, my name's Jewell, and I'll be your traffic guide all the way to College Park. As you travel, I'm turning off cameras and ensuring you have green lights all the way through. We'll piss off a few thousand commuters, but, hey, what's the use of being able to manipulate technology if you can't have fun?"

"Can you see us?" She looked down at the lady who seemed lost in her own work.

She glanced up for a moment and chuckled. "I can see your shoulder. The camera angle on this phone isn't the best. Thanatos, veer right at the next fork. I have your vehicle pin-pointed with GPS. I'll tell you when to turn, and unless we have some major problems or a really clueless asshole who decides to blow a light, you should be good to go all the way to your meeting in College Park."

"Thanatos?" She lifted her eyes to Dolan. "Why did she call you that?"

"It's just a call sign."

She leaned back into her seat away from the phone and away from him. *Thanatos.* She had heard that name before. Where? It was in college. There was something about the name. What she wouldn't give for her phone and a search engine. A call sign. Thanatos was his call sign. She listened as Jewell directed the vehicle. Every light was green as they traveled through the suburbs of Atlanta.

"My team is having problems accessing the next set of cameras. Eve, I need you to duck down. Now."

She glanced at Dolan before she folded in half, hugged her thighs and faced the floor.

"Three more cameras. Two more... standby. Last one. Okay, you can sit up. The next left and then you'll see our team. Black SUV parked on the right at the corner. I'm going into eagle eye mode. Dom Ops the line is yours in four, three, two, one..."

"Dom Ops has the con. Communications check starting with primary. Thanatos check-in," a deep voice boomed over the radio.

"Loud and clear. Arriving at rendezvous point. Do we have eyes on Tempest?" Dolan pulled their pickup over behind a black SUV.

Four men exited the vehicle. Oh, god, they looked like every television program she had ever seen depicting

SWAT guys. Black clothes, boots, caps and bulletproof vests. And there were guns. Rifles and pistols and every one of the men had more than one. She pushed back into the seat of the truck. *Oh shit.* Maybe she would have been safer at the farm with Joanne. Why did they need all those guns?

"What kind of trouble is your friend in?"

CHAPTER 18

Thanatos glanced at Eve. She seemed to have folded in upon herself when she noticed Guardian's team. He could understand why she would cower. The menace they exuded was palpable, but that couldn't be helped now. He turned the vehicle off. "I'm not sure, but we aren't taking any chances. Stay here." He exited the vehicle, giving a quick glance back to make sure Eve listened to his direction.

"What do we have, and why are we meeting out in the middle of the street?" He glanced at the men in front of him.

One of the men stepped up and started the brief. "We're announcing our presence. You'll see why. We've done three random drive-bys of the building that Dom Ops indicated our primary is located. This neighborhood is held by one of the larger gangs, one we know and have worked with in the past, but they are touchy on a good day. We did a drive-by with thermal. The building we're interested in has a smattering of heat registers that are indicative of humans. The building itself is condemned. Three floors plus a basement. Thermal could not register anything subterranean. The majority of all heat signatures are on the third floor."

He crossed his arms over his chest and nodded. "That means they have high ground and can see us coming."

A second man spoke up. "The question is who has this guy? If it's the Brotherhood, the gang that runs this particular set of streets, does he have market value? If he does, they won't waste him, and we can straight up pay for his release. If he doesn't have intrinsic value, the man's probably not their guest. If someone else is holding him and is confident enough to do so in the Brotherhood's backyard? Then those bastards are hardcore and will most likely put up a fight, which will bring in the Brotherhood. Either way, the best thing to do is to announce our arrival to the men who run these streets."

The first man nodded. "This guy is Hammond. He's our gangland specialist and liaison with the Atlanta PD. We haven't been able to pull him away full time yet, but we're working it. I'm Boxhaur. I'm the team lead and explosive specialist. This is Flynn. He's our weapons and tactics specialist, and that is Redford. He's IT and general all-around badass. I understand you're not familiar with the area."

He reached out and shook each man's hand. "No, I don't normally work inside the United States." He watched the recognition dawn on each of Guardian's men. Hammond was the only one who didn't make the connection and that was because he didn't have the clearance to know about the internal organization of Guardian.

"And the individual we're trying to retrieve? Is he a friend or foe?" Boxhaur asked.

"He was a friend. He's been off the scope a long time. His status as friend or foe is unknown." As much as it gutted him to say so, he wouldn't let a fellow Guardian go into a situation without having full knowledge. Withholding information like that got people killed. He glanced back at the truck.

"And who is she?" Boxhaur again.

"She is in my protective custody. We had to evacuate the location we were at quickly. The question is what to do with her now. She can't be left alone. She's considered a primary to Guardian."

Redford turned to stare at Eve and spoke as he examined her. "Is she friend or foe?"

"Friend," he growled.

A slammed Cadillac inched out of the neighborhood and drove up to their position. The darkened windows rolled down slowly. Thanatos wasn't the only person who had his finger on the trigger as they waited.

"Yo, man, what the men in black want in this neighborhood?"

Thanatos stared at the four people in the vehicle. The smell of marijuana floated freely once the window cracked open.

"Not a damn thing, man." Hammond sauntered toward the car.

"Yo, Ham man, dude, you know we ain't up to no shit. Not since them feds was down here looking at the Corner slugs. We been laying low, man. Ain't doing no time for no Corner crime."

"Not looking to jack you, man." Hammond glanced back at Thanatos. "Running this as a personal favor. No badges unless shit gets real. Got a friend who has a friend in trouble. Going in, get in our man, and get the fuck out. You got any watchdogs or lieutenants in the area, you call them off."

"Why would I do that, man?"

"No badges don't mean the bullets ain't real. Dead is dead, man."

"Somebody holed up on my streets and running something I don't know about? Yo, Ham, that shit can't be."

"I'm quoting gospel to you, Paradise. Have I ever been untrue?" Hammond crossed his arms and stared down the thug in the car.

"You always straight-up man. Where is this friend of a friend supposed to be? Let me know and maybe I take my peoples for a visit."

"And have one of your guys accidentally kill our friend? Nah, man. I would hate to have to take retribution."

"Fuck, man, you do that shit to me?"

"Not me." He nodded at Thanatos. "That man right there? He's bringing the reaper, man. I just get the fuck out of his way. Seems I can be blind when I need to be. What about you?"

The man in the car stared at Hammond for several long seconds before he shifted his gaze to him. Concessions were being given. The gang leader and Hammond were dancing a tune that combatants had been dancing since war began. The gangster wanted peace on his block. He didn't want to go to jail, and he didn't want to lose face. Hammond was giving him the opportunity to look away because it wasn't an official operation, at least according to Atlanta PD.

"It'll cost you, man."

"It always does."

"Seems me and my people are needed at the far side of the hood. Business, you know."

"I hear you." Hammond stepped back and the window wound up until they could see their reflection in the car.

"And that, ladies and gentlemen, is why we have Atlanta PD on our teams." The voice that came through their earpieces broke the tension. "We have a plan, gentlemen. Gear up if you haven't done so. Hammond, you will be assigned overwatch of Thanatos' primary. Boxhaur, Flynn and Redford will go in with Thanatos. We have satellite coverage for the next hour. Thermal imagery is online. We have occupied buildings next door. Use suppressors so the gen pop has no idea what you're doing. We will create a distraction so you can move in."

Bull-fucking-shit. He started to speak, but Hammond spoke over him. "You're going to need me at that location, especially if any of Paradise's men haven't been given the word to back out. Unless you want World War III, gang-land-style. The entire area is a powder keg. Just because I can promise Paradise a favor doesn't mean all his people will be so inclined. I know these people. Unless they see someone they know, someone who has a rep, this op will be riddled with holes, of the bullet variety." Hammond crossed his arms over his chest. "Call a patrol in to sit on the chick." He threw his chin back toward the truck and Eve.

"No." Thanatos barked his rejection. "No one here is coded to protect her the way I am. Check with my division, Dom Ops. I'm pulling rank." He glanced at the three Guardians in front of him.

"Stand-by," Dom Ops punched out.

Thanatos glanced at the cab of the truck. Eve had that cap pulled down, and she was tucked back into the seat, slouched down. Damn, from elementary school teacher to unwilling participant in a hostile retrieval of a possibly compromised Shadow operative. Just another hash mark added to the million reasons why she needed to be reassigned to a personal security operative or someone like Fury or Bengal who had walked away from the world— men who had the skills to keep her safe and the distance from the field to ensure the Shadow world didn't touch her. He should have let Bengal reassign her. What the fuck had he been thinking? He hadn't. He'd been reaching for a small bit of happiness and look what it fucking cost her. Too much. She was such a gentle creature. She should never have been brought into his shadow.

"Dom Ops to all parties, be advised we have inbound vehicles. Three SUVs four minutes out. Cyber is trying to slow them down. Hostiles. Thanatos, glue that woman to your six and keep her alive. She's worth millions on the black market if they take her or figure out who the fuck she is. Let's move!"

Fuck. "Dom Ops, explain hostiles!" He darted around the truck and opened the passenger side door.

"Two of the three license plates have been used during incidents on fringes of Stratus operations."

Son of a bitch! "Change of plans, you're coming with us."

"Why?" She squeaked as he caught her when she dove down from the truck.

"Bad guys coming in hot." It took twenty seconds to grab his rifle and extra ammo. With the boxes of ammo shoved into his pocket, he grabbed her hand and dragged her to the front of the truck. He spun and pointed at her. "You will stay at my back. Grab my jacket and don't fucking let go for any reason." He jabbed two fingers at Hammond. "He will be directly behind you. You will be safe, but this is going to get loud and dangerous. Do you trust me?"

She nodded, her eyes wide and her complexion a waxy white.

"I will protect you. Understand?"

She nodded again and reached out, grabbing the back of his jacket. That would have to do. He spun and nodded to Boxhaur. "Move!"

"What the fuck is Stratus?" Hammond shouted as he charged a round in his rifle.

"Big, bad shit," Redford bellowed as he took point. As a unit, they flew around the corner, and as a team they ran the block and a half to a corner where they stopped. He pushed back against the building and felt Eve suck up close to his side, her hand never loosening the grip she had on his jacket.

Boxhaur stared at each of them. "On my three, we move down two buildings. Tuck up close and tight to these structures. There is an alley. We use it to get to the back of the building. If they are expecting company, they will be watching out the front."

Thanatos nodded. He'd follow Boxhaur's lead, for now. The man counted down and they moved as a unit on three. Redford took the corner first. Single file with Eve glued to his back, they skimmed next to the brick buildings and moved quickly through the overgrown grass to their target. Redford, Boxhaur, and Flynn communicated with sign language. He agreed with the tactics they discussed, and when they glanced at him, he nodded.

Redford would take the point and enter the back. He would clear the first floor with Flynn. Boxhaur and Hammond would clear the second floor. Thanatos would move to the top floor but hold in the stairwell. If the SUVs that Guardian had detected were actually heading to this location, that would put four fighters in staged locations to delay and, if possible, repel any additional personnel.

There were at least four heat signatures on the third floor. Boxhaur signed the warning to Thanatos. He nodded his understanding. *Four men.* Hopefully one of them was Tempest, and he prayed to God his friend hadn't been compromised.

Redmond pulled open the back door and slid in, followed by Flynn. Boxhaur moved up to the door and waited. At his signal, Hammond moved from the rear to position himself behind the team lead. They entered.

Thanatos moved forward. When he got to the door he turned and whispered, "We are going in the door and up the stairs. Follow me and do exactly what I say when I say it."

"Okay." Thankfully, some color had returned to her cheeks and she seemed less terrified.

With his rifle in front of him, he rose to a crouching position and opened the screen door. They moved straight to the stairwell and silently climbed. A gunshot below them blew everything to hell. Thanatos grabbed Eve's hand and ran up the stairs. As he reached the top landing, the door opened into the stairwell. Rearing back, he kicked the door, slamming whoever was on the other side backward.

"Hold this." Thanatos shoved his rifle into Eve's hands. He pulled his automatic and kicked the door again and then plastered himself against the wall. The force of his kick shattered the old door's latch. A volley of gunfire erupted below them but there was nothing from the third floor or the man he'd kicked. Thanatos moved forward and grabbed the bottom of the door, pulling it open while keeping Eve behind him and out of range. He leaned forward quickly and peeked down the hall. Nothing. There were four doors that he could see, and all were open. He took a chance and leaned out farther. One room at the end of the hall had a closed door.

Shouts and a cascade of gunfire at the front of the building were his impetus to move. He leaned over and took the rifle from Eve, slinging it over his back. He pulled out one of his smaller automatics and handed it to her.

"I don't want this!" She hissed but took the gun. "I won't use it. I can't! I won't take someone's life!"

"I know you don't want it. This is the last resort only. Point it like you would your finger and squeeze the trigger." He thumped his chest with his free hand. "Point here, right here, and pull the trigger, but only if it's your last resort. If you follow me and stay close, you won't need to use it." He pointed his weapon down to the ground as he crouched and whispered as he rose, "Keep it pointed to the ground."

She nodded and crouched directly behind him.

"When I reach the door, you stay by the wall and watch down the hall to make sure nobody comes out of those doors. I have to clear each room. Do you understand?"

She nodded again and licked her lips, casting a glance down the hallway.

He moved forward, and she echoed his steps.

He stopped at the first door, and Eve pinned her back to the wall with her eyes pinging along the hallway.

He moved in and cleared the small apartment. One bedroom, small kitchen, one bathroom, two closets. They moved forward, zigging across the hall.

Second apartment cleared. Same setup, more drug paraphernalia, but same configuration.

Gunfire from downstairs was sporadic, and Guardian's comms were rife with talk. He tuned it out. He had to be able to focus to keep them safe.

They cleared all four of the smaller apartments.

He moved to the door that was closed and stopped

short, pulling her back so he could whisper, "I want you to stay right here. Don't move from this position."

He glanced down the hallway when he heard gunfire. It was getting closer and sounded as if the conflict was now in the stairwell. *Fuck him.*

"Change of plans. I kick in that door. You count to ten and then you come in. Stay low and move immediately to your left. There is a small archway directly behind this door. Get there and hide behind the small piece that sticks out. You understand me?"

She nodded. "To ten, go in, immediately to the left, archway, hide behind it."

"If anyone comes toward you, point that and squeeze the trigger."

Another barrage of gunfire sounded and running footsteps could be heard on the stairwell's tread. Thanatos stood up, centered himself on the door, lifted his foot, and smashed the thin wood inward.

He took out the first man with a single bullet through the forehead. The gun the bastard was holding dropped to the floor. He swung to his right and shot, clipping the second son of a bitch. Thanatos swung and double-tapped a third, but the bastard had pulled the trigger at the same time. *Fuck!* His leg exploded in pain. He'd been hit. He went down and rolled to his right, clearing the path for Eve. He saw a flash of metal and rolled again. The bastard he'd clipped was on him. He rolled and lifted onto his good knee. The bastard swung a blade his direction. He reacted. Gripping the knife, he forced it free from the man's grasp and with one sweeping slice, slit the throat of the attacker. He lifted his gun and put two slugs in the man's gut.

Tempest was tied and gagged in a chair that was angled into the corner. Tempest's eyes widened, and Thanatos spun. A man held Eve in front of him. He held a knife over her shoulder pointing toward her chest.

He lifted his handgun and pointed it at the bastard.

"Put it down or she—"

Thanatos squeezed the trigger of the gun. The sequence played in slow motion in his mind. His bullet drilled a hole in the motherfucker's forehead. Brain matter and blood splattered the back wall and coated Eve. The man's body contracted and then sagged, crumpling on top of Eve, his dead weight flattening her to the floor. Thanatos knew she was alive by her keening wail, but his priorities were to keep all of them alive.

He grabbed the knife recently used to try to gut him and sliced through the ropes and plastic zip ties that held Tempest to the wooden chair. He kept his gun trained toward the door.

The man in the chair barely resembled his friend. His skeletal structure tented his skin. His hair had been shaved and the scars and bruises on his face obscured the features of the man he used to be. Tortured.

"Can you walk?"

"I'd fucking crawl if it got me out of this hellhole. Give me a weapon." His friend's hand shook when he grabbed the lightweight automatic Thanatos offered him. Tempest checked the safety, flipped it off and slowly stood.

Thanatos limped over and helped Eve, who was struggling to push the dead weight of the man off her.

Pinned under him, blood and bodily fluids soaked her. After he flipped the man, he reached for her.

"OH GOD!" Eve felt the man's grip around her throat. A knife... she stopped breathing.

Dolan lifted his gun and pointed it at them.

"Put it down or she—"

The man that held her jerked at the same time as an explosion echoed in her ear. He pushed her to the ground, falling on top of her. Her shoulder hit the hardwood, forcing all the air out of her lungs. She opened her eyes. A bloody mass of hair flapped away from the man's skull. *No!* She pushed up against the man's weight, but her hands slipped out from underneath her. She blinked at the blood pooling around her palms before her lungs expanded and she screamed. She moved, pushing against the dead man's weight. *Help! God, please someone help him!*

She shoved the man's body. *Let him wake up. Please let him wake up.* Lifting, she managed to flip over only to have dead eyes stare back at her. The back half of the man's head hung from a skin flap and dropped onto her chest. *Oh God!* Her back squelched against the bloody floor. He *was* dead. *Oh god, he was dead!*

She sobbed and shoved against the body pinning her to the floor. Her world disintegrated under the dead weight of the dead man. Terrified, she screamed, or tried to, but she couldn't fill her lungs. She couldn't get away. Suddenly the body flipped off her. Horror struck and she skittered away from... God, Dolan. This wasn't the man she knew! His eyes held no warmth, no emotion. They were as dead as the man beside her. She rolled away and crawled across the apartment, slipping in the viscous blood covering the floor. Dolan made a move toward her. *No, he wasn't supposed to be this way! Not Dolan. Not him... God, please, he couldn't be a murderer.* Her hands, knees and feet slipped and slid from under her as she tried to get away. There was blood everywhere. Dolan reached out again. Oxygen finally filled her lungs, and she screamed, "Get away from me!"

She hit the wall and lifted the gun he'd given her into her hand, pointing the thing at him and then swinging it toward Tempest before moving it again to bear on his chest, just as he'd shown her. Her eyes fell to the weapon. "Oh my God!" She hurled the gun away from her and pushed further into the corner.

"Guardian Security!" Boxhaur's voice called from the hall.

"Clear!" Thanatos called back to him, not taking his eyes from Eve. She wiped at her face, smearing blood and bits of flesh and brain across her chin. Tears cleared a track down her cheeks, but what he saw in her eyes when she looked at him fucking shredded him. She was afraid of him. No, fuck that, she was terrified.

Tempest shuffled over and stood beside him. Tempest gave Eve a slow deliberate glance before he raised a bony hand to his shoulder. The hold seemed to steady him on his feet. "I couldn't compromise Guardian. I would never have violated protocols. I wouldn't have made it much longer."

Thanatos peeled his eyes away from Eve. "I'm sorry it took so long." There was no way to know what his friend had lived through.

Tempest closed his eyes and nodded before he drew a shaking breath.

Boxhaur and Flynn entered the room. He shot a glance past the men to the hallway. "Redford and Hammond?"

"Both dead. Guardian wants you back on comms."

"It was damaged." He'd been doing this long enough to know how to kill. He didn't need Dom Ops in his ear.

Boxhaur nodded. "Dom Ops wants you, the woman, and this guy in your truck and headed toward Maxwell Air Force Base."

"Roger that." He moved toward Eve to help her up.

She shrank back and shook her head. "No. I'm not going with you." Revulsion dripped from her words. "You killed those four men. Murdered them!" Her eyes were wild, searching for a way past them.

Boxhaur moved aggressively toward Eve, but Thanatos grabbed his arm. The man stalled but stabbed a finger at her. "*You* don't have a choice. You'll go willingly or I'll tie you up and throw you in the damn truck. I have two dead men downstairs. They aren't leaving this place. Do you understand they gave their fucking lives to make sure you and these men make it out of here alive? Get off your fucking ass and *move!*"

Wide eyed, Eve pushed to her feet. Thanatos snapped

forward and picked up the weapon she'd thrown away. He was over her temper tantrum, too. "Let's go."

Tempest shuffled forward. His tentative steps, little more than inches at a time, didn't bode well. He came up beside his friend and grabbed his arm, wrapping it around his shoulders to take his weight and get them going. Even with a bullet lodged in his thigh, he could move quicker than Tempest.

"You're bleeding. You need to get to medical," Flynn stated as he moved behind Eve, placed a hand in the middle of her back, and practically force-marched her from the room.

"I'll live. As long as I don't dig that damn slug out, it will be fine. The two and a half hours it takes to drive to Maxwell Air Force Base won't kill me." They made it to the top of the stairs where he dropped Tempest's arm and walked down two steps. He turned his back to his friend and looked over his shoulder. "Lean over, and grab hold of me."

"Thanatos..." Tempest stared at him.

The weakness in his voice was something he never imagined he'd hear. "Do it. We have to move."

Tempest leaned forward and locked his arms around his neck. The man was too fucking thin, just bones, but even so, the weight made his leg scream.

Boxhaur glanced back, his weapon raised and his eyes alert. He motioned for them to follow, so he clenched his jaw shut, stifled his reaction to the sensation of razor blades slicing through his leg and moved. He lumbered down the steps as behind them, Flynn pulled

Eve down the steps with an arm wrapped around her bicep.

He was damn glad they weren't on a higher floor; he'd have passed out. Blood was flowing at a steady rate down his leg, pooling in his boot. The squish of fluid each time he placed weight on that leg was almost as loud as Tempest's labored breathing.

They broke out into the sunlight before he straightened and slid Tempest off his back. He once again wrapped his friend's arm around him, and they hobbled back the direction they'd come only minutes earlier. Thanatos didn't look to see if Eve was following. Flynn had their six. He focused on Boxhaur and moved faster than he probably should have to keep up with the team lead.

That damn silver truck looked like heaven when he rounded the corner. He leaned Tempest against the side and opened the back seat door, stepping up to grab the medical bag. Two rolls of gauze and three ace bandages later, he'd slowed the blood flowing from the bullet hole in his thigh. He'd bled worse. He'd live.

Boxhaur had given Tempest a bottle of water and a protein bar. The man nibbled on the bar and sipped water.

"You good to travel for three hours?"

He shrugged when Thanatos glanced at him. "I've lived this long. I hope like fuck I can manage three hours."

He glanced at Eve. Flynn stood beside her as she wiped her face with a box of wet wipes. The distinct whine of sirens pushed him to move even though it was the last thing he wanted to do. "Tempest, up in the back-seat. Eve, I need you in the front."

"I'll sit in the back." She moved to get in the truck.

He caught her arm and held it when she moved to shake him off. "He needs to lie down. Stop thinking about your wounded sense of morality. If I hadn't killed that man, he'd have killed you!"

"What about the three others? You didn't give them a chance to surrender!" She screamed, her spittle hitting his cheek because she was so close.

"I've seen each of those men kill. I've witnessed them force brutalities onto innocent people, torture them... They would have killed Thanatos without a second thought, and then they would have taken you. What they would have done to you would have made you pray for death." Tempest's words were reed thin. The dark circles under his eyes and hanging skin from his skeletal features added emphasis to his words. "Please, I need to lie down." Tempest turned and tried to climb into the truck.

Thanatos limped forward and helped his friend. He turned toward Eve. She ignored his outstretched hand and used the handholds to climb up into the truck. He turned and stared at Boxhaur and Flynn. "If you ever need me, you reach out. I'm sorry about your men." It was probably the most pathetic thing he could say, but it was sincere.

"They knew the dangers. Redford's life was nothing but Guardian. Hammond? Atlanta PD cut him loose, and Guardian saved him from taking a fall that wasn't his to take. I think he stayed with the PD to piss them off more than anything. They were good men, and they were best friends. If one went without the other, I would have had problems. If there is a silver lining to this day, it was that they are together." Boxhaur's voice was thick. He nodded to Flynn. "We've got clean-up to do and evidence to collect."

"Roger that." Flynn lifted a hand and both men jogged away from the truck.

Thanatos glanced up at Eve. She stared down at him, her expression unreadable and her demeanor unapproachable. He shut her door and hobbled around to his side of the truck. As soon as his door shut his phone rang. He slid his finger across the surface.

"Same process as last time. Make a U-turn and follow my directions." He started the truck and put it into gear before turning around as instructed.

Eve glanced at the terrain. "Do I need to duck down again?"

"No." The single word came from a male, and not the woman who was guiding them.

Thanatos glanced at the face of the phone. "I have Tempest."

"I copy. Tempest, authenticate Earl."

A harsh cough from the back preceded a faint, "Gray."

"I need a bare-bones sitrep, now," the deep gravelly voice boomed over the phone.

"No offense, but who the fuck are you?" Tempest pushed himself up and grabbed the back of the seat, pulling himself closer to the phone. A deep rattle reverberated from the concave chest as the man drew a breath.

The screen switched from a blank canvas and Anubis' mug filled the screen. "You are online with Dom Ops, Cyber, me and Archangel. Archangel was the one requesting the information."

"Where is Alpha?" Tempest closed his eyes and dropped his head to his hands.

"I'm online, Tempest, working with Dom Ops on this one. Archangel has the lead." Another voice came across the line. That one he recognized. Alpha had run the Shadows for several years. Alpha would have been the only one in charge at the time Tempest went missing so it made sense he'd ask for his superior.

"I'd just finished the assignment in Malta. Made it to Hawaii. There was a woman wearing a pilot's uniform. She walked past me, I felt it. A hypodermic." Tempest stopped and an irritated groan pushed out of the back seat. "The next thing I know, I'm hanging in a cinder block room." He lifted his head and then his wrists. Scars circled his wrists. "They knew I was a Guardian. I don't know how. They didn't know anything beyond that. How was I compromised? My cover was solid." Tempest coughed and wheezed a bit. "Someone had to have told them."

"Darren Kowolski." Archangel's deep timber split the silence.

"Tango team leader?"

"Yes."

"Fuck. Why?" Tempest swallowed hard.

"We'll get into that when we have the time and you're feeling better."

"Okay. Know that I'm going to want to spend time with that son of a bitch."

"Noted. Thanatos, status?"

"Two dead. Boxhaur and Flynn are mopping up. I'm wounded, but I'll make it to Maxwell."

"Wounded how?" Archangel fired the question at him.

"A gunshot to the right thigh. No exit wound that I could determine. It was a fucking 9 millimeter. Who even carries that shit anymore?" He was bitching and, in reality, if the bastard had carried anything bigger, he wouldn't be driving the truck to Maxwell. He'd probably have bled out in that piece of shit apartment.

"Copy. Your primary?"

He glanced at Eve.

"Uninjured but traumatized by events."

She snorted and looked out the window.

"Bengal is in the air with medical personnel."

He glanced at the phone. Why the medical personnel? Things hadn't gone to hell when Bengal had boarded that flight. They had to have been added to the manifest because of Eve. Fuck.

"For what purpose?"

"Pull back your horns, Thanatos. We are soothing feathers that have been rumpled. No direct threat to your primary. Understood?" That was Anubis' voice.

Having a Shadow involved in the operations portion of their job made sense, and it just saved one hell of a lot of posturing. He scrubbed his face and nodded even though he doubted anyone could see him through the small camera on the phone.

"Turn right at the next corner." Jewell's voice came back online and guided him through the city traffic. Once again, they didn't stop as she manipulated the traffic lights and gave them turn by turn directions. By the time they left Atlanta behind them, Tempest and Eve were asleep. The adrenaline spike for both of them had no doubt waned, as had his. The phone vibrated on the console of the truck. He swiped his finger over it and noticed it wasn't a video call. He picked it up and held it to his ear.

"Authenticate Ocean." Anubis' voice came across the connection.

The new authentication threw him for a loop, but he responded, "Breeze."

"Sitrep. We have a medical doctor and psychiatrist who are Guardian employees, and a hematologist who is Federal, all en route with Bengal. The hematologist will ask Eve for blood samples and *that* will satisfy the CDC who wants to make sure she isn't contagious or carrying any of the biological strains Wellington's documentation indicated were developed. The CDC wants her in isolation."

He glanced at Eve. He figured after the events of today, she wanted nothing to do with him; nevertheless, they'd have to kill him before he'd put her in an isolation ward. She wasn't a lab rat to be caged—not any longer, no matter what she thought about him. He wasn't going to let that shit happen. His growl of dissent was clear. "We decline to follow that directive. She has been living in Minnesota for the last four years with zero indications of biological illness."

"Roger. That said, she will have to submit to some testing to prove she's normal. Then you'll be able to take her with you. I'm assuming you have another safe house?"

"No," he whispered. "I can't take her." He glanced at Eve. Blood splatter clung to her hair and dark brown spots still stuck to her neck and cheek. She'd seen exactly what he did today, and it had repulsed her. "She goes with Bengal."

"It was a rough situation. You couldn't leave her." Anubis sighed heavily. "How close was she?"

"She is covered in the blood and brain matter from a threat I took out with emphasis. She was pinned beneath his dead body while I dealt with three others."

He'd do it all over again. Not killing the son of a bitch would have been her death sentence, but in doing so, he also killed any chance at a relationship with her. He shook his head. Relationship? When the fuck had that idea snuck into his head?

"I'm sure she'll come around. You just need to explain it to her."

"I won't be doing that. She goes with Bengal. It's what's best for everyone."

"Bengal will be on the ground in twenty minutes. It's his decision. Call your contact who was going to meet him and tell him to stand down. Go to the gate. They'll have a patrol escort you through the cantonment portion of the base to the airfield."

Thanatos acknowledged his directions and signed off. He called Charlie. "Hey, Charlie, the situation has changed, and I won't need you to pick up the Guardian operative. You can go home."

"All right. You know the police left after about an hour. They wanted to search your place, but I wouldn't let them in without a warrant. Having a lawyer for a son is good for some things. I'm sorry he made that call. Wish like hell he would have talked to us before he called them."

"It isn't a problem any longer, Charlie. Chase did what he was required to do. He's an officer of the court, and if he hadn't reported it, he could be disbarred. I get it."

"You ain't bringing her back, are you?"

"No."

"I'm gunna hazard a guess you won't be back either. Ma and me figured we were your safe place. You came to us when you needed to be away from what you do."

He braced his left leg against the floorboard and moved his right. Pain snapped through his leg, but at least he could still move it. Thank god for cruise control or he'd be fucked. As it was, driving through city traffic was going to be an exercise in sucking up pain. "Yeah. Look, I'll be sending you and Joanne some documents. I'm giving you the place and enough money to make sure you're able to keep it up. Thank you for everything you've done for me."

"No. Damn it son, don't do that–"

"Goodbye, Charlie." He ended the call and carefully set the phone on the console.

"You're not going back."

He snapped a look at Eve. Her wide eyes looked too

big for her face, and he could read her concern from the other side of the truck.

He lifted an eyebrow but didn't respond to her statement. Killing Tempest's captors had severed whatever connection they had formed. It was best that anything between them stayed severed. Better for her. Better for him. He was stupid for playing house with the woman to begin with. Trying to reach out to her now? That was the definition of futility, especially as he would be walking... well, limping, away from her permanently. And wasn't that a shining example of this entire clusterfuck of an operation. She should have been assigned to another. Someone who knew how to deal with people.

"Why?"

He frowned before he remembered what she was talking about. Why wasn't he going back? Because he couldn't walk in that house and not think of her. He couldn't look out at the yard and not see her with those puppies. He couldn't walk to Charlie's for dinner without thinking of the time they spent looking at the stars. Why? Because he was weak and as much as it killed him to admit it, he couldn't go back because he cared for her, deeply, and the memories were too painful.

He concentrated on the road. No. There didn't need to be any more conversation between them. His mission ended at Maxwell Air Force Base. Eve was alive. Tempest was alive... barely, and what do you know, the lucky son of a bitch that *he* was, he'd fucking live, too. All things considered, this had been a successful mission. Until you counted the two men who had sacrificed their lives, and he did count them. He counted every person he'd ever hurt. Not his assassinations, those monsters were culled, but the people who he hurt with his actions. He'd started a list after his parents died. It had grown exponentially. Now, he could add three more names. Redford, Hammond, and Eve.

He blinked rapidly as he decelerated at the Day Street Exit off of I-85. He groaned, working the brake with his left foot and damn near passing out when he depressed the accelerator after the stop at the end of the ramp. Perhaps it was time for an exit strategy. He'd stay with Guardian until he found that bastard. Then, well then, he'd fly around the world and plant his feet in red dirt while marveling at blue skies. Out there past Alice Springs, he would live as far away from other humans as possible.

CHAPTER 19

The odor was what woke her. The stench of blood and filth that covered the man sleeping in the back of the truck. She kept her eyes closed and realized Dolan talked to someone on the phone.

"I won't be doing that. She goes with Bengal. It's what's best for everyone."

Was she the person he was talking about? Of course, she was. There shouldn't have been pain associated with those words or the dead tone that flattened his voice. But the weight that nearly crippled her in that third floor apartment hadn't eased. Why did she want to cry? To scream 'no', because she didn't want to leave him? There was no logical reason for her to want to stay with him. He... *murdered* those men. No 'freeze police', or 'put your hands up'... nothing. She watched him kick down that door and then...

She'd heard the snapping pop of Dolan's gun. He

hadn't given the man a chance. Tears threatened to fill her eyes again. She blinked them away and looked across the cab at Dolan. His jeans were saturated with blood, much like hers, yet his was from a bullet wound. The bandage he'd put in place was dark brown, soaked with his own blood.

"Yeah. Look, I'll be sending you and Joanne some documents. I'm giving you the place and enough money to make sure you're able to keep it up. Thank you for everything you've done for me."

She watched him end the call with Charlie. "You're not going back."

She hadn't realized she'd spoken out loud until he snapped his gaze toward her. The pallor of his skin emphasized the crescent shaped dark smudges under his bottom lashes. He raked his bloodshot eyes over her before returning his attention to the road. Dismissed, insignificant, unworthy, weak, betrayed, forsaken. In equal measure, the sorrow and misery each emotion inflicted bit into her almost nonexistent ability to keep from screaming. So instead of screaming she clenched her teeth together and struggled to breathe through her nose, praying she could keep the tears at bay.

Dolan was supposed to be one of the good guys. He was her knight in shining armor. They'd made love. He was supposed to be... hers! *'She goes with Bengal.'* He was handing her off like she was a bother... a hindrance. Damn it, he was leaving her, and she was so fucking mad at him. She was mad at him for everything! For killing those men, for making her want him, for being wounded and for not talking to her. She wanted to get out of the truck and walk away and never look back, but in the same measure she wanted to hold him and never let him go.

He pulled off the interstate just before the road ended and merged onto I-65. She heard his low groan when he moved his leg. The older section of Montgomery flew past her and they quickly approached an overhang and a brick building that declared it was an entry point for Maxwell Air Force Base. Four people wearing berets and uniforms of dappled gray, brown and green stood in the lanes of traffic. Oh, no. They all had machine guns. She grabbed the door handle of the truck.

Dolan slowed and rolled to a stop. One of the men walked over. "Can I help you?"

"I'm supposed to be escorted to the flight line."

"Your name?"

"Thanatos."

"Affirmative, sir. Do you need immediate medical assistance?"

"No, we just need to get to the aircraft that is waiting on us."

"Roger that." He stepped back from the truck and motioned to one of the other men, who immediately sprinted to a patrol car parked to the right of the traffic lanes. "Follow Sergeant Johannsen. Don't deviate from his escort."

"Copy. Thanks." Thanatos rolled up his window and fell in behind the patrol car. They drove down a tree lined avenue. Rows and rows of houses with neatly trimmed and manicured lawns gave way to bigger build-

ings and a more commercial area until she saw the
runway. They followed the patrol through several
warning signs and gates and stopped behind the patrol
car after they drove over what looked like a cattle grate in
the road. The individual in the car got out and circled his
car, inspecting it and especially the tires. He did the same
for the truck.

"What is he doing?"

She didn't expect an answer from Dolan, and he
didn't give her one. A response, however, did come from
the back seat of the truck. "FOD walk."

She craned her neck to look at the man behind her.
"What's that?"

He leaned forward, bringing a new wave of stench
with him. She put her hand under her nose and breathed
through her mouth, trying desperately not to offend him
and breathe at the same time.

"Anytime a vehicle comes onto the flight line there is
a danger of it bringing foreign objects with it. The
sergeant is looking to ensure there is nothing that could
potentially be sucked into a jet's engine. Foreign Object
Damage. FOD."

"Oh." She glanced to her left and to her right. There
were a few aircraft sitting across the vast expanse of
cement. When the patrol car started again, they turned
left and approached a massive sand colored building.
When they pulled to the front she gasped. A shiny black
jet was parked inside. There were various pieces of equipment hooked up to it and a large fuel truck beside it. Air
Force people wearing headphones were scurrying
around the outside of the jet. Thanatos pulled up to the

side of the aircraft, put the truck in park and shut it off, leaving the keys in the ignition.

Both men opened their doors, so she followed suit. She walked around the front of the truck and watched as a group of people exited the jet. She shrank at the sight of two of them—a blond man and a dark headed woman. The scrubs they wore brought bile up from her stomach. She slipped behind Dolan and the other man... Tempest.

Dolan extended his hand to the man who reached them first, but he was pulled into a bear hug. The two men said a few words she couldn't understand before the big man turned to Tempest. He enfolded the man gently in his arms. Tempest's shoulders shook, and he slumped as if his legs couldn't hold his weight any longer. The big man bent down and carefully lifted Tempest into his arms.

"Get him on board. Stat." The blond man in scrubs issued the orders right before he drew Dolan's arm over his shoulder. The man snapped his head around to her. "We're following you. Get going."

She jumped at his barked order. The woman wearing scrubs studied her before she plastered on an icy smile. She knew that look. She'd seen it her entire life, only now she knew what it meant. She wrapped her arms around herself and stepped quickly, following the man who was carrying Tempest.

The jet was nothing like she expected. It had furniture. Not rows of seats. The big man carried Tempest to the back. Not knowing what to do, she followed and watched as he carefully laid the man down on a bed.

Dolan and the blond who barked orders stumbled into the aircraft.

"See me after him, doc. I can wait." Dolan lowered into the first chair he came to and the doctor dropped down beside him. He did a quick exam before he nodded and headed back to where she was standing.

"Cooper, make yourself useful. Grab the medical kits. Zane, I need Wheeler back here now."

The woman she'd taken an instant dislike to pushed past her with several large bags.

The one he called Zane slipped past her, and as he shut the door, he told the doctor, "I'm on it." He pulled a cell phone out of his suit pocket and hit a button. As he put it to his ear, he caught Eve's eyes and pointed toward Dolan. "I need you to go up there and make sure he's okay." His gaze dropped to the floor. "Wheeler, report back immediately. They are already on board. What's your ETA?" The man listened and nodded. "Make it three minutes. Maliki needs your help."

She hadn't moved a muscle. The last person Dolan wanted near him was her and quite frankly, the last person she wanted to be near was him—until he hissed in pain and gripped the leather chair with bloody hands. She moved forward but Zane glowered at her and practically shoved her out of the way to get to Dolan.

He dropped to his knees and pulled off his suit jacket, slinging the material to the couch across from Dolan. "What the fuck happened?"

Dolan chuckled and then groaned. "Didn't they brief you?"

"Yeah, damn it, I got the gouge, but what the fuck happened?"

Dolan dropped back into the chair; his throat worked convulsively before he answered. "Stratus showed so we had to move faster than we wanted. I couldn't leave her, so she went with us."

Zane glanced over at her. His gaze swept over her. "Explain the blood spatter."

"Someone grabbed her while I was neutralizing the threat to Tempest. I took him out before he could take her out."

She lost control of her legs and flopped onto the couch next to her. He had, hadn't he? He'd killed the man who held her before he could use the knife on her. But, damn it, how did he know the man would actually carry through with the threat?

"Tempest?"

"Fuck, man, you saw him. Obvious signs of torture. He's been starved, beaten. I don't know how far down he went. I don't know if he can be trusted, if they turned him."

"We'll cross that bridge when we come to it."

A massive, black-haired man launched through the open door into the aircraft. Without preamble, she was back in that apartment. The guns, blood and death. She screamed and pushed back into the couch.

"Whoa, Eve, it's Eve, right? I'm one of the good guys."

The man reached toward her and she pushed away working herself over the arm of the couch. She dropped down to use it as a barricade. Dolan... where was Dolan? He'd half risen from his seat and their eyes met. Dolan's expression halted her movement. He looked exposed and raw.

He swallowed hard and closed his eyes. "She's scared, probably traumatized from today."

"Okay, well, we'll deal with that after we take care of you. We've met before. Several years back. Do you remember me?"

Dolan glanced at the man and nodded. "Go/no-go after a shit mission in Bosnia."

"Right. Now my specialty is the brain, but I'm going to help Maliki out and take a look at this piece of hamburger meat you got posing as a thigh. Sound good to you?"

Dolan dropped back into the seat and the doctor moved into position. "Zane, I need you to get me Mal's surgical kit." The man glanced up at Dolan, exposing a snake tattoo on the side of his neck. "I was never a surgical resident, but I'm going to get this shit off you and clean you up. Mal will come in and do what he needs to do to make sure you don't lose this stump. We clear on that?"

Zane barreled past her and after a quick knock on the cabin where Tempest had been taken he opened the door and slipped in, but her attention held on Dolan. "Can he really lose his leg?"

The doctor glanced at her as he unwound the bandages Dolan had wrapped around his leg. He sent a questioning glance up at Dolan who shrugged as if he couldn't care less. "Well, the obvious issue now is the damage done by the bullet. As you can see we are working without a surgical suite, so if Doc goes in for any reason, he's going to go in blind, which is dangerous as fuck on the ground, but in the air at thirty thousand feet, it is borderline stupid. I'm assuming he'll only do that if there is a real danger of him dying or losing the leg."

Zane raced back with the pack. "He's almost finished in there. Cooper will watch over Tempest until he's done with Dolan."

The dark-haired doctor nodded and pulled a pair of scissors out of the side pocket of the pack. The blood-soaked fabric fell away from the path of the razor-sharp shears.

Oh, God. With his leg exposed she could see the damage the bullet had done. The small entry hole was dark and gruesome, but the purple swelling worried her the most. It looked... angry.

A man entered the main cabin and paled at the site of the bloody strips of cloth on the floor by Dolan. "Sir, do you still want us to take off as soon as we get clearance?"

"Affirmative."

"Roger that. We've been cleared. We're rolling in three."

"Copy."

The man walked to the open door of the jet and hit a button. The stairs retracted and he shut the door, but she couldn't have said what the man looked like. Her eyes were tied to Dolan and only Dolan.

"Okay, Zane, help me get him onto the couch." The doctor looked at her. "Eve, I'm going to need you to help. I need you to remove some of the absorbent pads out of the backpack. They're right up on top. White packages about six inches by twelve inches."

She tore her eyes away from Dolan, who looked like he'd passed out. "No. He won't want me to help." Every fiber of her being knew he didn't want her close and that... that was her fault. No. It was his. He was the one who'd violated her trust and killed those men.

"Lady, he's almost unconscious. Now, I need all hands on deck. Get me those packs, but damn... don't open them. You're filthy. Zane, on three."

She glanced down at her hands and shirt. Dark stains of dried blood dotted her arms, and hands. Her hand lifted to her face and the tight pull of the dried blood on her cheeks. How could she have forgotten she was covered in blood?

The men bent down on either side of him and slid their hands underneath him, forming a seat for him. When Dolan didn't protest her involvement, she lurched forward and pulled the pack out of their way. Grabbing all the pads lying on the top of the kit, she waited until they stretched him out and then shoved them at the doctor.

"Hold on just a second." The man pulled out a smaller pack and opened it. He worked on a pair of latex gloves and nodded at Zane. "Pull that seam open. Don't touch the material, just give me access."

The doctor pulled out the pad and opened it before he carefully lifted Dolan's leg and positioned the pad underneath. "Zane give me the chlorhexidine."

"The what? I don't see anything like that."

"Shit... ahhh... is there any betadine in there?"

The big man dug past several paper and plastic

wrapped items. "Got it. Here." He grabbed a square pack and dropped the kit to his feet.

"Sir, we are ready to taxi. We need everyone to take their seats."

Eve's eyes shot up to a speaker above the couch.

"Good luck with that." Zane carefully opened the paper wrapping.

She watched the doctor wipe the skin around the bullet wound. The door to the bedroom flew open and the blond doctor in the scrubs snapped off his gloves as he jogged forward.

"How is he?" Zane asked the doctor as he grabbed a new pair of gloves.

"Severely malnourished, irregular heartbeat, dehydrated. I'll need a full body scan to determine everything done to him. I'm concerned about renal and pulmonary issues along with a host of other problems. I need to do a full work up on him. We can't be up in the air for four hours. I need a hospital, one where we can work on both of them. Jeremiah, I need an IV started. Lactated ringers to start. Let me see what we're working with here. Zane, take her and get out of our way. I'll call you if I need assistance, but right now you're both a liability."

The man grabbed her elbow and tugged her to the back of the plane, past the small bedroom.

"Stop that!" She pulled her arm out of his grip.

"Look, I know you've had a rough day, lady, but you are going to live. No matter what happens today, you are going to wake up in the morning. Those two men? That's not a given, so do me a favor and lose the drama queen attitude. You are either part of the solution or you are part of the problem. There are clothes in there and a shower. Clean up, give your attitude a check at the door and join us when you're ready to act like an adult."

"How dare you!" She pointed down a small walkway to the main cabin. "He killed men today without so much as a second's hesitation. Men who went with us into that house are dead. There were guns and... blood... and he fell on top of me! I couldn't get free." Her hands shook and she looked up at the man through tears. She sobbed and cupped her hands over her mouth before she sobbed again. "Oh, God. They're dead. All dead."

Strong arms circled her, and she fell into the man's chest and cried. She cried for the men who'd been killed, for the men who'd died trying to protect her. She cried because she couldn't have stopped any of the senseless deaths. She pulled on that man's shirt and tried to crawl into him. She needed someone to protect her, someone to keep away the world. No, not someone. "Dolan!" Her scream tore from the deepest recesses of her soul. How? How did it happen. She cried as she folded onto the floor. "He murdered them." Those strong arms still cradled her. They didn't let go as he rocked her or stroked her hair. They didn't let go when she finally stopped crying. They didn't let go when she tried to push him away.

Instead he held her tight. "Dolan did everything exactly the way he was trained. They all did. Those men fight a war the world doesn't want to acknowledge. They exist to wipe out the monsters who threaten our families and our country. Dolan is a man of honor, a man of principal and a man I am proud to call my friend. He isn't a murderer. We performed a federally sanctioned operation today. The man you and Dolan rescued with the help of our operatives in Atlanta had access to information that if exposed could cripple this nation. We had to retrieve him."

She swiped at the last remnants of tears. "He'd been gone for years. Dolan told me that. Why did they choose today to come after him?"

"That's a good question. We don't have the answers. Yet."

"I can never unsee what happened."

"Good. Remember it. Remember what that man was willing to do in order to save a friend and to save you. But don't let it be the only thing you see."

"What do you mean?"

"Before today, did you like the man you saw?"

Like? She'd fallen in love with him. The realization sent a shudder through her that did nothing to warm the aching cold that shrouded her heart. "Does it matter?"

"I think it does. Use the rest of this flight to ask yourself some really hard life questions, Eve. If he dies out there, what would that mean to you? Or, if he lives and he walks away, how would you feel? What would your life be like if he didn't exist? Where would you be now if that man hadn't been watching over you in Minnesota? Answer those questions, and then you need to talk to him."

"He stopped talking to me."

"I guess you have another question to ask then, don't you?"

"I do?"

"Yeah, ask yourself why he stopped." Zane released

her from his hold and stood up. "Take a shower, get some clean clothes on and come back out when you're ready."

She leaned against the exterior wall of the aircraft and stared at the small doorway Zane walked through. A psychedelic swirl of the day's events churned, a relentless assault that was now peppered with questions, ones she wasn't sure she could answer.

CHAPTER 20

Thanatos regained consciousness to the throb of jet engines and damn near levitated off the couch. "Fucking son of a bitch!" He clenched his eyes closed and tried to fist the leather under him.

"Welcome back."

"What are you doing, cutting the fucker off?" He blinked the doctor into focus.

"Stop whining, you'll live."

He watched Mal prep a syringe. "Your bedside manner sucks, Mal. What is that?"

"My bedside manner hasn't changed since the last time I patched your ass up." The doc looked down at him and pushed his collar out of the way, taking a look at the stitch job he'd done two years ago. A knife wound. "Fucking excellent work if I do say so myself."

Mal inserted the syringe into the IV port and depressed the plunger.

"What did you just give me?"

"A small dose of morphine. Just enough to take the

edge off, not enough to put you out. You lost a fair amount of blood so I'm also putting some liquid back in you." He nodded at the IV.

"Tempest?"

"He's resting." Mal looked at him and gave a small shake of his head. "He's alive."

"Shit."

"I'm in complete agreement."

"Eve?"

"She's in the back."

He grabbed the doctor's arm. "Don't let them take her, Mal. Don't let those fuckers use her as a lab rat. You got to promise me."

"You know we won't allow that. The doctor from the CDC is under constant surveillance. She won't be allowed to talk with Eve without a Guardian present."

"She saw shit today she never should have seen. I..." He dropped his arm and head and grimaced when the action flexed the muscles in his leg.

"Jeremiah will talk with her when he thinks she'll be receptive. Bengal is giving her some time to clean up." Maliki leaned back and scrubbed his face. "She is actually the least of my worries right now, even though she is the reason I was on the flight to begin with."

"What?"

"I was in DC. It seems I have a new partner for my clinic at the Rose. I was voicing my displeasure, in person. I have no idea why, probably my proximity, but Bengal pulled me into a meeting with that bitch from the CDC. It went downhill fast and the big boss got involved. We'd just finished a marathon session where Archangel tore that bitch a new one when Bengal got your call and pulled us out of the room. So, we were both shoved on the plane. Nothing new for me, but the CDC doc, Cooper? She about shit her pants."

Maliki's evil chuckle almost made him smile. The man was hard core and he'd been a member of Guardian for as long as he could remember. "No love lost between you, huh?"

Maliki snorted and closed his eyes. "None. But I'm glad I was available."

"Yeah, Tempest is in rough shape." He ached for his friend. He'd seen pictures of people who suffered through torture, but never had he expected to see his friend as a walking skeleton.

"He's only part of the picture here."

"My leg?"

"Yeah, well, you have been shot."

"Gee, thanks, I was wondering what the fuck happened."

The doctor chuckled before he leaned forward. "I don't believe any arteries were damaged. While you have lost blood, you got lucky. I can't see the bullet, so we'll have to go in after the damn thing and I'm not going to do that at thirty thousand feet. We're heading to the hospital Guardian built in South Dakota. It is an hour closer than my facility in Arizona. So, we've cleaned you up, administered some antibiotics, a mild dose of morphine and when we land, you're going straight into surgery. I'll pull that bullet out and sew you up. Good as new."

"Mal, can both Tempest and I make it an extra hour?"

The doctor cocked his head at him, concern creasing his brow. "Why?"

He threw a glance toward the back of the plane. "She's seen enough. Too much. She knows too much about the people in this aircraft and if she sees the complex and then the Rose, she could become a liability. She's been under supervision her entire life. Hell, she's never had a chance to live. If she learns much more, what will Guardian do?"

Mal chuckled. "The same thing they do to all of us that are injured or fucked up. They'll bring her into the fold and give her a home."

He tried to argue, but his eyes were getting heavy. "Bastard, how much did you give me?"

"Just enough to take the edge off. We're flying to South Dakota."

He lifted his heavy as fuck eyelids and snarled at the pain in the ass doctor, "I can wait."

Mal nodded and shifted his gaze to the back of the plane. "Tempest can't."

THE REST of the flight and the events that followed the aircraft's landing dotted his consciousness like a fog lifting and falling. He was hot. So damn hot. Where was Eve? He called for her several times, but no one was listening to him. They jostled him getting him off the plane. Lightning bolts severed that heat-soaked cotton that covered the edges of his world. "Fuck!" He tried to sit up.

"Stay down, asshole, or you'll tip over and land on the fucking tarmac." Maliki's voice then his face registered.

"Eve? Where's Eve? Mal, you got to make sure no one takes her. Eve?" Heat poured through his body. He grabbed Mal's scrubs and yanked him down. "You make sure no one hurts her. Eve!"

"Dolan. I'm here. I'm okay. I'm right here." A soft hand touched his cheek and her face appeared in front of him. "I'm okay. I'm here."

He grabbed at her and found her hand. "I'm sorry. I didn't want you to see. I wanted... I knew it couldn't happen, but I wanted you... I..." He groaned when the gurney he was on jolted. "They'll take care of you. Give you... what I can't."

He couldn't keep his eyes open, but he clung to her hand. He clung to the image of her above him in case it was the last time he'd see her.

"He's coming around."

He blinked his eyes open and squinted at the bright fluorescent lighting. The smells and sounds invaded his mind. Shit. Hospital. Hospital! "Eve?" He tried to sit up and regretted the move immediately.

"She's safe. Fury's wife took her to get some food and hopefully some sleep."

Bengal. He blinked to clear his mind. Mal, Bengal and Anubis. Fuck. He was in South Dakota. "Tempest?"

. . .

BENGAL CLEARED his throat before he answered. "Touch and go. He's holding on. I don't know how he survived as long as he has." He closed his eyes and let the regret that had been lingering wrap around his heart and take hold. He regretted so damn much. The pain of his actions and lack of actions hurt worse than his leg. "I waited too long to reach out."

"You violated every protocol we have." Anubis stared out the window as he spoke.

"I know. The result was worth any consequences you could throw at me." He only had one more thing to do before he let the shadows consume him. He could survive any sanctions Guardian threw his way, except confinement. But if his incarceration meant Tempest was alive, hell... a worthwhile exchange.

"Consequences." Anubis nodded and glanced at him. "Glad you are aware that those actions come with sanctions, because yours have already been decided."

Thanatos nodded. He was aware and he was willing to accept them. "What are they?"

"Not our place to tell you." Anubis glanced at Bengal, who nodded and then looked at the floor.

"Great. Love all the cryptic shit, but my patient needs his rest. Go spread cheer somewhere else." Mal moved between the two assassins and planted himself in front of a laptop that was on a rolling stand. He started typing before he blinked and looked over his shoulder. "Gentlemen, I don't care who the fuck you are outside these doors, inside them you are unwanted visitors, so get out."

"I love the way you think, Doctor Blue. I can tell your no shit policies and I are going to get along just fine." A gorgeous redhead walked into the room. He blinked at the way Anubis and Bengal shot out of the room.

"Oh, fucking goodie." Maliki snorted as he pounded the keys on the laptop. "My new partner."

"Grow up and get over yourself." The red headed doctor leaned against the footboard of his bed. "Is he always such a dick?" She nodded at Maliki.

He choked back a laugh and nodded. "Worst bedside manners in the world."

"Fuck you." Mal shot the words at him while he typed.

"No thanks." He closed his eyes, not really wanting to get involved between the two doctors.

"Your loss," Mal flung the words back at him.

"While I'm enjoying your little convo here, I came back to let you know that Eve has eaten and is sleeping."

His eyes popped open at the mention of Eve's name. "The doctor from the CDC?"

"Won't be getting anywhere close to her. She's staying down at the Twin's place."

"Twins?" He sent her a quizzical glance.

"One of them is married to a co-worker of yours. She sends her best and wanted me to tell you that you were stupid as fuck for getting shot. Our Joy has an eloquent way with words."

"Joy." So that was the name Moriah was using. He, Anubis, Bengal, and Moriah—all in the same place. What were the odds of that shit happening?

"Yeah, and my husband says you're a fucking moron for breaking protocol, but I think he is glad you did. The man next door wouldn't have lasted much longer if you hadn't."

"Husband?"

"Yep. He's coming by to see you later. Won't do it when there are so many people around. He's... antisocial."

Maliki snorted a laugh. "Understatement of the year."

"Damn, and here I was going for the decade." The woman chuckled and lifted a hand. "Get some rest. I understand we'll all be traveling west in a couple of days." She left without a backward glance.

He rolled his head on the hard as a rock pillow. "Why don't you like her?"

"Her? I don't have a problem with her." Maliki continued to type.

"You sure as fuck act like you do." He closed his eyes and focused on the tentacles of regret that continued to wind their way through his chest.

"Long story that I won't bore you with. How's your pain?"

"It's there."

"Obviously, I just sliced you open. Do you need more meds?"

"No." There was nothing that could mute the pain he was feeling. Very little of it was physical. The discomfort of the surgery wasn't even registering.

"Don't be a macho fuck. If you hurt, tell me."

He snapped his eyes open and pegged Mal. "There is nothing you can give me for the kind of pain I feel. Good enough for you, asshole?"

Mal's chin kicked up and his eyes widened. He blinked and nodded. "That I understand loud and clear."

He closed the lid on the laptop and crossed his arms over his chest as he stared out the window. "Want some unsolicited advice?"

He swallowed hard and closed his eyes. Advice? On how to do what exactly? Extract his fucking heart and sew up his chest? "Not really."

"Tough. That woman, she's been raised in a petri dish. Sure, she's had a few years among the rest of the world, but from my briefings, they believe the limited freedom she'd been given had been constructed and monitored. Her world has exploded. Give her time to let the pieces fall back to earth, then help her put the puzzle back together. You'll regret it if you don't."

He lifted his lids and glanced at the man staring out the window. "Personal experience?"

Mal looked at him. His blue eyes were clouded, but he nodded. "Wounds heal differently for different people. Scars on the inside sometimes fuck us up worse than the scars you can see. She's going to need support and help."

"I can't be that for her." He'd already proven that. Look what he'd cost her already.

Mal sighed and headed for the door. "Okay. So, I've revised my official clinical diagnosis, and I'll have to update my notes. Remind me to put in the records that you are fucking stupid and blind as a bat. Damn horses and water and all that shit."

He shook his head and stared up at the hospital ceiling tracing the lines in the tile. No one knew Eve like he did. He'd seen the terror and abject rejection in her eyes when she was in that apartment. No one understood he'd destroyed her innocence and polluted her awe for all the wonderful things in life. Putting distance between the monster he was and the beauty she deserved was the only thing he could do. Those coils around his heart tightened another notch. He glanced down at his leg and the bandage around the surgical site. He'd be up and around in a day and out of here in two. He wasn't going west. He was going dark.

CHAPTER 21

Eve pulled on the clothes that had been left in the small guest room, but she was glad to be out of the scrubs she'd changed into on the aircraft. The jeans weren't too bad of a fit. They were a little tight and about four inches too long. She'd rolled them up and slipped her feet into some leather mules sitting beside the clothes. The long-sleeved t-shirt was soft and too long in the arms, so she pushed up the sleeves. There was a toothbrush and toothpaste she'd made use of after her shower. She'd braided her freshly washed hair. The jets in the shower made her feel clean, unlike the trickle of water from the aircraft's tiny shower. She opened the door and followed the sound of voices. She'd met the twins and their wives when Ember had brought her down to the house, but she was so exhausted she barely remembered slipping into the sheets and closing her eyes.

She'd spent far too long in bed after she'd woken up, and then lingered in the shower. The events of the past days played in a hodge-podge display in her mind. The carnage and death yesterday interspersed with Dolan's acts of kindness when they were at the farm. Reconciling the two people, Dolan at the farm and the man in Atlanta... She had no idea how to do that and her heart hurt so damn bad. Why? Because he was leaving, and she'd never be able to understand the whys behind the differences. She stopped just outside the kitchen door and wiped at tears. How could he leave? How could she tell him not to? She had no idea what was going to happen to her, and she needed him, and hated that she was still afraid of him, too.

All talking stopped when she entered the kitchen. A fluffy, white dog hopped over to her and danced on his hind feet, pawing at her legs. She bent down and petted the fluff ball when a huge brown cat with a crooked, bobbed tail pushed its way between her and the dog. She laughed at the motorboat purr that started up the second she touched the cat's wiry fur. "Well, you're not very patient." She stroked both of the animals and glanced at the people in the kitchen.

"Cat doesn't like Sasha getting any attention." A small woman stood and walked over to her. "I'm Joy. I'm married to Dixon; the fluff ball is Sasha, and she's mine. That is Cat. She belongs to Drake, Jillian's husband."

"Hey." The other woman waved from the counter where she was washing dishes. "We didn't wake you up, did we?"

"No, I've been awake for a while." She continued to pet the animals, but asked, "Has there been any word from the hospital?"

"Oh, damn. Yeah, sorry. Mal got the bullet out. He'll be fine." Joy lifted a coffee cup. "Want some?"

"No, thank you. I don't drink coffee."

"Holy fuck. A unicorn, they do exist." Joy laughed at her own joke and pointed to the refrigerator. "All kinds of stuff in there. Glasses are in that cupboard. Help yourself."

She stood and walked carefully around the animals to the cupboard and the fridge, pouring herself a small glass of OJ.

"I've got a breakfast casserole in the oven. We didn't know when you'd wake up. Are you hungry?"

She sipped the OJ and considered the question. She hadn't eaten yesterday. The night before, she and Dolan had only played at eating dinner and ended up making love in the kitchen. Making love. With those words her mental war sent another barrage of images and that killed her appetite. "Thank you, but I'm not really hungry."

"That's okay. Hey, Jill, can you give us a second?"

"Sure, I'm going to head to the lab. See you tonight."

The lab? What kind of lab? She glanced sharply at Jillian and side stepped her as she left the kitchen. Joy sat down at the table and motioned for Eve to sit, too. She recognized it for what it was—an order, not a suggestion. She set her glass on the table and sat down. The cat launched into her lap and tried to curl up, but she was so big Eve had to hold her to keep her from falling, which she was grateful for, because she knew she was close to losing it again. The need to scream had been building since the moment she'd opened her eyes this morning.

"Jillian is a mechanical engineer. Her 'lab'," the woman made air quotes, "is more like a barn on steroids, but she has some cool shit she's working on."

"Oh." She swallowed back a bit of the panic and focused on the cat in her lap.

"So I understand you saw some epic shit yesterday?"

"Yeah."

"Okay, just so you know, I hate this shit." Her eyes popped up to the smaller woman. "I don't do the touchy feely, heart-to-heart thing. I barely do people, so I'm going to cut through the shit."

Eve stopped petting the cat and stared at the woman across from her. She nodded, wary of the intensity that radiated from her.

"Thanatos has baggage, but we all do. Don't tell me you don't, because I know all about what happened to you. That man has served his country and saved untold lives by doing what he does. Granted, that shit yesterday was not his typical MO, but he's deadly and efficient. It is what he gets paid to do." Joy leveled her dark eyed stare at her. "You've got two options here. One, you suck up the angst and the drama and you decide you love that man or two, you decide all this shit is too much for you and you walk away."

Eve shook her head, tendrils of anger at the audacity of the woman's words started to spread. "Suck it up, huh?"

"Yup." The woman took a drink of her coffee.

"Fuck you."

The small woman's eyebrows popped, and she threw

back her head, letting loose a hearty laugh. "Oh, girl, you do not want to throw down with me."

"Really? Fine, then mind your own business."

In an instant, Joy was on her feet and in her face, shouting. "He is my business. He is one of the few people in this world who are my business. He has tortured himself his entire adult life looking for the motherfucker who killed his family, raped him, and left him for dead. I know that anger. I know that hatred. I know that need for revenge, but that man? He turned that rage on himself and has held it inside for a lifetime. He doesn't think he is worthy of love. He doesn't think anyone would be willing to take a chance on loving him because he doesn't feel worthy!"

Eve stood, sending the cat to the floor and the chair flying backward. "How the fuck do you know that?"

"Because I lived it. I existed in the same hatred, the same rage, the same self-loathing. I know him because I am him. But you know what saved me from imploding? My motherfucking husband saved me! He believed in me when I couldn't believe in myself. He loved me when I couldn't see anything worth loving. He trusted me with his heart, and he saw me, not the assassin, not the badass adult, but the woman who was crying out for someone to love her. He was the only one to see me. Thanatos let you in. You saw the real man. You saw him."

"I..." So many things ran through her mind that she couldn't string a sentence together.

The smaller woman huffed. "Yeah. Whatever. The fucking scene you saw yesterday will be nothing compared to the devastation you will cause if you fuck this up and walk away from him. For once in your life, stop being a victim. You'd be amazed how powerful you are." She stood up and walked to the sink with her coffee cup. "I'm going to the hospital. Do you want to come?"

Eve dropped her eyes to her hands. She had to sort through the nuclear bomb blast that just happened. Yes, she wanted to go, but... that man's blood hitting her face, the coppery smell of the blood she still couldn't rid herself of. The words, 'she goes with Bengal'... so much to sort through, to try to understand. So many people telling her what to think, how to act, how to feel, she just... couldn't. She shook her head slowly.

"Right. Don't leave the house. You're safe here but that woman from the CDC is somewhere on the ranch and, as much as I'd like to let that bitch have a go at you right now, there is a voice in the back of my mind telling me that wouldn't be right. Stupid fucking conscience. That is also my husband's fault." She paused at the doorway. "I'm serious. Don't leave this fucking house. Understand?"

Eve nodded and listened to the woman walk out. The crooked tail cat padded across the kitchen floor and hopped back up into her lap. The loud squeaky purr covered the sounds of her losing her mind while her heart continued to shatter.

"I don't know what to do." One hand held the cat as the other stroked the wiry molted looking fur. "It looks like you've had a hard life, too." An ear with a piece missing twitched in agreement. The animal rolled and exposed her belly, swatting at the braid that hung down her shoulder.

A soft knock on the front door of the house startled

both her and the cat. The animal rolled off her lap and fell gracefully to the floor, trotting out the door. She didn't move. It wasn't her house. She cringed at the sound of heavy footfalls.

The dark-haired doctor from the plane leaned against the door frame. "Hey, how you doing today?"

Eve shrugged, because she had no way to answer that question. "How is... ahh, Tempest?"

"He's not good, but he's a fighter. May I sit down?" He nodded to the chair across the table from her. She shrugged again because she really didn't care, nor did she want to talk to anyone.

"You've had a rough couple of weeks, huh?" He leaned back in his chair and linked his fingers over his stomach.

Eve closed her eyes and shook her head. "No, look. I'm not going to do this again. Just give me your sermon, and leave me alone, okay? I just don't have the energy."

"Sermon?"

She snorted. "Yeah. Tell me how you think I should feel. Tell me what you think I should do. Everyone else has."

"Is that right? Well, then they're all assholes."

She lifted her eyes to look at him. The snake tattoo on his neck peeked out of his collar and more ink covered his forearms. He was an unusual looking doctor.

"They meant well." She was sure they did. She just wasn't sure what *they* thought she should do was what she should do, and didn't that sound like a dog chasing its tail?

"Did they? That's debatable. They probably wanted

what they felt was best for their friend, not taking your feelings into consideration. *That* I can believe." He stood and went to the cabinet where the coffee cups were, pulled one down and poured himself a cup before he sat down again. "I'm sure what you saw yesterday has been haunting you."

"Haunting." She echoed the word. Yes. Haunting was the perfect word. "The man I saw yesterday, he isn't the same man I've known. He murdered a man in cold blood. He isn't the man I thought he was, but I can't stop remembering what he was like at the farm. It was like he was a different person. When he shot that man, his eyes were... dead. There was no emotion. No regret, no fear... nothing. I just don't know how to put the two halves of him together. I don't know what to do." She watched the cat pad back into the kitchen.

"Who says you have to?"

"What?" She swept her gaze back to the doctor.

"Who says you have to know what to do? I mean eventually, yes, you'll have to have a plan, and you'll have to move forward, but that doesn't have to happen today." He took a sip of the coffee and stared at the contents of the cup. "For now, it is enough to acknowledge that all the events happened. When you're ready to talk, to discuss how you feel, to work through the emotions that are screaming for attention, then you move forward."

"How?"

"You mean how do you move forward?"

"Yes."

"One small step at a time."

"I have nowhere to live."

"Not true."

"I can't live here, in this house."

"I wasn't suggesting that. There are numerous options here at the ranch, or you can go elsewhere. Guardian will set you up. Make sure you're safe."

She didn't try to stop the snort of disbelief.

"You don't agree?"

"You'll have to forgive my skepticism. I was almost killed yesterday."

"Ah." The man nodded and took a sip of his coffee.

Eve narrowed her eyes at him. "Ah, what?"

"Nothing." The cat jumped up in his lap and stretched out, hanging off the edges of the man's lap.

"It was something. What did I say?"

The man leaned forward. "You said you were almost killed yesterday."

She nodded. "I was."

"I'm just confused."

"About what?"

"Well I listened to the audio recordings of the events yesterday."

She frowned and tried to connect the dots, but she couldn't. "And?"

"You told off Guardian when they suggested you not accompany... ah... Dolan."

"I didn't know he was going to murder those men."

"I'm sure he didn't know that either."

"But he did kill them."

"Yes, he did. The first man was a wanted felon. He'd escaped custody four years ago. He was convicted of killing a woman and her husband for their car. Then he drove to his parents' house and killed his family. He was arrested, tried and convicted. He overpowered and killed two guards during a prison transport and escaped. The second man was a surprise. He was Russian Bratva. That is their mafia. He was in the country illegally and is a known entity. His specialty is torture.

"I understand Tempest was tied to a chair when you entered the room. Guardian believes he would have died yesterday at the hands of that man. The man who grabbed you? He was a thug. You know, the usual convictions for assault and armed robbery. He was awaiting trial for rape. Usually they don't get out on bond for those types of crimes, but money talks and the people who were holding Tempest have all kinds of money. Dirty money. So, yes, Dolan killed the men."

She stared at her fingernails as his words registered. "He didn't give them a chance."

"No, he didn't. He assessed the situation and took action."

"That doesn't make what he did right."

"I'm not saying it did. You feel he acted hastily."

Eve dropped her head to her hands and closed her eyes. "No."

"No?"

"No." She tipped her head up to look at the doctor.

"You just said he didn't give them a chance. To me, that would mean he acted hastily."

She shook her head. No. Dolan had moved with economy of motion. There was no haste as he kicked the door in, or when he moved two steps forward and shot the first man. Then the second man. She closed her eyes.

She thought the man was going to kill Dolan. Instead of moving the direction Dolan had instructed, she'd come into the room. If she'd done what he'd told her... She drew a long shaky breath and looked at the man across from her. "If I hadn't been there, if he hadn't had to worry about me, they would have handled everything differently, right? The way they did everything would have been different."

The doctor leaned forward. "I don't know. I'm not one of them. Neither are you."

"Yeah." She exhaled as she agreed. "I couldn't do what they do."

"Neither could I."

"You're a psychiatrist?"

"I am."

"I think I'm going to need some help dealing with all of this."

"I can do that, or recommend someone who can help you work through the last week's events, but may I suggest you go back farther?"

She glanced up at him and lifted her eyebrows. He knew. Of course he knew. "I'm dealing with that."

"Are you?"

"Poorly, but yeah. I'm trying."

"Getting help isn't admitting defeat. It is admitting you need help."

She chuckled, "Wise words."

"I'm full of them. Do you know how long you are staying here?"

She shook her head and looked around the kitchen. "I really don't even know where I am."

The doctor chuckled. "Well, you are smack dab in the middle of nowhere, and we love it out here. I know Guardian's bosses are flying in this morning. As soon as they land, I'm sure they'll bring you up to speed on what's going on. Until then, would you like to go for a walk? I hear Frank has two new colts."

"Horses?"

"Yep. Wanna go look?"

"I'd... yeah, I'd like that." She stood and watched as he assisted the ragdoll of a cat off his lap. "Do you think Dolan wants to see me?"

"I think you should give it a day or two. Right now, his mind is probably just as jumbled as yours. He has a lot to put into order, too, you know."

"It was a very hard day." She could only imagine how killing those people affected him.

"True, but I'm not talking about yesterday."

"Then what are you talking about?" They moved to the front door at a snail's pace.

The doctor smiled and shook his head. "Things, just things. Come on, let's stretch your legs and go see those colts."

CHAPTER 22

Thanatos heard the men walking down the hall before he saw them—at least three of them by the sounds of the treads on the floor. The head of his bed was elevated, and he'd washed earlier so he was presentable for his firing squad. He recognized Alpha and Fury. The family resemblance between them and the big man who came in next was impossible to miss. The older man following them? He didn't know him, but the deference the other men paid him told him he was the Saint. The one that moved on from Archangel a few years back.

"Dr. Blue has indicated a full recovery is anticipated," the older gentleman said as he shoved his hands in his suit pants.

He nodded. He recognized the fine tailoring of the bespoke suit. He had several closets full of the same type clothing. Not that he'd seen any of those clothes during this assignment. Not that he'd ever see them again. He'd exposed himself and Guardian when he reached out to

Tempest. They could put a bullet in his head now and be justified.

"I understand Tempest is alive today because of the... extreme measures you employed to make contact with him." The man leveled his stare directly at him.

"I'd do it again." To hell with the dance. He was going to take full responsibility for his actions.

The man nodded and looked down at the floor. "Noted." The word was said as he stared at his Italian leather shoes. "I believe we have some other information for Thanatos?" He looked over his shoulder at the biggest of the King brothers.

The man nodded and then shut the door behind him. He took off his glasses and pinched the bridge of his nose as he spoke. "The DNA confirmation you were looking for has been confirmed. We traced the family line and found them."

Thanatos sat up and winced. "Where?"

"With the exception of one woman, the family is dead. Buried in a plot in Maine. She had one brother." He pulled a picture from his pocket and stared down at the photo for a moment before he handed it to him.

He stared at the offering. It wasn't close enough for him to see the man. Not taking it, he shook his head. "He can't be dead." Damn it, he wanted to kill that bastard.

"This man died three years ago. He was stabbed in a bar fight. According to the sister, it was a gruesome and painful death." He moved forward and placed the picture on the side of the bed. Thanatos sent a quick glance at the men standing around him before he licked his suddenly dry lips. He picked up the photo and stared at the image facing him. His head began to shake. No. This had to be wrong. He flipped the photo around. "This isn't him."

The men looked at each other. "It was a familial match to the sister. A brother. Her only brother is this man and he is dead."

"Unless she has another brother she doesn't know about." He grasped at straws, desperate to find a reason.

"We've scoured the family's background. There is no one else." The big guy shook his head. "The only other alternative is the DNA collected at the crime scene was mixed up with another case?" It happened all the time with old, unsolved cases that got jockeyed from evidence locker to storage facility, especially one as old as his family's.

"So, I have nothing." The emptiness of that revelation gaped in front of him.

"Gentlemen, a minute?" Fury's request from near the door turned all eyes.

They nodded and in a single file left the room. Fury shut the door behind them.

The man pulled a small chair out and flipped it, straddling the thing and crossing his arms over the back. "What were your plans after you found this bastard?"

He held the picture of the man who looked nothing like the bastard who'd killed his parents. "Head south and disappear."

Fury nodded and was silent for a moment. "We're working a new concept at the Rose. We're bringing in established teams and either integrating a Shadow onto the team, or in some cases developing a Shadow from existing personnel. We're also looking at reducing the size of the teams. No more five-man crews. We want to go smaller, more agile and less detectable. The training will be intense and brutal and geared toward Shadows."

He rolled his head toward his old friend. The gray at the man's temples was the only indication of the passing years. "How does this concern me?"

Fury shrugged. "Anubis is staying here in the same job. This secure facility will still be an information and operational base for Shadows, and it will still be used for Dom Ops and Personal Security Operative training, but only after they've been through the Rose. Recurring training will happen here, as well as rehab. The medical facilities here are much more sophisticated than what we have at the Rose."

"Again, I don't understand how this concerns me."

Fury leveled a stare at him. "There are consequences for breaking our rules."

"Ones I am prepared to accept."

"So be it." He stood up and opened the door.

The three men who had been waiting outside filed in.

"He is prepared to accept the consequences of violating our security protocols."

This was it. He braced himself and lifted his chin.

The older man nodded. "So be it. Thanatos, as a punishment for violating the security of the Shadow community, for reaching out using unauthorized channels and possibly compromising the integrity of our communications, you are hereby ordered to serve a term of not less than five years at the Rose, working for Fury. May God have mercy on your soul."

He sat straight up and growled as shards of stinging heat sliced through his injured leg. "Wait, what?"

Archangel explained, "We've developed new technology. The old dead-drops are being mothballed. Granted, a few months sooner than we would have preferred, but we have a global system we can hijack and infiltrate without anyone knowing who we are or what we're doing. A year ago, I'd have strung you up by the balls and cut them off for that stunt. Now? I'm mildly irritated at having to ask my sister to rush through the implementation because she's a royal pain in my ass, but we have ways to work around the loss of the dead drops. Besides, you got Tempest back for us. Your redress to Guardian is to work with that asshole and try to keep him out of trouble."

"Fuck you very much."

Fury flipped him the bird.

"What if I decide to walk away?" He'd head to Alice Springs, to that red dirt and just get lost in the vastness of Australia.

"You seem to have forgotten you compromised our protocols. At this point you are not allowed to walk away. Besides, you're currently on an assignment," Alpha said as he reached for the door. "We never stop before the mission is over."

He glared at his old boss. "Eve? I'm not following. My responsibility is over. You required I see her to safety. She is safe.

"There are three known entities who want her. One of them, unfortunately, is domestic."

Thanatos stared at each man, moving his eyes from

one to the other. He saw the determination, the fierceness in each one.

"Over my dead body." A vow. To her, and to them.

EVE SAT VERY STILL. The small conference room Dr. Wheeler had brought her to was at the front of the hospital. She'd held Dolan's hand when they were unloading him from the airplane yesterday until they'd given him something to knock him out. She knew where his room was. She knew how to get there from here, but what she didn't know was how to say the words she needed to say.

She jumped when the door opened. Two men walked in. One was absolutely massive, the other, well he was big, too. She swallowed hard and fisted her hands tightly in her lap.

"Eve Salutem, my name is Jason King. I run Guardian Security. This is Gabriel. He is my boss."

She nodded at the men. "Will you tell me what is happening?"

"Absolutely. May we?" The bigger man gestured to the chairs on the opposite side of the table. She nodded again and watched as they unbuttoned their suit coats and sat down.

"I'll start at the beginning–"

"That would be appreciated." She interrupted him, and that was rude, but they owed her an explanation.

He nodded and cleared his throat. "About seven weeks ago, a man, Benjamin Wellington died. To put it mildly, he was an abomination. To date, over two thousand deaths can be attributed to the biological weapons he has made."

"Yes, my alleged benefactor. Did he use my blood to develop those weapons?"

"No. We thought so, initially, but no. The strains concocted in his laboratories were not based on your blood."

"Then why... I was..."

"From what we now understand, your genetic markers are unique. You are, for a lack of a better explanation, resilient. When you were exposed to the biological elements he used in his weapons, your body's immune system fought the elements and won. You are the antidote, not the cause."

She stared at them absorbing the information. "How was I born with this... ability?"

The men exchanged glances before the older one nodded. Mr. King returned his gaze to her. "Wellington made you. He impregnated females who he'd injected with his chemicals. From the documentation we've recently discovered there were five live births, but only you made it to adulthood."

"Why did he let me go? Why wasn't I kept in the hos–, the research facility where I grew up?"

"This is just an assumption, but based on his last words, we believe he was impressed by your resilience. You do realize you were never out of his control, correct?"

"What do you mean? The monthly trips to the doctors?"

"That and the people he put in your life to watch you."

"People?"

"Indeed. Lori Hutchinson. We became suspicious when she alerted the police about your absence and 'abduction' less than a day after you and Than... ahh... Dolan departed the area. Then when the national news suddenly became interested, we looked into why. I believe you two started teaching at the same time?"

"Yeah, we did. Her husband Mark is the football coach."

"We believe both were assigned to watch over you."

"What? No. How can you say that?"

"We followed the money." That comment came from the older gentleman.

"So she was paid to be my friend?"

Mr. King answered this time, "No, she was paid to watch over you for Wellington, as was her husband. We have statements from them."

She wrapped her arms around her waist. "Oh, my god..."

"But, there is good news." The older gentleman spoke into the silent room.

"Really? What's that?"

"One, you are no longer in that environment. Everything you do or choose from this point forward is made as a person responsible for your own destiny." He drew a breath and leaned back against the chair. "And you have several decisions to make."

Her eyes snapped to Mr. King. He nodded his head. Both men's brows furrowed. That didn't bode well, now did it? "What decisions?"

"First, there is a doctor on the premises from the

CDC. Based on intelligence we'd originally uncovered, there was a chance you were being used as a... Typhoid Mary for Wellington. Since then, and I'm talking within the last twelve hours, we have found reliable and verifiable information that shows you were being used for building antidotes, not the disease. Regardless of the new information, the CDC would like a blood draw." The older man held her gaze and asked, "Will you consent to the federal government drawing blood from you to study?"

"Would this be a one-time event?"

"We can insure that."

"How?"

"You'll disappear and they won't be able to find you. Easy."

"Disappear?" She heard the wavering in her own voice. What did that mean?

Mr. King interrupted, "You'll be relocated and given a new identity, one that no one can trace."

She covered her mouth with her hand and dropped her eyes to the tabletop. A picture of the CDC doctor's malicious smile and the coldness in her eyes formed in her mind. She shook her head. "I don't want her to do it. She can monitor, but she doesn't touch me."

Both men seemed to relax in their chairs. "Done. We can ask one of our people to do the draw."

"What are the other questions? You said there were several."

"Ah, yes." The older man leaned forward. "We need to talk about your future."

"But I get to decide, right?"

"Absolutely."

"Fine, I have several requirements." She nodded her head. This was her life she was talking about. She wanted time to make sure she got it right this time.

"As long as the conditions aren't illegal or immoral, I guarantee to make them happen." The older gentleman smiled, and the action transformed his face. She smiled back. For the first time in her life, she planned on living.

CHAPTER 23

Thanatos stood at the edge of the Rose compound. The setting sun colored the desert with hues of orange and pink. Occasionally, at night, he could pick out darker shades of red. Shades that reminded him of the red dirt of Australia. He'd be able to go there some day. Alone. He shoved his hands into his jeans pockets and stared into the emptiness. The Arizona desert wasn't empty. It had its own beauty, if you looked for it, but he wasn't looking.

He lifted his eyes and picked out the first star in the heavens. His mind went back to those evening strolls he and Eve would take from Joanne and Charlie's back to his house. Fuck, he missed her, so damn much.

Archangel had returned to his hospital room not three hours after he'd left and informed him Eve was no longer his assignment.

"What do you mean?"

"She was very specific. She didn't want you responsible for her protection. We've assigned her to someone else."

He closed his eyes and dropped his head back onto the bed. The tiny sliver of hope he'd clung to vanished, and in its place anguish rushed forward. What did he expect? She'd seen him, the true him, and she couldn't accept him.

"However, that does not release you from your obligations to Guardian. You'll be on your way to the Rose tomorrow. Fury and his family and Maliki will accompany you."

He nodded in response. He'd fulfill his obligations to Guardian. He'd existed before. Finding his way back to that place where no one mattered was going to suck, but he knew the path to take.

He dropped his head and ambled a bit further out past the edge of the compound's camera and sensor system. Five miles. He walked out into the desert every night. It was his only solace. The training had started in earnest a week ago. Five months from the day he'd flown into the Rose. Fury was a demanding and exacting leader. He fell into the role as the man's second with little trouble. Probably because he trusted Fury with his life. Fury was one of the few he'd follow to hell and back... at least for the next four years and seven months.

Darkness was falling and cloaked the desert, bringing cooler temperatures with it. The extremes of the desert were comforting in their regularity.

Stopping in the twilight, he cocked his head and listened. An animal... the padding feet and soft panting along the trail he'd used to enter the desert. A fucking wolf or coyote. He reached for the automatic he carried holstered on his belt. The desert was a dangerous place and almost everyone in the complex was armed. Hopefully, the animal would hear him and skirt around. He didn't want to kill it, after all, he was the one encroaching.

He kicked a rock against an outcropping, hoping the noise would startle whatever was approaching. The sounds stopped for a couple of seconds and then the damn creature started running toward him. He drew the pistol and aimed it down the path. The thing that saved it was the neon pink collar. He lowered the gun and stared. A German Shepherd pup, about six months old. One ear flopped precariously while the other stood straight up. Paws the size of platters and a head that should have unbalanced the gangly body trundled forward. He watched in disbelief as the animal loped toward him. The dog danced around him and yipped before racing back down the trail, only to turn and race back to him. He bent down and extended his hand to the animal. It snuffled around his hand and gave it a slimy bath with the foot long tongue dangling from the side of its mouth. He grabbed the collar and found the tags. He squinted in the quickly disappearing light. *Liberty.*

"Libby! Libby, come here, girl!" Dolan's back went ramrod straight. Eve! He let the dog go and watched it streak down the path. "Good girl."

He heard the dog's collar jangle as it raced back to him. It danced around him and whined as he watched a vision walk out of the dark. "Hello, Dolan."

He blinked, because he had to be seeing things, but no. She was there, in front of him. "What the hell are you doing here?"

"Okay. Jeremiah said you might be mad. We talked about that."

His blood boiled and he ground out, "Jeremiah?"

"Doctor Wheeler. He's a psychiatrist that's been helping me work through a lot of my issues. I've been working on me." The dog whined and danced over to her.

"Liberty?"

"Yeah, she's mine. Mr. Marshall gave her to me as a present. I've been living at the ranch for the last five months." She leaned down and stroked the animal's coat. "She is going to be way bigger than the dogs that Joanne raises, but I didn't care. She's perfect. Well, except for this ear. For some reason it doesn't always stay up."

She looked up at him and smiled. He tried to pull air into his chest and failed miserably. "Why are you here?"

"I came to see you."

"Why?"

"Because we have unfinished business?" She walked over to him. "Because there are words left unsaid."

"I have nothing to say." Nothing that she'd want to hear. She'd left him, and now she'd showed up to drive home the fact that she hated him? Fine, he could let her have her closure. It wasn't like he could bleed any more than he already had. "But I'll listen to what you believe needs to be said."

"Okay." She lowered her eyes to her feet for a moment before she rolled her shoulders back. "I'm living my own life now. Nobody is making decisions for me."

He swallowed hard. Good for her. Damn, he was happy to hear that. He managed to nod at her when she cocked her head at him.

"I don't like what you do for a living. Or rather, did. I can't abide it."

He closed his eyes and shook his head. Fuck, this was harder than he'd ever imagined. Hearing exactly what she thought of him was going to kill him. His words were barely whispered, but they were close enough for her to hear him, "I am what I am, Eve."

"And you aren't that man any longer. You don't do that anymore. That's what Mr. King told me. Was he right?"

"I'm not currently doing those missions."

"What we had... was it a game or a pastime to you?"

His head snapped up and he glared at her. "What?"

"What was between us. Was it real for you?"

"As real as it gets." The truth was all he had to offer her. It was all that was left of him.

"Why were you going to send me with Bengal?"

"When?"

"When I woke up in the cab of the truck, you told whoever you were talking to that I'd go with Bengal. Why?"

"Because I saw the terror in your eyes. The fear you had of me. I wasn't going to keep you with me only to have you hate me even more." He absently reached down and stroked Libby's head when she sat beside him and leaned on his leg.

"I've worked with Jeremiah a lot about that day. I think my abject fear of death played heavily into my reactions. Well, actually he thinks that, and I agree with him. See, I always thought I was ready to die, because they always told me I would, sooner rather than later. But being resigned and fearing death are two different things. I'm working on that. I've got a lot of things left to work out."

"Like?"

"Like whether or not you'll take a chance on me even though I'm still messed up?"

He stopped breathing. "Take a chance?"

She nodded. "I've got to say it again, because this is a deal breaker for me, I cannot be with you if you continue in your old line of business." She crossed her arms and the look of defiance in her eyes was probably the most beautiful thing he'd ever seen. Perhaps that day in Atlanta hadn't permanently damaged her. It was his hope, no... his prayer.

He lifted a hand to his neck and rubbed it. A warm feeling started somewhere deep in the icy pit that used to house his heart, but if she needed honesty, he'd give her the unfiltered truth. "If I find the man who killed my parents, I will go after him."

"If you go after this guy, you're no better than he is. Don't. Please don't."

"I *am* no better than he is."

"The man who protected me *is* better than that. The man I was with in Alabama, who made love to me and took me on picnics *is* better than that man."

"He killed my family."

"Then let him rot in jail, but let justice prevail. Let the past go. I want you with me. With all my soul, I want to stay with you, here, but I will walk away if I have to. I will. Don't make me go. Please, don't hold onto the hatred of the past. Hold onto me instead."

She leaned into him and his arms enfolded her. Her warmth and softness invaded the coldest parts of him. The parts he'd never dreamed he'd allow another access to filled with a vivid illumination, one that eradicated any shadow and gave him a lifeline. A chance. He only needed one. The one chance he'd prayed for all those months ago.

He buried his face in her hair and drew a deep breath of heaven. He pulled her into him tighter. God help him, he'd never wanted to let her go. "I don't know if I can be who you want me to be."

"You already are."

He could hear the tears in her voice, but he knew this was his one chance with her. He had to be completely honest. "There is so much you don't know about me."

She pulled back and framed his face with her hands. "Unless it has anything to do with us, I don't want to know. I can't change your past or mine."

He stared at her for a moment. "I don't know what the future will hold. There could be missions. If Guardian asks me to go, I will."

"You work for Gabriel, right?"

"Indirectly."

"He told me he would honor your request not to do what you used to do, but *you* have to ask him, and you have to articulate why. He said no one could make the decision for you."

"It is all I know."

"It really isn't. The man I love is so much more than a job description."

"You love me?"

"I do."

"But... you haven't lived. You haven't experienced life."

"And you know what I figured out? Neither have you. Maybe it's time we learned how to do that?"

"Are you sure I'm who you want?"

"I've worked through my emotions for the last five months, and I know I'll have to continue with therapy, but one thing I didn't have to discuss, that I didn't have to examine was the fact you were all I wanted. Take me back to the compound, Dolan."

She leaned in and he met her halfway. The softness of her lips and the temptation of her taste launched him into the stars. Only this time he wasn't searching for answers, he was holding them for the woman he loved.

HE FILLED a bowl full of water and laid out a blanket in the front room for Libby while Eve used the bathroom and cleaned up from her trip. He patted the pup on the head and slipped into the bedroom, closing the door behind him. His clothes were off by the time he reached the bathroom door. He opened it and took in the sensuous sight. Through the fogged glass of the shower stall he could see her silhouette, her curves and her long dark hair, but little else. He moved across the marble floor and opened the glass door, allowing steam to billow out past him. She ran her hands over her hair, slicking it back before she opened her eyes and smiled at him. "I'm glad you're here, I'm having problems reaching certain spots." She looked up at him and pulled her bottom lip between her teeth.

"Which spots?" He pulled her into him and walked them both back into the warm water.

"This one." She lifted his hand from her hip to her breast. He lowered and kissed her thoroughly as he worked her nipple to a pebble. He bent down and used his mouth to caress, stroke and scrape the other. Taking his time, he worked his way back up her chest and long neck to her mouth. Against her lips he asked, "What other spots do you need help with?"

She pulled him down into another kiss and grabbed one of his hands, directing it to her sex. He split the folds and found her with his fingers. Her hot center was slick with desire and he fucking needed to be inside her. Her leg lifted and he grabbed it at the same time as he cupped her ass and lifted.

She squealed and grabbed onto his shoulders, slipping and grasping again. He pinned her to the cool tile of the shower wall, and she squirmed, laughing at the sensation. He moved her legs and centered under her while consuming her in a kiss. He relaxed his hold enough that she slipped down a few inches. The second he breached her, he shuddered and stopped. He was so close, too close. He pulled away from her mouth and drew deep pulls of air.

Her hands pushed his wet hair from his face and lifted it. He blinked the water out of his eyes and gazed at the woman who had been forced into his life and had changed everything. He tilted his hips and slid home. Her mouth dropped into a small O shape and her eyes fluttered shut. A deep crimson blush covered her chest and crept up to her cheeks. He moved inside her and lost all restraint. His hips pounded into her. His thoughts of slow gentle love making... he stopped and snapped his eyes to her.

"What? God, why did you stop? Please don't tease."

She moved to kiss him again, but he leaned away. What a fucking idiot he'd been.

"What's wrong?"

He shook his head slowly from side to side. He was such a stupid asshole. "I love you."

The confused look slid from her face. "Yes, I know, but it is good to hear it out loud."

"How did I get so lucky?"

"Make love to me." She moaned as his hips snapped forward and then bit at the corded muscle at his neck. His eyes damn near rolled into his brain. He wedged her against the tile, wrapped one arm around the small of her back to keep her angled perfectly and grabbed her ass, lifting and lowering her with as much force as his hands and hips could generate. She was a picture of wanton desire, her eyelids half closed, her hands holding her breasts, twirling the nipples. She snaked a hand between them and holy hell, she fingered where they were joined. His orgasm blew fast and sharp. He fought to stay upright as he rode through his body's release. Eve's shout and clenching suction struck and damned if he didn't see fucking spots even though his eyes were open. He leaned into her and braced an arm and his forehead on the tile beside her. "Holy hell, woman. That almost killed me."

"Yeah, but what a way to die." She rolled her head to look at him.

He chuckled and carefully dropped her to her feet.

He'd killed many people in many ways, but death by orgasm hadn't been among his repertoire. He moved the water spray and pulled her into him again. "I will wake up every day and strive to be the man you deserve. I'll try to be the person you see. I love you."

"You already are the man I deserve and the only man I'll ever see. I'm yours."

"Yes ma'am, you are..." He whipped a towel off the towel bar and wrapped it around her, pulling her toward him. "At least two or three more times tonight."

EPILOGUE

Tempest sat on the covered porch of his small house in the desert. He surveyed the compound. Nothing was moving this time of day, at least above ground. He stuck his feet out into the sunlight. With so little body fat, his internal temperature fluctuated radically on good days. On bad days, he froze even in his own house where the thermostat hovered at eighty degrees.

A dirt devil off in the distance caught his eye. The whirlwinds weren't uncommon, and the compound had hunkered down during a couple massive dust storms. The first one proved that the underground facilities needed filtered air systems the dust and sand couldn't suffocate. That brought out people from the other training complex. He wasn't sure where it was, but Moriah lived there. He smiled at the memory of seeing her with the man she married. She was happy and that was something he never imagined he'd ever see.

The ghost of a smile faded. He wasn't trusted with

any information, which he expected. What he didn't expect was how the alienation affected him. He wasn't part of... anything. He did his PT and came back to the small house he'd been given to live in. He watched the others go about their daily lives. He knew things happened in the underground facilities, but he wasn't allowed to know what. Hell, he didn't actually know exactly where they were. The desert. That was a no brainer, but where? The vehicles that entered the complex were too far away for him to see the tags and he didn't have the strength or the willpower to wander across the complex to figure it out.

He watched the dirt devil dance closer. Each day his strength returned. Each day he inched closer to the man he used to be. He'd been debriefed. Guardian knew what information he'd released and when. He'd need to heal physically and go through the mandated counseling before he would be allowed back into their folds, but he was a patient man. The alternative, not being a part of Guardian, was unacceptable, because when you no longer existed in the light or in the shadows, where did a soulless life force linger? His lip ticked up in a sneer.

The End

ALSO BY KRIS MICHAELS

Kings of the Guardian Series

Guardian Defenders Series

Gabriel: Book One

Guardian Security Shadow World

Anubis (Guardian Shadow World Book 1)

Asp (Guardian Shadow World Book 2)

Lycos (Guardian Shadow World Book 3)

Hope City

HOPE CITY - Brock - One City, Countless Stories

Everlight Series

An Evidence of Magic (Everlight Book 1)

An Incident of Magic (Everlight Book 2)

STAND ALONE NOVELS

SEAL Forever - Silver SEALs

A Heart's Desire - Stand Alone

Hot SEAL, Single Malt (SEALs in Paradise)

Hot SEAL, Savannah Nights (SEALs in Paradise)

ABOUT THE AUTHOR

USA Today and Amazon Bestselling Author, Kris Michaels is the alter ego of a happily married wife and mother. She writes romance, usually with characters from military and law enforcement backgrounds.

Made in the USA
Las Vegas, NV
05 November 2023

80299546R00174